AMERICAN HIPPO

AMERICAN HIPPO

SARAH GAILEY

A TOM DOHERTY ASSOCIATES BOOK

New York

AMERICAN HIPPO

Maps by Tim Paul

Edited by Justin Landon

A Tor.com Book
Published by Tom Doherty Associates
175 Fifth Avenue
New York, NY 10010

www.tor.com

Tor® is a registered trademark of Macmillan Publishing Group, LLC.

The Library of Congress Cataloging-in-Publication Data is available upon request.

ISBN 978-1-250-17643-1 (trade paperback)
ISBN 978-1-250-17642-4 (ebook)

Our books may be purchased in bulk for promotional, educational, or business use. Please contact your local bookseller or the Macmillan Corporate and Premium Sales Department at 1-800-221-7945, extension 5442, or by email at MacmillanSpecialMarkets@macmillan.com.

First Edition: May 2018

CONTENTS

RIVER OF
TEETH

FOREWORD

In the early twentieth century, the Congress of our great nation debated a glorious plan to resolve a meat shortage in America. The idea was this: import hippos and raise them in Louisiana's bayous. The hippos would eat the ruinously invasive water hyacinth; the American people would eat the hippos; everyone would go home happy. Well, except the hippos. They'd go home eaten.

Much to *everyone's* disappointment, Congress didn't follow through on the plan, and today America lives a cursed life—a beef life, with nary a free-range hippo within the borders of our country.

Reader, this is an actual, literal thing that almost happened. The hippos are not a metaphor. You should investigate hippo ranching for yourself; as much as I'd like to call this novella the definitive text on the matter, it is most assuredly fiction. With that in mind, I caved in to my desire to make this a hippo-cowboy romp and fiddled with some dates. I shifted everything back by about fifty years, and took some liberties with what technology existed at the time in order to fit the story to the time period. I regret nothing: it was worth it for the hats alone.

For actual facts about hippo ranching, check out Jon Mooallem's fabulous piece in the *Atavist Magazine* ("American Hippopotamus").

Yours in dreams of the America that Might Have Been,
Sarah Gailey

Chapter 1

Winslow Remington Houndstooth was not a hero.

There was nothing within him that cried out for justice or fame. He did not wear a white hat—he preferred his grey one, which didn't show the bloodstains. He could have been a hero, had he been properly motivated, but there were more pressing matters at hand. There were fortunes to be snatched from the hands of fate. There were hors d'oeuvres like the fine-boned young man in front of him, ripe for the plucking. There was swift vengeance to be inflicted on those who would interfere with his ambitions. There was Ruby.

Winslow Houndstooth didn't take the job to be a hero.

He took it for the money, and he took it for revenge.

The scarred wooden table in front of him was covered in the accoutrements of The Deal. The two-page contract, signed and initialed in his cramped handwriting. The receipt for disbursement of funds. A set of five photographs that had been culled from several dozen files: his team, selected after hours of arduous negotiation. There was a round-faced woman, her hair set in a crown of braids; an ink-dark, fine-boned rogue; a hatchet-nosed man with a fussy moustache; and a stone-faced woman with a tattoo coiling up her neck. The latter two were concessions he was already braced to regret. And finally—never last, only ever *finally*—there was Houndstooth himself. The photo didn't do him justice—he noted that the part in his hair was off-center by at least two centimeters—but he was wearing his finest cravat in the picture, so he'd call it a wash.

And then of course, there was the fat sack of money.

He counted out the thick gold coins, his eyes flicking to the photo of the hatchet-nosed man once every few seconds, and he waited. Now that the negotiations were over—now that his rate and his team had been established, and the money had changed hands—the small talk would begin. It was always the same with these government types. They were deeply confused by the juxtaposition of his vague accent and his eyes. His country's accent. His parents' eyes.

"So, where are you from?"

Ah, yes. There it was. They could begin the requisite dialogue about where he was from and where he was *from*. Houndstooth didn't look up from the coins.

"Blackpool." He could have made his tone frostier, but being in the presence of such a lovely stack of hard money warmed him like a milky cup of Earl Grey.

When the agent didn't immediately respond, Houndstooth paused in his counting, placing a mental finger next to the number "four thousand."

The agent was staring at him with such blue eyes. Such *attentive* eyes. "You don't sound British," the agent said quietly. Houndstooth found himself intrigued by the catch in the young man's voice.

"Yes, well," Winslow Houndstooth replied with a crocodile grin. "I suppose my accent's almost gone by now. I've been in Georgia for some time. I came to the States to be a hopper, and once I tasted my first Georgia peach"—he reached across the table to touch the agent's arm, scattering the photos—"it was just too sweet for me to leave."

The federal agent's cheeks reddened, and Houndstooth's smile grew. He didn't move his hand.

"I do so *love* the peaches down here."

—◆◆◆—

Winslow Houndstooth left the federal agent's office an hour and forty-seven minutes later, smoothing his hair with an elaborately carved comb. He eased the door shut behind him with a small smile.

That young man would need to take a nap for the rest of the afternoon.

The sack of gold coins was heavy, and he divided it evenly into each of Ruby's saddlebags. She could have carried the weight on one side easily—eight thousand dollars in U.S. government gold would hardly wind her—but it pleased him to know that he was flanked by four thousand dollars on each side.

He swung himself into the kneeling saddle on Ruby's back. She grunted at him.

Ruby had settled her bulk deep into the water-filled trench next to the hitching post. She wasn't made for long periods standing on land, although her breed could do it for longer than most. The Cambridge Black hippopotamus was the finest breed in the United States: sleeker, faster, and deadlier than any other hippo on the water. Ruby wasn't bred for meat; she was a hopper's hippo, meant for herding her slower, grazing cousins.

Ruby was onyx-black and lustrous; she looked like a shadowy, lithe version of a standard hippo. She stood five feet tall at the shoulder, about the height of a standard Carolina Marsh Tacky—although horses, Tackies included, were rare ever since the Marsh Expansion Project had rendered their thin legs a liability on the muddy, pocked roads. Her barrel chest swung low to the ground over short legs, perfect for propelling her through marshy waters when her rider needed to round up wayward hippos on the ranch. She grumbled on land, but could carry Houndstooth up to ten miles overland between dips in the water—another marker of her superior breeding (her cousins could only do six miles, and that only under duress). Fortunately, she was rarely out of the water that long.

"I know, girlie. I shouldn't have left you out here by yourself for so long. But you know I just can't resist blue-eyed boys." Houndstooth patted Ruby's flank and she let out a little rumble, standing under him and dripping freely for a few moments. She lifted her broad, flat nose briefly and yawned wide. Her jaw swung open by nearly 180 degrees, revealing her wickedly sharp, gold-plated tusks. They gleamed in the late-afternoon sun. She snapped her mouth shut and lowered her head until her nose nearly brushed the ground as she prepared to head home.

"Yes, alright, I know. Let's go home, Rubes, and you can keep your judgments to yourself. We need to pack up."

Houndstooth swayed with her rolling gait as she began to trot. He rubbed a loving hand over her leathery, hairless, blue-black flank, feeling the muscles shifting under the skin. Ruby was sleeker than most hippos, but not by much. Though her live-stock cousins had been bred for marbling, her sub-Saharan ancestors carried little excess fat. Their rotund shape belied merciless speed and agility, and Ruby was the apex of those ancient ideals: bred for maneuverability, fearlessness, and above all, *stealth*. She was dangerous in the water: no gulls dared to plague the marshes she wallowed in, and if one was so foolish as to try to rest on her back, it would quickly be reduced to a cautionary tale for other gulls to tell their children.

"Eight thousand dollars, Ruby. We'll be able to buy our own little patch of marshland, maybe get you a bull." Ruby huffed, her nostrils—set squarely on top of her nearly rectangular snout—flaring with impatience. Her round ears didn't turn toward the sound of his voice, but they flapped irritably. Houndstooth chuckled. "Of *course* I'm joking. You're past breeding age anyway, Ruby-roo."

It was another thirty minutes to the marshside tavern where Houndstooth had a room. It would have been forty by horseback, but Ruby's trot was quicker than a horse's, even with her frequent detours to dip back into the river. Houndstooth knew when he'd picked her out that she'd grow up to be more temperamental than a slower hop would have been, but her agility had made her spirited temperament worthwhile.

She'd saved his life enough times that he figured she'd earned the right to her opinions.

When they got back to the tavern, Houndstooth unlatched the kneeling saddle and the saddlebags from Ruby's harness and set her loose in the marsh. "I'll see you in the morning, Ruby. We'll head out around dawn, alright?" She waited, already half-submerged in the water, for him to rub her snout. Her ears twitched back and forth, impatient, and she blew a bubble at him. He laughed, earning a long, slow blink of her slanting, hooded eyes. "Okay, alright, I know. You've got places to be, grass to eat." Houndstooth crouched and put a hand on either side of her broad snout.

"You're my girl, Ruby-roo," he cooed, rubbing her whiskers. "And you're the best gull-damned hippo there is."

With that, Ruby sank into the water and was gone.

— ◆◆◆ —

Houndstooth propped his feet on a chair as he watched Nadine work the room. She was in her element: sliding full mugs of beer down the gleaming bar, promising to arm wrestle drunk patrons, letting customers buy her shots of whiskey to share with them (she always poured herself iced tea and pocketed the cash). He loved to see her efficiency. He'd told her many times that she would make an excellent hopper, but she always said she preferred to herd malodorous beasts that paid in cash.

She dropped off a steaming mug of Earl Grey—brewed from his own personal supply—and straightened his hat. "Where've you been, Winslow? Out with some new girl?"

He winked at her, and she tapped the brim of his hat to set it back askance.

"Ah, some new *boy*. Green eyes or brown on this one?"

"Blue," he said, toasting her. "Blue as the Gulf, and twice as hot."

He pulled out a silk handkerchief and bent to polish a scuff on his left boot. His timing was fortuitous. As he bent down, the door to the tavern burst inward and a man nearly the size of Ruby barrelled inside.

"What jack-livered apple-bearded son of a horse's ass," the man bellowed, "let a fucking *hippo* loose in a private marsh?"

Houndstooth did not remove his boots from the chair as he waved his silk handkerchief over his head. "Yoo-hoo," he said in a high falsetto, before dropping his voice down to its usual baritone. "I believe I'm the jack-livered apple-bearded son of a horse's ass you're looking for." With the hand not holding the square of paisley silk, he unbuttoned his pin-striped jacket. "What would you like to say to me about my Ruby?"

"That's your hippo?" the man said, crossing the now-silent room in a few sweeping strides. As he came closer, Houndstooth did a quick calculation. He added the bristling beard to the muscles straining at a flannel shirt and the shedding flakes of marsh grass, and he came to the obvious conclusion: marshjack. The man, it was safe to assume, spent his days scything marsh grasses to send to inland ranches. His accent was unplaceable, a combination of tight-jawed California vowels and loose Southern consonants. Houndstooth decided that he must have come South during the boom and taken up marshjacking after the bust. "That tar-skinned brass-toothed dog-eating monster out there is yours?" The man looked down at Houndstooth, who was still in his chair. "Who the hell let you on a hopper ranch, anyway? I'd like to have a word with the damn fool what thought to let you—"

"Dog-eating, did you say?"

"That's right, you yellow-bellied bastard," the man growled. "That monster of yours done *et my Petunia*."

"And what," Houndstooth inquired, easing his feet off their perch, "was your Petunia doing in that *private* marsh? Certainly not helping you hunt ducks on private property, I would hope?"

Everyone in the bar was watching them, speechless. Nadine leaned forward over the bar—the private marsh in question was her property, and so were the ducks that swam in it. The ducks she raised from eggs and sold at the market in order to pay the taxes on her bar.

"That ain't none of your business, you slick fuck," the marshjack spat. "What's your business is that my Petunia's dead because of your painted-up hippo *bitch*."

He swung his arm. Houndstooth registered the glint of metal.

What happened next happened very quickly indeed.

Houndstooth dropped forward out of his chair and into a crouch, and the knife sailed over his head.

The marshjack's momentum carried him forward and he stumbled, his leg brushing Houndstooth's shoulder as he put out a hand to catch himself before he could hit the ground.

Houndstooth straightened, fitted his right fist neatly into his left hand, and used his full weight to drop the point of his elbow onto the back of the marshjack's skull.

There was a crack like a branch snapping. The assembled crowd in the tavern made a collective "ooh," and the marshjack fell onto his face. By the time he managed to roll over onto his back, Houndstooth was standing over him. He twirled the marshjack's long, ivory-handled knife in his hand as the marshjack's eyes eased open.

"Well, old chap," Houndstooth said in a carrying voice. "Seems you tripped and dropped your knife." He flipped the knife in the air and caught it without taking his eyes off the marshjack. "Not to worry, I've caught it for you." He tossed it again; caught it again. The marshjack's eyes followed the spinning blade.

Houndstooth crouched over him. "Now, here are some things you ought to know. One: Ruby is not painted. She's a Cambridge Black hippo, and I'd guess that's why she was able to sneak up on your dear departed Petunia. Bred for *stealth*, you see, but she can be territorial. I'm not surprised that she '*et*' Petunia, if the dog was in her waters." He tossed the knife from hand to hand as he spoke, almost lazily. "Two: Her tusks are plated in gold, not brass. It's my gold. I took it, chum, from the type of men who like to steal ducks. So you see, it *is* my business why you were in that marsh, because my Ruby-roo can always use more accessories." The marshjack tried to track the knife, but one of his pupils was dilating and he seemed to be struggling to follow the movement.

"And number three, my dear man." Houndstooth reached down and gripped the bridge of the marshjack's nose between the thumb and forefinger of his left hand. The marshjack's eyes stayed on the knife, which was now twirling baton-like between the fingers of Houndstooth's right hand. "I thought you'd want to know that they *don't* let me on hopper ranches. Not anymore." His voice dropped to an intimate murmur as the knife flashed in his hand. "But I'll be *happy* to address your concerns myself."

In one fluid motion, Houndstooth inserted the knife into the marshjack's left nostril and slit it open. Before the marshjack could so much as choke on his own blood, his right nostril had been similarly vented.

Winslow Houndstooth straightened and wiped the blade of the knife clean on his handkerchief. He dropped the square of ruined silk onto the marshjack's face just as the man raised his hands to clutch at his filleted nose.

"I'll help you clean up the sawdust tonight, Nadine. Sorry about the mess." Houndstooth stepped over the marshjack and shot his cuffs, raising his voice over the marshjack's moans. "Oh, and I'll be paying out my room this evening. I've got a business trip to go on and I think I'll be a while."

Nadine set two glasses on the bar and poured a measure of whiskey into each as the bar patrons slowly began to converse again.

"Where ya headed, Winslow?"

He took a photo out of his breast pocket. The hatchet-nosed man glared up from it, his wispy moustache abristle. "The Mississippi River, sweet Nadine." He tossed the marshjack's fine ivory-handled knife in the air; it flipped end-over-end five and a half times before dropping, point down, through the hatchet-nosed man's left eye. Houndstooth clinked his glass against Nadine's. They each downed their whiskey, and Houndstooth gave Nadine a wink and a grin to go with the burn in both their throats. "And what a fine river it is."

Chapter 2

Nobody ever suspects the fat lady.

Regina Archambault walked through the market with her parasol over her shoulder, plucking ripe coin purses from pockets like fragrant plums from the orchard. Her hat was canted at a saucy angle over her crown of braids. Many of her marks recognized her, the visitor they'd sat next to at church or at a fete. They greeted her by name—and then their gazes slid off her like condensation down the side of a glass.

And she helped herself to whatever she deemed that they didn't have a use for. Rings, watches, wallets, purses—the peacock feather from the back of a particularly lovely bonnet. They never seemed to suspect that a woman whose dresses were custom-made to fit over her broad body would have nimble fingers. That she would be able to slip past them without drawing attention.

"Archie! Oh, Archie, you dropped your handkerchief!" A young gentleman in a beautifully felted bowler hat ran after her with a flutter of pink clutched in his outstretched hand.

"Now, Aaron," she said, archly but in low enough tones that they would not be overheard. "You know full well that is not my 'andkerchief. I did see one just like it for sale in the general store, though." Aaron flushed, and he smoothed his downy moustache with a nervous forefinger. Archie stepped with him into the entrance of an alleyway, where they could be away from prying eyes.

"Well, Archie—that is, Miss Archambault—that is—I just supposed that I might—"

Archie reached out her hand and took the handkerchief. "Aaron, mon amour—you know we mustn't let anyone see us together like this. Why, think how they'd *talk*." Her fingers rested on his for a moment as she took the little scrap of pink from him.

He leaned toward her. "Archie, I have to talk to you about our *plan*. I think my parents suspect something, and I won't be able to get away tonight after all."

His father, the stern patriarch of the wealthiest family in New Orleans, certainly did suspect something—he suspected quite a bit, if he'd read the anonymous letter Archie had sent him. She pressed the pink handkerchief to her lips and summoned tears to her eyes—just enough to brim prettily. "Oh, mon ciel étoilé, but I must go first thing tomorrow! And you must come with me, and we *must* buy the tickets this evening! I suppose— you'll just have to give the money for the train tickets to me and I'll buy them, and I'll—I'll 'ide one in the knot in our tree for you to collect when you can join me. You *will* join me, won't you, mon amour? You . . . you remember the tree I'm talking about?" She dabbed delicately at her eyes with the handkerchief and fluttered her lashes at him.

"Oh, yes, Archie, I—I remember. How could I forget where we—" If he had been any pinker he'd have been a petunia. He pulled an envelope from his vest pocket and pressed it into her hands, looking over both of his shoulders as he did so. "Here's the money for the train, and . . . I'll see you at the station, then?"

Archie pressed the handkerchief to her eyes again, so he wouldn't see her roll them at his ham-fisted attempt at stealth. "A kiss, Aaron. For luck." She kissed him hard—a better kiss than the boy would likely ever get again in his life. She kissed him thoroughly enough that he wouldn't notice her fingers dancing through his pockets.

"I'll see you at the train station in two days, my love."

She waved her handkerchief at him as he crept out of the alley, and she tucked the fat envelope of cash into her reticule. The poor little overripe peach of a boy—she marvelled at the way he walked, with the confidence of someone who's never been hungry or cold or heartbroken before in his life. When he was out of sight, she examined his pocket watch. A fine piece—it would fetch a fine price. Just *fine*.

She straightened her wide-brimmed straw hat and left the alley, gathering her skirts around her. She turned down a side street, away from the crowd, and walked to a broad old dirt road. A dog ran between two of the pecan trees ahead of her. Other than him, she was alone, and she walked down the middle of the road, parasol dangling from her wrist, holding her skirts up with one fist and her hat down with the other.

As she walked through the pecan trees to the marsh dock, the hidden pockets in her overskirt thumped against her leg.

As she scanned the water for Rosa's white ears, Archie whistled—a tune she'd heard from a busker in the marketplace. She couldn't remember the words—something about a hopper and a debutante—but the melody was catchy.

A stream of bubbles moved across the surface of the water. *Aha*.

"Rooo-saaa," Archie sang in her lilting alto. "I seeee-youuu!"

A white blur erupted halfway out of the water and rushed the dock. Archie swept her hat off, spread her arms and set her legs in a wide stance as the three-thousand-pound albino hippo splashed toward her at full speed.

"Bonjour, ma belle fille!" Archie cried. "Mon petit oeuf douce, 'ave you been having fun while maman was at the market?"

Rosa skidded to a stop a few inches in front of the dock. Archie tapped a long finger against the hippo's broad white nose.

"You, ma cherie, need to get sneakier. You're too easy to spot!"

Rosa shoved her snout against Archie's drooping skirts. "Yes, fine, 'ere—" Archie unclasped her skirts and pulled them off, revealing close-fitting red pinstriped riding breeches underneath. "—I got you a pastry, cherie. I know that cruel veterinarian says you shouldn't, but we don't 'ave to tell 'im about this, do we?"

Archie pulled a slightly squashed turnover from the pocket of her skirt and held it out to Rosa's nose. The hippo's pink eyes remained unfocused, but she turned unhesitatingly toward the smell of the tart. Her mouth swung open, and Archie dropped the turnover onto her tongue.

"Aren't you scared she'll bite you?"

Archie whipped around, startling the sallow, bone-thin boy behind her so much he nearly fell off the dock. She grabbed his arm and hauled him away from the edge of the planks.

"Of course I'm not scared," she said, still gripping the boy's arm. "I've 'ad Rosa since she was just a petit 'op. She would no sooner bite me than she would join the Paris Opera. Sneaky little urchins who follow me, on the other 'and—" She smiled and brought her face close to the boy's face, close enough that she could have bitten the brim of his cap. "She eats them up without a thought."

The boy swallowed hard but was not foolish enough to wriggle out of her grip. "Please, ma'am, you *are* Miss Regina Archambault, aren't you? They told me to look for the, uh, the—"

"The fat Frenchwoman with the albino 'ippopotamus?" Archie deadpanned.

"Uh, yes, miss. I—I have a letter for you. Please don't feed me to your hippo, ma'am, I didn't mean to sneak—"

He raised a trembling hand with an envelope in it. Her name was written on the outside in familiar, spiky lettering. Archie released his arm.

"Well, then, that is something else altogether." She grabbed the letter. "Would you like to pet a 'ippo, boy?" He looked nervously at Rosa's tusks. "She will not eat you. Not unless I tell 'er to. Just make a lot of noise as you walk up, so you don't startle 'er—'er eyes, they are not so good."

The boy glanced between Archie and the pink-eyed hippo. "I've never heard of a blind white hippo before."

"Well," Archie said, "the 'opper that bred 'er was going to kill 'er when 'e saw. 'What use is a blind 'ippo?' 'e said. But I knew better—she is the finest 'ippo in all the world."

The boy stared at Rosa, awe plain on his face. "Her name's Rosa?"

Archie ran her thumb under the seal on the envelope. "*Oui.* Let 'er smell your 'and, then you can scratch behind 'er ears."

As the boy approached the beast, tentatively placing a small hand against her snout, Archie read through the letter.

"Well, well," she whispered to herself. "Winslow, you old connard," she said, not looking up from the letter. She murmured to herself as she read it through again. "Ferals . . . eight *thousand* . . . a full year? Non, that can't be—oh, oui, I see now . . ." She turned to the boy, who was staring at Rosa's tusks with rapt fascination as he rubbed her nose. She looked him over, taking in his dull, patchy hair and his anemic complexion. She wondered if he slept in the streets, or if he hadn't escaped the orphanage yet.

"Miss Archa-Archim—"

"Call me Archie."

"Miss Archie? You said you had her since she was just a hop, right?"

"Oui," Archie replied. The boy was looking up at her with shining eyes, one hand resting on Rosa's nose. Archie lowered her voice conspiratorially, just to watch his face light up. "Hoppers, you see, we apprentice for years—then we choose a hop, when the time comes. We sleep beside them, we feed them, we sing to them. We're with them every moment of their lives, from the time the cord is cut to the moment they're fitted with a harness."

The boy's eyes were wide. "So that's why you're not scared of her?"

Archie laughed so heartily that the boy began to look sheepish. "I'm sorry, boy, it's just—I couldn't imagine being less frightened of sweet Rosa." Rosa, hearing her name, yawned wide, showing off her teeth. The boy stared into Rosa's massive mouth, his face aglow with awe.

"How do you get her teeth so white?"

Archie smiled. "I brush them. Would you like to see?"

The boy nodded, reaching out a now-fearless finger to touch one of Rosa's gleaming tusks.

"I'll show you, if you run a little errand for me. I need a telegram sent to a Mr. Winslow Houndstooth. Can you remember that?" She told him the message she wanted sent to Houndstooth, and she gave him a coin to get her a map of the Mississippi River.

"Be back here in two hours, and I will show you 'ow I brush her teeth. Hell, I'll even let you 'elp me pack up 'er saddlebags."

The boy put a hand on top of his cap, as though afraid it would fly off in the wake of his excitement. "Oh, boy, Miss Archie, I'll be back faster'n you can spit!"

He ran down the dock, his feet flying up behind him. Archie smiled, and turned back to Rosa, who was waiting patiently to see if another turnover would be forthcoming.

"Well, cherie," Archie said, folding her laden skirts over her arm. "It would appear that Winslow is calling in our old debt. I suppose I could argue that I owe 'im nothing after what 'appened in Atlanta—but what's a favor between friends, oui? 'E's got a job for us, my Rosa. How would you like to be a rich 'ippo?"

Rosa grunted, lowering herself farther into the marsh. Archie pushed her skirts into a half-full saddlebag, then slipped off her shoes and sat on the dock, dangling her feet in the water. She rubbed a wet foot over Rosa's half-submerged nose. "Eight thousand dollars. Just think, Rosa. Think of the pastries I'll buy for you."

Chapter 3

Hero Shackleby did not read the letter when it arrived.

They didn't read the second letter either.

They read the third, but only because it was hand-delivered.

Hero sat in their rocking chair, watching the tar-black hippo with the gold-plated tusks amble up the road. It would stop in front of their house, to be sure. Hero didn't look up from the sweet tea they were stirring as the hippo came to a stop at the bottom of the front steps.

"You can pop her in the pond with Abigail. Gate's around the side there."

The man on top of the hippo didn't respond, but dismounted and walked around the side of the house. Hero listened as Abigail greeted her new pondmate, as the man in the peacock-blue cravat cooed to—ah, yes. "Ruby," he called her. Abigail was a Standard Grey—not too far off from a meat hippo, but considerably smarter. She would be friendly to Ruby. She was friendly to everyone. *Hospitable,* Hero thought.

Hero stirred the iced tea, tasted it. *Not quite there yet.*

Ruby's rider came back around to the bottom of the front steps. He put his boot on the first step, then stopped, his chin tilted toward Hero's face. "Might I join you?"

"S'why I've got a second rocking chair," Hero said, assessing the man out of the corner of their eye. He was tall, immaculately dressed. He had cheekbones that sliced right through the thick, golden afternoon sunlight. He walked up the steps deliberately, watching Hero. Watching Hero's pistols.

"Don't worry," Hero said. "I won't shoot you. Sweet tea?"

"You haven't been reading my letters," the man said.

"You're English. Lancaster?"

"Blackpool. You haven't been reading my letters."

"And you haven't accepted my hospitality," Hero said, gesturing to the unoccupied rocking chair and the sweet tea sweating on the porch rail in front of it. "Please, won't you sit?"

The man sat. He looked like he wanted to sit on the edge of the rocking chair, but it was canted so that he had to sit all the way back. He held his hat in his hands. "My name is Winslow Houndstooth. I got your name from the federal agent who gave me this." He dug into his pocket and held out a thick gold coin with an eagle on it. "He said you'd want this job."

Hero sipped at their sweet tea, ignoring the proffered coin. "Hot this summer. They said it would be cooler, but I'd say it's a sight hotter than it was this time last year."

Houndstooth tapped the coin against the arm of his rocking chair. "I wouldn't know. I've never been to this part of Louisiana before. Rode here all the way from New Orleans. And that after the steamship ride along the Gulf."

"Your Ruby must be tired as a hog after a boil."

"She seemed happy to get into the water. Your Abigail looked damn bored in that pond, though. I bet she'd like the work." He pulled an envelope from his jacket pocket and handed it to Hero.

"I'm retired." They considered Houndstooth over the rim of their glass. "But I'm glad you came to tell me about this 'job' in person. Like a gentleman."

Houndstooth's eyes found Hero's. "Shackleby. That's an honest name. Are you an honest person?"

Hero smiled, close-lipped. "I'm not a liar. Ask me anything and I'll tell you the truth."

"Is that sweet tea poisoned?"

Hero's smile broke into a broad grin. "I thought you'd never ask." They picked up the second glass of sweet tea from the porch rail, took a sip, and set it back down. "See? I'm just fine."

Houndstooth didn't touch the glass.

"Abigail is bored," Hero said after a moment. "She's not used to living in one place, to having her own pond all to herself. She loves it. Has her own little dentist-bird." Hero leaned their head back against the rocking chair and fanned themself with the letter. "But she's bored. I haven't saddled her up in months. It's just been the two of us, all alone, plus the milkman once a week. And I don't even drink milk."

"Hero." He seemed to be rolling their name across his tongue. Hero caught themself staring and looked away. "Hero, I'm supposed to get you to accept this job. I accepted this job with the understanding that I would have a demolitions expert on board."

Hero sipped their sweet tea and watched Houndstooth fiddle with his hat. "I'll need some convincing. So. Convince me." They tried not to blink while they said it, knowing that it sounded for all the world like a line. Houndstooth's eyes snapped up, and he swallowed hard. Hero rubbed a tapered forefinger through the condensation on the outside of the pitcher of sweet tea.

"Well," Houndstooth said in a low voice. "There's the money. Eight thousand dollars. Gold, not bonds."

"Hmm." Hero ran their finger down the side of their throat, letting the cool water cut through the heat of the afternoon.

"Then there's the job itself," Houndstooth said. "Clearing the feral hippos out of the Mississippi. You'd live up to your name, if we managed it. We'd be heroes, Hero."

"Mmmhm." Hero leaned back in the rocking chair and crossed their legs, right over left. It would be something, to be a *hero*. A decent way to end a career that had gone on too long.

Better than simply fading off the scene, like they'd planned. They tapped their nails on the arm of the rocking chair, one-two-three-four.

"And then, of course, there's the team. It would be you and me—" He paused for a moment. "—Archie the Con, Cal Hotchkiss, and Adelia Reyes."

Hero sat forward at this last name. "Adelia Reyes? I thought I heard she was—"

"Yes," Houndstooth interrupted. "But she'll still do the job. She never turns down a job."

"Well." Hero sat back, folding their hands in their lap. "It sounds like you've got quite a team already. Without me. So why would you need me, Winslow Houndstooth? Why do you want to pull me out of the retirement I've been so thoroughly enjoying?"

Houndstooth stood and turned on his heel, leaning his back against the porch rail. His hand rested next to the untouched sweet tea, which had begun foaming softly. He looked down at Hero, his gaze unwavering.

"Because," he murmured. "I think you want it."

Hero was thankful that their skin was dark enough to conceal the hot flush that was climbing their neck.

"I think you've only been retired for a year, and already, you'd poison a stranger just to break up the monotony." Houndstooth knocked the sweet tea off the porch rail. It hissed as it ate through a rosebush. He leaned forward, still holding the porch rail. "I think you'd enjoy working this job a lot more thoroughly than you've enjoyed sitting in that rocking chair."

Hero looked at Houndstooth's burning eyes. "Is that what you think?" they asked, and sipped their sweet tea to relieve their suddenly dry mouth.

"Yes. That's what I think. That," he said, tilting his head to one side, "and I've got some things I need blown up. From what I hear, you're the one to do it."

Hero set their glass down and stood, clapping their hands decisively. "Well, then." They walked inside, and emerged a few moments later wearing a battered leather Stetson and clutching a large, bulging duffel.

Houndstooth laughed. "I thought it would take more convincing than that!"

Hero walked toward Houndstooth until their boots touched. The laughter on Houndstooth's lips died. They were nearly the same height, and their noses were less than an inch apart. Hero could smell the sweet iced tea on their own breath.

"Ask. I know you're wondering. If we're going to work together, you may as well ask."

Houndstooth swallowed. "I . . ." He paused, looking down at Hero's mouth, then looked back at their eyes. "How did you drink the poison? Without it killing you."

Hero blinked. That wasn't the question they had anticipated. "I'm immune. Small doses. Every day."

Houndstooth smiled. "Well. That's the only question I need the answer to." He sat back down and unfurled a map of the Harriet on the table between them. "Shall we plan a route? I think we should be able to get into the marshes by midmorning, and then we can collect Cal before meeting up with the rest of the crew. . . ."

Hero let themself smile as they sat across from Houndstooth and began studying the map. This *would* be more fun than retirement.

Chapter 4

Houndstooth watched out of the corner of his eye as Hero stretched their arms high over their head. The popping of their spine as they twisted made Ruby startle; her tail flapped irritably in the water of the marsh.

Hero and Houndstooth had been riding since dawn. The day's ride had been filled with long, easy silences and the slow, steady rhythm of Ruby and Abigail's treads through the water. The shadows were growing long as the sun began to dip, and Houndstooth had just started to doze off when Ruby's flicking tail splashed water down the back of his shirt.

"Ah! Damn." He wiped his brow with his handkerchief. The day was hot; the air was thick enough that even the mosquitoes seemed to be flying a little slower. Houndstooth swatted at one that was trying to find its dinner on the back of his neck; then he reached back into his saddlebag, pulled out two pears, and tossed one to Hero, who caught it without looking.

"Show-off," he said with a small smile.

"Sleepyhead," Hero drawled back.

Houndstooth was about to object, but interrupted himself with a huge yawn. He tried to cover it by biting into his pear, but Hero was already laughing at him.

"Keep me awake, then," he said through a mouthful of pear. Hero raised their eyebrows and Houndstooth felt himself blushing. Hero let it lie for a moment before answering.

"Alright, if it's my job to keep you stimulated. Let's talk about your grand . . . caper."

"It's not a *caper*, Hero. It's an operation. All aboveboard. All very well-planned and prepared-for."

"And what's the plan?" Hero asked.

Houndstooth coughed. "I was hoping you'd help me come up with that."

Hero bit into their pear, spat a seed. "You're funny." They said it without smiling. They tossed the top third of their pear into the water in front of Abigail, who snapped it up without missing a beat. Abigail crunched and swallowed the pear, twitching her ears.

"That I am," Houndstooth said cheerfully. "Have you ever been to the Harriet before?"

"No," Hero said, "I'm not one for gambling."

Houndstooth looked at them sidelong. He dipped his hand into his saddlebag and scooped out a little pouch of the white saddle-resin all hoppers used to keep their kneeling saddles from sliding around on the slippery, hairless backs of their hippos. He dipped his finger into it and drew a long oval with open, fluting ends on Ruby's inky shoulder, where Hero could see it. He drew a thick line across the top third of the oval, where the narrowed end flared open again—the dam that had turned the Mississippi into the Harriet. Not quite a lake and not quite a marsh, the Harriet was a triumph of engineering, but the ferals trapped within it rendered it a national embarrassment. The riverboat casinos that dominated its surface did little to alleviate the distaste with which most of the country considered the entire region.

"So, if this is the Harriet, then this is the Gate." Houndstooth drew another line across the bottom third of the oval. Hero snorted.

"You're not much of an artist, are you?"

Houndstooth glowered at them. "This is the Gate," he continued. "It keeps the ferals inside of the Harriet, so they can't get out into the Gulf. The Gate at the bottom of the Harriet and the dam at the top keep the ferals penned." He smudged white on each side of the circle. "Unbroken land to the east and west for a few miles in all directions keeps the ferals from traveling to other waters."

"So, it's . . . what? Twenty miles overland in every direction?"

"Give or take," Houndstooth said with a shrug. "It's enough land that the ferals can't make it across. I'm sure a few try every year, and die in the process. Either way, the Gate extends far enough inland to discourage them from making a serious attempt at migration."

"Do they want to leave?"

Houndstooth chewed on this. "I doubt it," he said after a minute. "They've been there for a few breeding generations. It's all they know. And other than the riverboats, it belongs to them."

Hero nodded. "Alright. So this plan that you're expecting me to come up with is supposed to motivate these dangerous, well-entrenched animals to migrate *south*."

Houndstooth grinned at them. "That's right. Per the federal agent who hired us, all we have to do is get them through the Gate," he said, drawing a line from the middle of the oval out through the bottom line on the crude map. "And then they're in the Gulf, and they're not our problem anymore." He drew the white line of resin all the way down Ruby's flank and into the water, making Hero laugh. Their laugh was infectious, and Houndstooth found himself laughing too as he splashed marsh water onto Ruby's back, rinsing the map away.

"What does the Coast Guard think of this plan?"

Houndstooth shrugged. "They're not the ones paying me."

"And what do the riverboat casinos think of it?"

"That's a good question," Houndstooth said. He settled his hat low over his eyes, and the two sank into the easy silence of the humid afternoon.

There would be plenty of time for Hero to learn about the Harriett, Houndstooth thought. Plenty of time for them to learn about the man who had shaken enough hands and bought enough half-destroyed land to practically own the surface of that feral-ridden puddle.

Travers.

If he had a first name, nobody seemed to know it. If he had a soul, Houndstooth had certainly never glimpsed it. Travers had seen an opportunity when the Great Hippo Bust of '59 rendered half the marshland in Louisiana worthless. He'd made his first fortune purchasing parcels of land for pennies apiece and reselling them to the Bureau of Land Management for use in developing the Harriet. The only caveat had been that he would have unfettered, exclusive business rights on the water, and the right to deny access to any nongovernmental person seeking entry via the Gate.

It was a story that most hoppers didn't know, but then most hoppers hadn't done business with Travers. Unless they'd spent time on his riverboats, most hoppers didn't know how much he relied on the vicious, hungry ferals that infested the Harriet. There had been a time when he would have paid handsomely to have even hungrier beasts in those waters.

There had been a time.

Hero interrupted Houndstooth's blood-soaked memories of the most dangerous man in Louisiana. "So, we're getting the ferals out of the Harriet because—why?"

"Trade route," Houndstooth murmured without looking up. "The dam is crumbling already—there's a huge crack down the middle, and it's less stable every year. The plan as I understand it is to tear it down and reopen the Harriet to trade boats that need to get down to the Gulf. But the boats won't go through if there are ferals eating their deckhands. So, they've got to go."

"Ah, right. That's not what I meant," Hero said. "I meant why are *we* doing it? What's in this for you?"

Houndstooth missed the comfortable silence. He swayed back and forth on Ruby's back, listened to the lapping of marsh water against her barrel chest. Abigail nudged Ruby with her shoulder. Ruby grumbled and ducked her nose under the water, and Houndstooth felt the pressure of Hero's patience settle over him.

"Have you ever had anything that you feel like you'd die without?" Houndstooth said it so quietly that it sounded like a prayer. "Something that you've put everything into—your whole life, all your heart? Have you ever had anything like that?"

There was another long minute of silence as Hero thought it over. Ruby blew bubbles in the water with her nose. On the shore of the marsh, a trio of fat frogs hopped into the water. Abigail glared at the shore primly, affronted by the commotion.

"I don't think I have," Hero said. They sounded distant, but when Houndstooth looked over, they were patting Abigail's flank with a small smile.

"I had a ranch once." Houndstooth watched Hero out of the corner of his eye, from under the shadow of his hat. He was ready for them to be skeptical, ready to have to prove his credentials. Hero didn't look back at him; they simply braced their hands on the pommel of Abigail's saddle and tilted their head back, their eyes half-closed. Houndstooth managed not to stare at the bead of sweat that ran down the side of Hero's long throat. "A breeding ranch."

"Takes time, saving up for a ranch," Hero drawled without opening their eyes.

"Fifteen years," Houndstooth replied. He found himself watching the water to keep from watching Hero. Ruby left barely a ripple in her wake; the mosquitoes that landed on the water didn't move out of her path. "It took fifteen years of work to buy the land. I started when I was seven years old, bottle-feeding sick hops at my uncle's ranch outside Atlanta every other summer. My father wouldn't pay for my passage across the ocean, so I worked throughout the year to get the money—I did whatever I could, short of stealing." He swallowed back memories of his father's reaction the one time he'd attempted to pick a pocket. "One year, I just didn't go back home. I stayed, so I could work the ranch year-round."

"That's when you knew," Hero said. It wasn't a question.

"That's when I knew," Houndstooth answered. He took his hat off and used it to scoop up a patch of mostly clean water, dumping it over Ruby's back to keep her skin from drying out. "I was the best breeder in the country, you know. Back before my ranch burned. Could have been the best in the world."

Hero didn't ask what had happened. They rode in silence for another thirty minutes or so as the sun dipped low, kissing the tree line. They set up camp a few miles outside the Harriet Gate. There would be no fire that night, but the air was warm enough that they didn't need it. They laid out their bedrolls and sat, listening to the cacophony of nighttime insects and frogs singing. They passed a flask of whiskey back and forth while Ruby and Abigail splashed and grumbled in the water, looking for good patches of grass to dine on. The sky went grey; a few bright stars announced themselves. There was no moon, but the star-filled sky cast just enough light for Hero and Houndstooth to see each other's outlines.

After a few more minutes, Houndstooth grunted, leaning back on his bedroll and propping himself up on his saddlebag.

"I'm going to kill the man who burned down my ranch, Hero. You should know that."

Hero stared hard at him. "If that's what you have to do to make something right," they said. "If you feel ready for it."

"I've been getting ready for years, Hero," Houndstooth murmured. "He's been hiding from me on the Harriet. And I've been waiting for the need to kill him—the hunger for it—to die down. But it hasn't. And now?" He patted his saddlebag. "Now I have a warrant to get onto the Harriet, and not even Travers can turn me away at the Gate."

By way of an answer, Hero held out the flask. Houndstooth reached up for it. He misjudged the distance in the dark, and his fingers closed over Hero's wrist. They both froze for a moment— then, Houndstooth slid his hand up over Hero's. His fingers felt their way slowly past their hand, past their fingers, over their fingertips, finding the flask.

Houndstooth unscrewed the top of the flask, taking a long drink. Then, finally: "I wish you could have seen it. The ranch."

Hero's murmur only just carried over the hum of insects that rose around them. "Tell me."

It was the kind of story that couldn't have been shared by daylight. Houndstooth told Hero about the ranch—about the hard year he spent preparing the land he'd bought near the Harriet, about the harder year he spent getting his hands on good breeding stock. As the darkness thickened and solidified, he told Hero about sleepless nights spent nursing newborn hops back from the brink of death. He told them about hiring his first ranch hand, Cal—the man they were on their way to collect. He tried to show them a scar he'd gotten from his very first breeding bull—a thick rope of shining skin that cut across the inside of his bicep and ran almost all the way to his collarbone. He unbuttoned his shirt to show Hero where it met his shoulder.

"I can't see it," Hero laughed. "It's darker than the inside of Ruby's belly out here, Houndstooth."

Houndstooth set down the nearly empty flask and grabbed Hero's hand. "Here," he said, and before he could think he had pressed their fingertips to the scar. His breath caught.

"Are my hands cold?" Hero whispered.

"No," Houndstooth murmured back, as Hero's fingers traced the full length of the scar where it met his shoulder. He could smell the sweet whiskey on their breath.

"What happened?" Hero asked, their fingertips still on Houndstooth's collarbone.

"Well, the bull was trying to kill a nine-month-old hop, and I—"

"No," Hero interrupted Houndstooth. "What happened to the ranch?"

For the space of three of their shared breaths, the only sound was the buzz of night insects and the flap of Ruby's ears in the water. Then, just as Hero was preparing to draw a breath to apologize for asking a question they knew they shouldn't have, Houndstooth answered.

"He burned it down." His voice broke on the word "down," as though he couldn't quite hold the notion that the ranch was really *gone*. He lifted his hand and impulsively placed it over Hero's.

"I woke up one night, middle of the night. I'd been in . . . in the birthing barn." He cleared his throat but didn't stop telling the story. His fingers tightened briefly over Hero's. "I'd been in there all night, working through a difficult labor. It hadn't looked good— I almost lost the mother three or four times. My hands were white and wrinkled from being underwater so long, trying to shift the hop into the right position to come out. But then, like nothing had ever been wrong at all, that mother just up and pushed out her hop. It was small, but it swam right up and poked its head out of the water and took its first breath, no problem. It was a healthy, perfect little girl-hop. The cow was looking at me like she didn't know why I thought I needed to interfere." He let out a breath that was almost like a laugh. "I was so exhausted, I fell asleep right there on the marsh grass beside her.

"When I woke up, the barn was filling with smoke. It smelled . . . wrong. I'll never forget it, Hero." He was nearly whispering, and Hero leaned a little closer to hear him. His voice was thick with the memory. "I stumbled outside and tripped over the hop, the one that had just been delivered. The mother was nowhere in sight—but then, I could hardly see anything, the smoke was so thick. There was sweat in my eyes, it was so hot, and the fire . . . the fire was *everywhere.*

"I picked up the hop and ran. She was small, small enough for me to carry, and too new to wriggle like they do. I got to the edge of my marsh and set her down in the water—her skin was already getting dry—and then turned to run back and put the fire out, but—" He stopped midsentence, and Hero could hear him trying to find the words.

"It was too late," they murmured.

Houndstooth sniffed hard. He squeezed Hero's hand once, hard, and then let it go. He leaned back on his bedroll, resting his head against his saddlebag again. After a few minutes, he went on.

"I couldn't go back through the fire. The marsh grass was just dry enough, and there was a wall of flames between me and the paddocks. I couldn't see through the fire and the smoke, but I could hear them," he said. "The air smelled like . . . like *meat,* Hero. It was all wrong. I could hear them thrashing, bellowing. I could hear the hops. I could hear them burning. A hundred in all, hops and mothers and bulls, and I stood there and listened to them die." His voice broke, and there were another few minutes in which they both pretended his tears were silent ones.

"I stayed there, as close as I could be without choking on the smoke, and I watched it burn. All the hippos I'd spent my life breeding—gone. Dead." He fell silent.

"What about the hop?" Hero asked after a moment.

"Ah, well, of course," Houndstooth answered, his voice still thick. "She started nudging at my ankles around dawn, as the flames died down. She was hungry enough that she started trying to suckle on the toe of my boot. She raised up well enough, didn't she?"

"She sure did," Hero answered. "Jesus, Winslow. A hundred hippos." They whistled long and low. "That must've been a helluva ranch you built."

"It was," he replied. "It really was." He laughed mirthlessly. "But after it burned? I had nothing left but bad debt. I had to sell the parcel to Travers to get out from under it." Houndstooth spat into the water. "And look at me now. What do I have to my name? A bedroll and a grey hat and Ruby. The last of her line. And her getting older every day."

Hero put their hand near the edge of their bedroll. Their pinky finger brushed against Houndstooth's. He didn't pull his hand away.

"A few weeks from now, that won't be all you'll have," Hero murmured.

"No?" Houndstooth said, linking his pinky finger with Hero's.

"No," they replied. "In a few weeks, you'll also have revenge."

Chapter 5

"They don't have hoppers in California, asshole. They don't have *hippos* in California."

"Well, Alberto," Cal Hotchkiss said to the balding off-duty ranger, shifting his toothpick from one side of his mouth to the other, "that's your opinion."

The four men around the table were not looking at each other. They watched the cards in their hands as though nude women were painted on the fronts of the cards, instead of the backs. They were not wreathed in smoke—the riverboat casinos did not allow smoking in private suites—but three of them chewed on unlit cigars. Cal Hotchkiss preferred his toothpick.

"It's not an opinion," the tall black man in the black hat chimed in. "There's no hippos in California. No rivers. No marshes. Means no hippos."

The men accepted cards from the dealer, who kept his eyes downcast as he slid them across the felted top of the table. They slid the cards into their hands, muttering to each other about the Sacramento River and whether it featured marshes; none of them knew, and Cal declined to educate them. Alberto sniffed. He leaned toward the window, holding onto his grey felt hat, and spat a thick stream of tobacco into the water. A moment later, a soft splash sounded.

"You know what they do have in California?" The man in the black hat took a sip from the mint julep that rested on the felt in front of him. "Adelia Reyes."

For a moment, none of the men seemed to breathe. The only

sound was the creaking of the giant wheel that propelled the riverboat slowly forward.

The moment passed.

"Never heard of her," Alberto said. "Edvard, you heard of her?"

The fourth man at the table—a squat Swede in a bolo tie—shook his head. "If I had heard of her, I sure as shit wouldn't want to hear of her again."

Cal Hotchkiss didn't say anything at all. He laid out his cards. The rest of the men at the table seemed to exhale as one as they each acknowledged defeat. Cal reached out one long arm and hooked it around the pile of chips in the center of the felt, reeling in his winnings. He lifted his bowler with one hand and ran his fingers through his damp, white-blond hair. The breeze coming in from the open window just behind his chair ruffled the fine wisps of his moustache. "Well, gentlemen. I win again." He lifted his hat high in the air, and a dark, doe-eyed waitress wearing a breathtakingly low-cut corset slid over. She leaned close to him, her perfume wafting around the table.

"Yes, Mr. Hotchkiss?"

"I'd like a drink, Cordelia. And then I'd like for you to come and sit in my lap."

"Right away, Mr. Hotchkiss."

She walked out of the small room to fetch a drink from the main floor of the casino, and the other men at the table watched her go—all of them except for the man in the black hat.

"Going to take her to bed with you, Cal?"

"Nah." Cal shrugged, slipping his winnings into the pockets of his jacket. He looked sharply at the man in the black hat. "Mr. Travers wouldn't like it."

The man in the black hat smiled. "Of course. It's nice to meet you, Cal Hotchkiss. Name's Gran Carter, U.S. marshal." He flipped up his jacket to reveal the silver star that hung from his belt buckle.

"I know who you are."

"Then maybe you know why I'm here."

"Maybe I don't give a shit."

The pit boss walked past the doorway and the dealer made eye contact with him. A moment later, the dealer had melted away from the table, leaving the four men alone with the dregs of their drinks. Alberto turned to Gran Carter. He was more than a little drunk. "Look here, Mister Marshal, I ain't done nothin' wrong here no how, an' I've got a badge too, see, I'm a *ranger* for the Bureau of Lan' Management, an' I fancy I've got even more pull here than the likes of—"

Gran Carter clapped Alberto on the back hard enough that he choked midsentence. "You're alright by me, friend. I'm not here for you, and I'm not here for the casino, and I'm not here to stop Mr. Travers from throwing cheats into the river. Hell, I'm not even here to make Mr. Hotchkiss shave that embarrassment of a moustache." He reached into the breast pocket of his jacket. All of the men around the table reacted instantly, drawing pistols and pointing them at the U.S. marshal in the broad black hat.

"Woah there," he said, holding up his hands. In one of them, he held a photograph. The men around the table put their guns away—all except Cal, who merely lowered his. He kept one hand on the gun. The other hand reached up unconsciously to stroke his patchy blond moustache. At that moment, Cordelia arrived with a tray and handed a glass of honey-brown liquor to Cal. She perched in his lap like a cat sitting on a fence post, her eyes fixed upon his unholstered revolver.

Carter set the photograph on the table and slid it toward the center of the felt. "That there's Miss Adelia Reyes, gentlemen. I happen to know that she was on the Harriet eight or nine months ago, and I'm guessing she talked to some people here. She owes me a conversation. I'd be much obliged if y'all'd look over that photograph and tell me if you've seen her."

None of the men took the photograph, but their eyes all locked onto it the same way they'd been watching their cards before the game had ended. The sepia photograph showed a woman with burnished bronze skin and the cool, steady gaze of a contract killer. She stared out of the photo with hawkish, predatory eyes; a tattoo of a thorny vine coiled its way up the side of her neck and into her hair.

"Well," said Edvard. "I think I'd remember it if I ever saw a lady like that. What'd she do that a marshal's looking for her?"

Alberto rubbed a thick rope of scar tissue on the back of his left arm. "I'd imagine she killed a man."

Carter looked at Alberto with that unwavering smile. "You'd imagine right."

Cordelia leaned over the table to look at the picture, then opened her mouth as if to speak. Cal Hotchkiss rested his hand on her hip, his grip tight. She closed her mouth without speaking.

"Well," Carter said, pushing back from the table and standing without taking the photograph. "I'll be around if you need me."

Edvard and Alberto stood together and walked over to the bar, shooting glances at Carter as he sauntered toward the exit. Cal watched him walk away, then stood. Cordelia toppled from his lap. He grabbed a wad of cash from the center of the table and thrust it at her. "For the drink. And the company. Go on and tell 'em downstairs that I'll be along shortly to pick up my Betsy."

"No need," a cheerful voice rang out from just behind them. "I've already moved her into a paddock for some quality time with my Ruby."

Cal whipped around so quickly his hat fell off, leaving Cordelia to gather the bills he'd dropped. In the instant it had taken him to turn, he'd grabbed his revolver off the table and unholstered a second, smaller gun from his belt. He had both pointed at Winslow Houndstooth with the hammers cocked back by the time his hat hit the ground.

"Now, Calhoun, that's no way to greet an old partner." Houndstooth strode toward Cal, plucking his bourbon from the table and sampling the bouquet deeply before taking a long, slow sip. Behind him, Cordelia slipped out of the room. "Oh. That's very fine, indeed. You still have excellent taste."

"You here for me, Houndstooth?" Cal growled. "If you think I'll go quiet, think again." He shifted his toothpick back and forth in his mouth.

Houndstooth laughed. "Nothing like that, Cal, my old friend! I'm here to work with you again. Partners. Just like old times. Just like back on the ranch." Houndstooth flicked open a long, thin stiletto blade and twirled it between his fingers like a baton. "You remember the ranch, don't you, Cal? The one you worked on, right up until it burned to the ground on the same night you ran off to work on the Harriet? A fine coincidence, that."

Cal started to edge toward the door. Houndstooth stepped swiftly between him and the exit. "Love the—is it a moustache you're working on? We really must catch up, Calhoun, old chap. I've been wanting to have a *chat* with you for some time now."

A cough sounded from the door. They both turned, and the air in the room went cold. Hovering in the doorway was a sleek little stoat of a man, his pencil moustache slicked across the top of his lip like a drunk draped across a chaise longue. His seersucker suit was fitted to him so impeccably that Houndstooth's breath caught for a moment in his throat.

"Gentlemen. I trust you're both familiar with the rules of my casinos." The man's voice was smoother than the bourbon his bartender poured for high rollers.

"Mr. Travers," Houndstooth said. "I wasn't going to hurt my old friend Cal, here. Just showing him my new knife."

"And a fine knife it is," Travers responded, inclining his head. "It would be such a shame if it were to get wet. And your pistols, Mr. Hotchkiss—I don't imagine they stand up well to submersion?"

Cal and Houndstooth stared at each other for a long moment. The boat creaked as they watched each other. Travers cleared his throat, and they both lowered their weapons.

"Very good. Now, I'm sure you gentlemen would like to have a civilized discussion over drinks at the bar? On the house." He waved an arm toward the door. The two men hesitated, neither wanting to walk in front of the other—but after a beat, Houndstooth put his grey hat on, tipping it to Travers.

"I'll be waiting for you with a whiskey, Calhoun, old friend. We've got business to discuss."

He walked out without a backwards glance. Cal made to follow, but Travers put out a hand before Cal got to the door. Cal stopped before Travers so much as touched him.

"Now, what precisely do you suppose he's doing here?" Travers murmured, his voice as silky as a snake's belly sliding over a bed of marsh grass.

"I got no damn idea," Cal growled. Travers considered him for a long, silent minute. "I said I don't *know*," Cal said, his eyes flicking away from Travers'. "And whatever it is you're thinking you'll ask me to do about it, I ain't doin'."

In just three unhurried steps, Travers crossed the room and was behind the chair near the window, where Cal had been sitting. He stooped, looking like a heron that had spotted a fish. When he straightened, he was holding three playing cards. He held them up where Cal could see them. Cal's face didn't so much as twitch. Travers dropped the cards onto the felt of the table and spread them out with the manicured tip of his index finger.

"Three queens. Were these insurance against losing, or did they come in handy at some point while you were fleecing my customers?"

Cal shook his head as his lips went white. Travers held up a quelling finger.

"Shhh, no, don't try to lie to me, Mr. Hotchkiss. You were cheating. You were *stealing* from me. Oh, yes, I know, you weren't stealing my *money*, Mr. Hotchkiss—but you've tarnished my name. You've put my reputation into question, and you've made me look foolish." His voice hadn't risen above a murmur, but it dripped with menace. He whipped the silk pocket square from his jacket and, turning to the open window, laid it across the broad sill. "You realize that this is your second warning?"

Cal nodded.

"And you realize, don't you, that there will not be a third warning?"

Cal nodded again.

"Let's just be sure, why don't we? It always pays to be thorough. Come here."

Cal shook his head again, unable to form words. His face had turned a peculiar shade of grey. Travers gestured with one elegant hand, then unbuttoned his cuffs and began to roll up his sleeves.

"Come now, Mr. Hotchkiss. *Cal.* Let's not waste time. Your friend is waiting, after all." He finished rolling up his sleeves, then checked to make sure they were of equal lengths. That done, he snapped his fingers. Cordelia entered, holding a domed silver tray. She did not look at Cal as she passed by. She set the tray on the gaming table near where Travers stood, where he could reach it without moving away from the window.

"Thank you, Cordelia, darling." Travers smiled at her with warm eyes. She smiled back, tentative. He nodded to the door, still smiling, and she left, ignoring Cal's desperate attempt to catch her eye on her way out. After she'd disappeared from sight, two massive men stepped in from the hall—Travers' security. They turned away from the room, so their backs filled the doorway. Cal let out a strangled sound like an aborted whimper.

"Mr. Hotchkiss," Travers said. "I don't have all day. Do not make me ask you again."

Cal crossed the room with slow steps. Sweat beaded on his brow as he watched the covered tray. The only sounds in the little gaming room were his shaky breathing, the creak of the steamboat wheel, and the lapping of the Harriet.

Travers uncovered the little silver tray. There, on top of a folded maroon napkin, lay a gleaming, curved hunting knife—Cal's hunting knife, taken from his room on the boat. It had been cleaned and honed since he had seen it last. The edge of the blade was so fine that his eyes couldn't quite rest on it.

Travers picked up the cards from the felt-topped table and laid them down in a neat row on the square of silk he'd laid across the windowsill. He rested the tip of one manicured index finger on the center card.

"Are these your queens, Mr. Hotchkiss?"

Cal swallowed hard, a muscle twitching in his jaw. He nodded. Before he had finished nodding, Travers' hand flashed out, and Cal's face slammed into the windowsill. His right cheek was pressed against the three queens. Travers' hand was smashed flat against the left side of his face, holding him against the sill. The corner of the top card pressed against the right corner of Cal's lower lip, sharp. The tips of Travers' fingers dug into the flesh of Cal's face, his grip as firm as bone.

Travers slowly bent his head until his eyes were level with Cal's. The heel of his hand ground painfully against Cal's jaw.

Travers picked up the knife.

"Are these your queens, Mr. Hotchkiss?"

Cal made another strangled sound. Sweat dripped into his eyes. He finally managed to open his mouth wide enough to rasp the word "Yes."

Travers brought the knife to rest just under Cal's left eye, then traced it along the top of his cheekbone, just lightly enough to leave the barest red scratch. Cal felt a single tear work its way out of his right eye. It fell through the open air, all the way down to the water.

"Look," Travers hissed. And Cal did.

He looked down, following the path his tear had taken. He couldn't move his head, but he strained his eyes. His breathing hitched as his gaze found what Travers wanted him to see: the ferals.

The water swarmed with them. They stayed near the *Sturgess Queen* during daylight hours, while the sun warmed the water around the riverboat to a temperature they could abide. They circled it hungrily, waiting for someone to cheat or brawl or get handsy with one of Travers' girls. Waiting for Travers' security staff to hurl someone overboard, so they could fall, flailing and screaming, into the water.

Cold sweat ran down the small of Cal's back as he watched the ferals look up at the boat, impatient for their next meal.

Travers let him sweat for a full minute before he asked the question a final time. "Are. These. Your. Queens."

Cal choked out the words. "Yes, Mr. Travers, sir."

There was a flash of movement. Cal's left ear felt suddenly hot, searing hot, and then there was pain, blue-white and filling the left side of his head. He spasmed, but Travers' hand gripped his face, and he could not lift his head from the windowsill. He could not lift it even as blood filled his ear, muffling all other sounds in the room—even as it poured down the front of his face, stinging his eyes. He tried to draw breath to scream in pain but ended up sputtering, choking on a mouthful of his own blood.

Travers held him there with a firm hand, taking slow, deep breaths. He held the knife out in front of him, over Cal's head. Balanced on the edge of it was the lower half of Cal's left ear.

Eventually, Cal stopped thrashing and was still. His breathing was labored and ragged; blood covered his face, stained his collar, pooled around his cheek. It would have run down the windowsill, but for the square of silk that just barely managed to contain the puddle of blood. Travers lowered the knife so Cal could see his ear, as delicate as a magnolia petal.

"I don't give third chances, Mr. Hotchkiss," Travers murmured. He licked a fleck of saliva from the corner of his mouth with the pink tip of his tongue. He twitched the knife. The severed half-ear landed directly in front of Cal's eyes.

Travers finally released Cal, but the blond man didn't stand up right away. Travers grabbed the purple napkin from the silver tray, and used it to wipe his hands clean before dropping it on Cal's head.

"You should get cleaned up," he murmured, staring at the bleeding man with flat, passionless eyes. "I expect Mr. Houndstooth will be waiting for you. Oh, and Calhoun?" He waited for Cal to straighten and look at him before continuing. "Not a *word* to Houndstooth." He pulled a linen handkerchief from his back pocket with a flourish. He used it to pick up the piece of Cal's ear that still lay on the windowsill; then, he wrapped the ear up with quick, delicate motions, and dropped it into his breast pocket.

Cal's eyes were locked on the pocket that had half of his ear in it. "Yes, Mr. Travers, sir."

"Very good." Travers turned and left the room without another word. Cal stared after him, clutching the purple napkin to what was left of his ear. After a minute or two, he swore under his breath. He left the room, still pressing the napkin to the side of his face. Houndstooth was waiting for him.

Chapter 6

The Harriet Inn was the only bar in the slim mile between the Gate and the Gulf with its own pond. All the hoppers that came through town stopped there sooner or later to enjoy the excellent service and the brutal atmosphere. The darts were sharp and the drinks were strong. Cal and Houndstooth arrived together, and, without speaking to each other, they spread themselves out at a low, scarred table. They ordered the first round, and several mugs of beer arrived well before anyone else did.

Houndstooth lit a long, slim, black cigar, and blew a stream of smoke at Cal, who chewed his toothpick as though it had wronged him.

"So," Houndstooth said. "You quit?"

"I got all the smoke I needed ten years ago." Cal smiled around his toothpick. The smile did not extend beyond the corners of his lips.

Houndstooth ashed his cigar directly onto the tabletop. He stayed at the Harriet Inn as frequently as any other hopper, but he felt no affection for the place. It was only ten years old, and it still smelled to him of smoke and burning hops. It rested on the grave of his old ranch: Travers had used the land to build the Harriet Inn, so that anyone too drunk to get home from the Harriet had a place to lose the remainder of their money.

"You know," Cal said in a conversational tone, "if I didn't need the money to pay off Travers, I'd just as soon kill you."

Houndstooth took a pull on his cigar and let the smoke curl

out of his nose. "Really?" he asked. "Because I could just as easily *not* find Adelia for you. I'm sure she'd rather not be found. Especially not by a man she went *fugitive* to avoid."

Cal bit his toothpick in half. He did not respond.

Twenty minutes of thick, heavy silence later, toward the butt end of Houndstooth's cigar, Archie walked in. She sat on the bench with her back against the wall, avoiding the too-small chairs that surrounded the other three sides of the table.

"Well, hot damn. If it isn't the great Regina Archambault," Cal drawled, putting unnecessary emphasis on "great" as he fingered the bandage that covered his left ear.

"Call me Archie," she said, not looking at him. "Winslow, do you 'ave another one of those cigars to share? I've been on the road all goddamned day."

As Houndstooth pulled his cigar case out of his pocket and cut a fresh one, the door eased open. Hero slid in, melting easily into the shadows of the dimly lit bar, and slipped into a chair.

"Well, that's it. We're all here."

"Un moment, s'il vous plaît," Archie said. She whistled a few short, high notes, like birdsong. A towheaded boy poked his head into the bar. She signaled him, and he perched on the bench next to her.

"This is Neville. 'E is my assistant."

The table was still for a moment; then, everyone looked at Houndstooth. Archie addressed him directly, ignoring Cal and Hero.

"I trust 'im, Winslow. The boy knows where 'is loyalties lie. Plus, 'e knows that if 'e ever betrays us, I'll gut 'im like a one-legged 'op. Isn't that right, Neville?"

Neville nodded strenuously, looking only at Houndstooth.

"Well, if you trust him, Archie, then I suppose he can stay."

Archie ashed her cigar onto the floor, satisfied.

"Well," Houndstooth said. "Let's all get to know each other. You all know me, so I'm not going to introduce myself—forgive me, Neville, you'll just have to figure me out on your own time." Neville nodded again, with vigor.

"Archie," Houndstooth said, gesturing with the stump of his cigar, "is the finest con either side of the Mississippi. Her meteor hammer can take down a charging bull faster than anyone I've ever seen. She's saved my life nine and a half times."

"Ten," Archie said, grinning around her cigar.

"Nine and a half," Houndstooth responded with a smile. "Also, she's got a connection to a certain U.S. marshal of whom we don't want to run afoul." Cal looked as though he had a comment to add. Archie levelled a pitiless stare at him, and he thought better of it.

"Hello, Archie," Hero said, extending their hand. "I've heard so much about you."

Archie shook Hero's hand. "Charmant," she said, and to the surprise of everyone at the table, it sounded for all the world like she actually meant it.

"From what I've been told," Houndstooth continued, "Hero there could blow up a bank vault using a pile of hippo dung and a cup of water, and they could make it look like an accident. Plus, they could poison a hummingbird and it would dip its beak twice before it dropped. They're smarter than I am, which is saying something. And they're—" He coughed, took a sip of his drink. "They're, ah, they're just a great team member."

"What kind of a name is 'Hero'?" Cal muttered around his mangled toothpick.

"It's my name," Hero responded.

Cal spat splinters into the sawdust on the floor, then selected a fresh toothpick to maim. Archie raised her eyebrows. "And who is this charming young man?"

"Calhoun Hotchkiss," Houndstooth said archly. "He's the fastest gun in the West."

"I'm the fastest gun anywhere." Cal responded with the speed of deep-seated bitterness over the title.

"He's also the only one of us that's ever dealt with ferals," Houndstooth added. "Aside from Adelia Reyes, if we can find her. He's spent years working on the Harriet. He knows everything there is to know about it. He's stupider than he looks, but he shouldn't hold us back too much."

"And what about you?" Cal retorted. "What do you bring to the table, you smug fuck? Who made you the boss?"

Houndstooth was evidently ready for this question. His hand flicked, and before Calhoun could flinch, there was a tiny click on the table in front of him. All the eyes at the table fell on the sliver of wood that suddenly lay in the puddle of condensation left by Cal's beer.

Cal reached up and felt for his toothpick, which had been sliced cleanly in half.

Houndstooth rested both his hands on the tabletop. One of them held the same stiletto blade he'd drawn on the riverboat.

"I'm the boss, Calhoun Hotchkiss, because I'm faster than you. I'm smarter than you. I'm *better* than you. And I'm the one who can send the telegram that will get you paid at the end of this. So here's what's going to happen: you're going to get us into the places that only your reputation can get us into. You're going to shoot fast and you're going to shoot straight. You're going to be helpful and respectful. If you don't do those things, then you don't get paid. Is that clear?"

Cal drew a fresh toothpick from his pocket and inserted it into his mouth, saying nothing.

"Good," Houndstooth responded. He glanced around the bar. It was empty but for them and the bartender. "Now, we need to find the fifth member of our crew." He slid a photograph into the center of the table—the same photograph that Gran Carter had left sitting on the felt of the poker table earlier that day. Adelia Reyes stared unsmiling out of the photograph. Everyone at the table examined the photograph, but it was Cal who reached for it first. He looked at it for a long time, swallowing hard; then he set it back in the center of the table and stared at his hands for a few minutes, clearing his throat every few seconds.

"You're all familiar with Adelia Reyes. She's been missing for seven months."

Cal coughed. "Seven and a half."

"Right," Houndstooth said, frowning at Cal. "Seven and a half months. She rides two hippos: a Standard Grey and an Arnesian Brown. She switches between the two so she doesn't have to rest either one—so we'll probably find her near the water somewhere. Can't travel overland with two hippos for long."

Neville, who had been silent until that point, raised his hand. Archie gave him a quelling look, but he kept his eyes fixed on Houndstooth, who, after a long minute, waved a hand at the boy.

"Sorry to interrupt, Mr. Houndstooth sir, but I've seen that woman."

All eyes at the table swivelled toward Neville.

"You've what?" Hero and Archie said at the same time. Cal looked at the boy with an intensity so sharp it put Winslow's knives to shame.

"I've seen her. Just now, outside. She was . . . well, she was at the tobacconist, sir. She looked . . . a little different from how she looked in that photo, sir. She spotted me 'n Archie, and while I was putting Rosa up in the pond out back, she came by the water to visit, and she—" He met Cal's eyes and paused.

"She what, Neville?" Hero asked gently.

"Um, well." Neville turned to Houndstooth. "She came by the pond, and she took a look at Ruby—that's the hippo with the gold tusks, right? She looked inside Ruby's mouth and asked if I knew who rode her here, and I said I didn't, and then she looked at the other grey in the pond, the one with the nasty scars? She talked to that one for a while."

Cal sucked in a breath at this and looked back down at his hands. A little blood had started to soak through the bandage over his ear.

Houndstooth sprang up from the table and made for the door. Archie gave Neville a little shove. "Go after 'im, now. Show 'im where you saw 'er."

But before Neville could get up—before Houndstooth made it across the bar—the door burst open. A woman walked in and stood, silhouetted in the doorframe until the door swung closed behind her.

She took a few steps forward, into the light, and looked over the crew assembled around the scarred old table.

"Well," Adelia Reyes said. "Well, well, well." The most brutal contract killer of the late nineteenth century folded her hands over her distended belly and winked at Calhoun Hotchkiss, before settling her gaze on Houndstooth. "I'd be willing to bet you're looking for me, Mr. Houndstooth."

The crew assembled at the table watched as the outline of a tiny foot pressed at Adelia's shirt. She pressed a hand to it. "Shhh, mija. Mama's working."

Calhoun slid sideways off his chair and fell to the sawdust on the floor, unconscious.

"Hello, Adelia," Houndstooth said. "How would you like to make eight thousand dollars?"

Adelia pulled out a chair, not minding too closely whether

the chair's legs smacked into Cal's head. She sat with her legs spread wide to accommodate her belly, resting a foot on Cal's neck. She smiled at Houndstooth, her hands stroking the shifting mass of her stomach.

"Well," she said softly, "what's the job?"

Chapter 7

It was quiet in the swamp. Deep quiet—the kind that's defined by the buzz of insects and the lapping of water and the thick wet heat of the day. The shade of the willow and sycamore trees that grew along the edge of the water dappled the golden light, but their shade wasn't enough to cut through the weight of the heat. The hoppers rode slowly, easily—they shared an unspoken need to enjoy the calm of the swamp. It would be their last peaceful day. Soon, they'd reach the Mississippi Gate, and the chaos would begin.

Adelia rode Stasia, her heavily armored Arnesian Brown, without a saddle. She rode cross-legged, one hand wrapped around her belly; the other gripped the pommel of Stasia's harness. Stasia, an exemplar of her breed, snapped at birds that flew too close to her snout. She grumbled at sticks that bumped into her legs, and squinted suspiciously at the other hippos. And yet, for all her aggression, she seemed devoted to Adelia—Adelia, who swayed with Stasia's rolling gait, occasionally singing nonsense to her in lilting tones. "Stasia, my Anastasia, Ana Aña, Aña-araña . . ."

Neville rode next to her on her second hippo, Zahra. He knelt awkwardly in the borrowed saddle, but Zahra—an aging Standard Grey, nearly identical to Abigail save for the livid bolt of white across her brow—followed Stasia gamely, ignoring the way the boy pitched to and fro in the saddle.

"Miss Adelia, this is so *hard*," he said, out of breath from struggling to maintain his balance. "How come you can do it without even a saddle?"

"I have been doing it since I was in my mother's belly," she replied with a wisp of a smile. "When my little niña is born, she will ride with me, and she will be just as strong as I am. Stronger, perhaps."

"What if it's a boy?" Neville asked, clutching at the saddle.

"It won't be a boy."

Neville stared at her for a few moments without speaking, his eyes lingering on her belly.

"You are wondering about the father," she said, unsmiling. Neville stammered an incoherent denial, his blush destroying his credibility.

"There is no father," Adelia said. "There is a man who gave me the child I wanted from him."

Neville stared hard at his hands. "Alright ma'am," he whispered, mortified. She grinned at his embarrassment.

"I am not ashamed, boy. I have no need of a husband. This girl will have no need of a father. Perhaps a second mother, someday—but if not?" She shrugged. "It makes no difference."

A sharp whistle sounded from behind them, where Archie rode her diamond-white Rosa. Neville twisted in the saddle to look at her, then caught himself on the pommel as he nearly tipped out of the saddle. Adelia whistled back without looking away from the water ahead. Archie's rich, deep laugh carried over the sound of the hippos' splashing progress through the shallows of the swamp.

Ahead of them, Cal, Houndstooth, and Hero rode abreast. Ruby slid through the water like a shadow between runty brown Betsy and Hero's grey Abigail. Shy, sweet Betsy bumped out of the way with a sidelong glance at the sleek black hippo, but Abigail didn't seem to notice her. Ruby came close enough to Abigail that Houndstooth's leg brushed against Hero's. Hero startled.

"I didn't—I didn't hear her get so close," they said, holding their hat on with one hand.

"Well, you wouldn't, would you?" Houndstooth said. "Some things just sneak up on you like that."

Hero tried to stop the smile that spread across their face, but it was too late; Houndstooth was already grinning back.

———

As dusk settled over the marsh, the hoppers clustered closer together. Houndstooth rode in front. Behind him, Adelia, Archie, and Neville clustered together. Hero and Cal rode behind, occasionally shooting wary glances at each other.

"So, I've been wondering," Adelia said. "What is that for?" She pointed at the coiled chain that Archie wore on her hip. "It looks like the strangest bola I've ever seen. I can't imagine using it to disable a man, much less a charging hippo."

Archie smiled. "I adore your idea of small talk, Adelia. This is my meteor 'ammer." She patted the smooth metal ball that swung beside her thigh. "I will show you 'ow it is used sometime. I think you will like it."

"It's really somethin', she showed me on the way here," Neville piped. "She swings the chain around her whole entire body and then she just turns and whips it and *pow!*" He slapped Zahra's flank. The hippo didn't seem to notice. "It just *crunches* whatever she aims it at!"

"I hope I don't have a need to see it in action," Adelia said, "but I would love to see a demonstration." She looked at the meteor hammer and for a moment, genuine affection ghosted her features. "At any rate, we should find a place to tie up," Adelia said. "It's unwise for us to be in the water after sundown."

"Oui," Archie said. "And we should go over the plan for this caper before we turn in."

"Why?" Neville asked.

"It's not a *caper*," Houndstooth replied, sounding irritated. "It's an *operation*. All aboveboard."

"Well, we still need to go over the plan," Adelia snapped.

"If you see a dry patch I don't," Houndstooth said, slapping at a mosquito, "you go right ahead and point it out."

"There was a petit island a mile back or so," Archie mused, "but too small, I think, for all of us."

"Why can't we be out after dark?" Neville asked again.

"Too small for *your* fat ass, maybe," Cal called from the back of the group. Archie's fingertips played over the revolver that hung from her hip.

"He's not worth the bullet," Adelia murmured to her.

"Why shouldn't we be out after dark?" Neville piped.

"I could stab 'im, perhaps," Archie said, giving Adelia a wry smile.

"Si, but then the blood would ruin your lovely blouse."

"Excuse me," Neville said again.

"Strangulation, then. The cleanest death of them all," Archie continued, ignoring him.

"Ask Hero for some poison, maybe?" Adelia and Archie both laughed. Hero smiled from under the brim of their hat. Neville looked back at Hero, eyes wide.

"You have a lot to learn, boy," Hero drawled. "Never stare at someone you're scared of."

Archie smiled over at Neville. "Are you scared of Hero?"

Houndstooth chuckled. "I'd imagine he's scared of all of us."

Hero fanned themself with their hat. "Oh, son. You shouldn't be scared of us. Us, you'll see comin'. No, what you want to be scared of," they said, looking at the boy with a wicked gleam in their eye, "is the *ferals*."

Neville clung to Zahra's back. "I ain't scared of hippos." His voice shook a little.

"Well, young man, there's hippos and there's hippos," Cal said. "Now, Zahra there, she's a sweet thing. Raised by people from when she was just a little hop. Slept next to her hopper's raft every night, ate from her hopper's hand every day. Loyal. Loving. But a feral?" He laughed mirthlessly.

"Let's not scare the boy," Houndstooth said. "He won't be seeing any ferals anyway. They're all between the Gate and the dam, and he won't be going in there with us."

"You never know," Cal intoned.

"Is . . . is that why we have to find a place to camp before nightfall? Because of ferals?" Neville asked.

"That, and Cal is scared of the dark," Archie said loudly. "So let's 'urry it up, oui?" She snapped her fingers twice and Rosa surged ahead, nudging her white nose against Ruby's coal-black flank.

They found an island just as the sun dipped below the horizon. The hum of insects intensified as the last light of the day died, and the hoppers guided their steeds toward the little hump of land that rose out of the water. Archie whistled to Neville. "Would you care to give Rosa's teeth a brush before we turn 'er loose for the night?"

Neville grinned, his sweat-damp blond hair falling into his eyes, and he held up a leather pouch. "I've already got her toothbrush, Miss Archie!" He splashed down the riverbank, cooing to Rosa. The white hippo had already begun to wander away from the sandy bank of the islet. She had been riding all day, and was reluctant to come back to the shore before she'd eaten. The sound of Neville's coaxing entreaties for her to come back for a brushing drifted through the stillness of the dusk, blending with the buzz of cicadas.

"'E is a good kid," Archie said ruefully, settling onto a log beside Hero.

"He's too green to be out here," Hero responded. They pulled out a pocketknife and began scraping the bark off a fat stick.

"Ah, 'e'll be fine. I couldn't leave 'im behind," Archie said. "Rosa, she likes 'im too much for me to tell 'im no, when 'e asked to come. Just like Houndstooth. I could never say no to 'im, either."

The sounds of Houndstooth and Cal arguing over where to start the fire drifted to them through the warm night air.

"You really care about Houndstooth, eh?" Hero asked.

"I could ask you the same question, couldn't I?" Archie responded with a grin. Hero looked up, not returning Archie's smile.

"You know, when I first met Houndstooth, 'e had just had 'is 'eart broken. 'Is dream—it was in ashes. I watched 'im meet someone, a woman. I watched 'im fall in love with 'er."

Hero's brow furrowed, but they did not interrupt.

Archie waved her hand vaguely. "She ran off with a postman. They were going to go north, to the cities. Tried to take Ruby with them, but of course Ruby, she would not go. She is devoted."

Hero considered Archie. "So . . . what happened after that?"

"Ah," Archie said. "Houndstooth started to sow 'is wild oats. As for the girl? Well, I will not say. Houndstooth . . . 'e does not need to know what I did to the girl when I found 'er trying to steal Ruby. But I will tell you this"—Archie looked at Hero, her face serious—"what I did to 'er will look like a kindness, compared to what I will do to anyone who breaks 'is 'eart like that again."

Hero stared into Archie's eyes, unblinking. "I understand."

Archie clapped them on the shoulder, hard, smiling warmly. "I know you do. I can tell. I just 'ad to say it—you know 'ow it is.

Ah, don't be too scared. I think you are good for 'im! You should see 'ow 'e smiles at you when 'e thinks you are not looking. Plus, you keep 'im from thinking 'e is the smartest in the room."

Hero smiled, ducking their head; then, they looked up, the smile suddenly gone. "Did you hear that?"

"What," Archie said, "are they finally just comparing their cocks and 'aving done with it?"

But Hero was already on their feet, running to the water's edge.

They were too late.

By the time Hero had reached the riverbank, Neville was half-submerged in the water. There came a fierce splash, and the boy surged into the air before landing, caught, in the gaping mouth of the feral bull.

He hung in the mouth of the beast, stunned. His left leg hung between the bull's front tusks, the angle wrong. It bled freely, and his blood spilled over the hippo's whiskers. Archie covered her mouth with both hands when she caught up with Hero as though to catch the boy's name even as she shouted it. Cal and Houndstooth looked up and came running. The bull was still for a long, thick moment. Then, with a lightning-quick twist of its thick neck, it snapped its jaws closed.

The boy was dead. There could be no question, even before the feral bull shook him below the water. Archie turned away; Hero put an arm around her, shielding her as much as possible from the bloodied swamp water that sprayed the shore. Cal and Houndstooth stood frozen a few yards from the water's edge, empty-handed. Cal's toothpick dangled from his slack lower lip.

They did not see Adelia coming.

Neither did the hippo.

It wasn't until the beast was bleeding that Houndstooth registered her standing next to him, her arm outstretched toward the hippo as though she was offering it a handshake. Houndstooth looked from her to the bull, which twitched and writhed spasmodically in the frothy pink water.

He put a hand to his pocket, as though he'd find anything there; but of course, it was empty. The long, slender, ivory-handled knife he'd taken from the marshjack back in Georgia was gone. A mere inch of the handle still protruded from the bull's eye socket. The rest of the knife was buried in the beast's brain. A trickle of blood spilled over the hippo's cheek like tears as it gave a final thrash, and then sank below the surface of the water.

As the ripples stilled, Adelia lowered her throwing arm.

"That," Cal said quietly, "is why you shouldn't be in the water after sundown."

Chapter 8

Dragging the hippo's carcass out of the lake wasn't easy, but it had to be done: Rosa, Ruby, Betsy, and Abigail wouldn't approach the shore with the bull's blood pinking the muddy water. Zahra and Stasia were nowhere to be found, but Adelia seemed certain that they'd return at dawn so long as the bull's carcass was gone.

Fortunately, none of the hoppers was a stranger to dead hippos. Archie insisted that she be the one to wade out into the swamp—insisted that it was her fault the boy had been in the water in the first place. She secured a length of rope around her middle and made her way to the hippo while Cal and Houndstooth watched the water, ready to haul her back in if so much as a bubble surfaced nearby. She girded the beast with five separate ropes before splashing back to the shore. They all hauled him onto the sand together, dragging him far enough inland that their hippos wouldn't be disturbed by the smell of their mad, dead cousin. Had they been on a ranch, they'd have butchered the carcass and sold the hide to a tannery; as it was, nobody could bring themselves to take a knife to the creature that had so efficiently slaughtered young Neville.

The exhausted hoppers dried themselves around the fire, not acknowledging the fact that none of them would volunteer to wade back into the river to find Neville's body. Cal was the first to break the silence.

"I think it's time you told us the plan, Winslow. You *do* have a plan?"

Archie looked at him, hollow-eyed. "Yes, 'oundstooth, what is the plan?"

Hero was the one who answered. They reached into their bedroll and pulled out a map of the Harriet, spreading it on the ground a safe distance from the fire and weighing down the corners with empty, whiskey-sticky mugs. The map showed the lake, enclosed parenthetically by the dam to the north and the Gate to the south. The feral's usual territory, near the center of the lake, was marked with a large red circle; the safe travel routes, by blue arrows. The rest of the marks on the map were incomprehensible at first glance.

"Dynamite," Hero said, pointing to a concentric series of red X marks on the map. "Here, here, and here—all around the northern perimeter, just far enough from the dam to be safe. A series of controlled explosions that will drive the ferals toward the Gate." They pointed to the next row of X marks below that. "Then another series, here, and another here, just south of that one. The idea is to keep the detonations behind the ferals, driving them closer to the Gate, not giving them a chance to double back."

"Like a funnel. A hippo funnel," Houndstooth added.

Archie examined the map, nodding. "And we will have the Gate open, right? So they just scoot out into the swamp and then head down to the Gulf?"

"Exactly," Hero said. "We close the Gate behind 'em, spend a few weeks rounding up any stragglers—and then sit back and enjoy the Harriet for the rest of the year."

"And how does the Coast Guard feel about this?" Archie asked.

"Don't worry about it," Houndstooth said peevishly. "The Coast Guard isn't where the money's coming from, so they're not our problem."

"You don't think we should be concerned about the Coast

Guard?" Archie said, incredulity lifting her brows. "Not even a *little* concerned?"

"What, are you Alexander Hamilton's great-great-grandniece twice removed or something?" Houndstooth snapped. "It doesn't *matter*, Archie."

Cal sniffed, wiping his nose on his sleeve. "More important question: who's gonna light the fuses?"

Hero pulled two small black boxes out of their saddlebag, holding them aloft when Cal tried to grab one. "These," Hero said, "are remote detonation devices. I just push this button, and . . . boom."

Cal looked extremely dubious. "Hop shit," he said. "I've never heard of a *remote* detonator."

"That's because I invented them," Hero responded icily.

"I've seen them work," Houndstooth confirmed. He stared at Hero with an admiring smile. "They're amazing."

"Why two?" Archie asked. Hero smiled, enigmatic.

"Always have a backup plan, Archie."

Adelia stared at the map, her lips moving silently for a few moments. Then she frowned, her hands pressing against her belly. "This is a good plan. It will work, so long as you don't get eaten."

Houndstooth cleared his throat. "Hero will be riding Ruby while they set the charges." He said it with a hard look at Hero that spoke to many arguments over this decision. "Ruby can dodge the ferals' notice, and Travers', too."

Adelia glanced at him sharply. "We don't want this Travers to know what we are doing, is that right?"

Houndstooth nodded. "We'll be sticking to the islets, camping without a fire, laying low as we can. Until the job is done. We don't want to get on his bad side, Adelia. Travers is not a man whose eyes you want on you, if you're disrupting his business."

Adelia nodded as she rose from her crouch, rubbing her

lower back. "He sounds dangerous. We should be vigilant." She grabbed her bedroll. "We should also be rested. Goodnight." Without another word, she stalked away from the fire. Archie caught Hero's eye, her brows raised. Hero shrugged in reply.

"She's right," Houndstooth said, rolling up the map. "We should sleep. We ride at dawn—we want to get through the Gate without drawing too much attention to ourselves."

Cal grabbed his bedroll, walking in the opposite direction from the one Adelia had chosen. "Five hoppers on six hippos," he said, loud enough to be heard by all the hoppers. "Shouldn't draw too much attention at all. Real subtle-like, this crew."

Adelia took the hippo's tusks during the night, presenting the cleaned and polished ivory to Archie before dawn.

"I couldn't sleep anyway," she said, bracing the small of her back, her eyes on the water. "The niña kicks me awake."

Archie watched the water, too, rather than watching Adelia's face. Her eyes shone. "I suppose he's still at the bottom."

Adelia shrugged. "There are alligators here, I think. They would not bother us while we are riding, but who can say? I'm sure they get hungry, too."

Archie turned white and went back to polishing Rosa's saddle. Adelia stayed watching the water, chewing her lower lip, until Houndstooth's sharp whistle cut through the morning mist. They left the islet behind before the sun had finished rising. Not a one of them looked back.

The Gate was a thirteen-mile-long grate dividing the Harriet from the southern tip of the Mississippi River. It stood as a testament to Man's Victory over Nature—a brand seared into the landscape, marking it as the property of the federal government. It crossed the narrowest part of Louisiana's Mississippi River and extended inland by six and a half miles, just outside the overland range of all but the most determined ferals.

The openings in the grate were alligator-wide and fish-tall, designed by the finest engineers the government could subsidize to allow everything but boats, hippos, and law-abiding men to pass.

By the time the hoppers arrived at the Gate, the sun was high and hot overhead, and all five of them were dewy with sweat. The Gate bowed toward them in places, the metal warped in the shape of rampaging feral bulls that had seen something worth having on the other side of the grate, but it was intact, and still looked strong. Debris floated in the water around the grate— sticks and leaves that hadn't been cleared by the crew of old soldiers who manned the outpost. Rosa picked through the water around the sticks, lifting her nose high in the air. Archie nudged her forward, peering at the grate. Ruby nosed at the sticks freely, searching for anything that appeared edible and ignoring Houndstooth entirely. Betsy, meanwhile, bowled through the flotsam, kicking up waves of water that soaked Cal to the waist and sent leaves flying at the other hoppers.

As they neared the outpost, they were greeted by the warning report of a rifle. A ranger peered down at them from one of the four high towers that dotted the thirteen-mile-long Gate, his face shaded by a broad-brimmed, sweat-stained hat with a Bureau of Land Management badge affixed to the brim.

"Alrigh' down there," he shouted. "Let's see your badges, just hold 'em high, now. No trouble."

Houndstooth produced a waxed wallet instead. He removed a large sheaf of paper and waved it in the air with one hand, cupping the other around his mouth.

"We don't have badges, but we have a contract with the federal government. We've got free passage."

The ranger peered down at them, mopping his creased brow with a well-worn kerchief. Then, understanding bloomed across his face. "Are you the same Houndstooth what Alberto let through t'other day? Thought he told me you was a British fella."

"Yes, yes, that's me," Houndstooth called back up with a barely perceptible sigh. "Winslow Houndstooth, at your service, my good man. Would you terribly mind letting us through?"

The ranger spat brownly over the side of the Gate, well away from the five riders. "Sure enough, sure enough. Where'll you be staying?"

The voice that answered from beyond the Gate was smoother than a newborn hop's underbelly. "Not to worry, Harold. They'll be staying with me."

The ranger startled so violently that his hat fell off, dropping thirty feet from the tower. Hero caught it neatly, spinning it in their hands.

"Yes sir, Mr. Travers, sir," the ranger said, a quaver in his voice.

"Real subtle-like," Cal muttered to Houndstooth, his hand rising to touch the bandage over his left ear. Then he raised his voice, inclining his head toward the small, sleek man on the other side of the Gate. "Mr. Travers. What a fine surprise this is."

Chapter 9

Travers rested comfortably in the center of his raft. He was surrounded on four sides by hulking men who trained rifles on the water, watching for ripples. "Calhoun. Mr. Houndstooth. Ladies." Hero made a disgruntled sound, and Mr. Travers tipped his hat to them in particular with a cough. "*Et alia.* I look forward to hosting you on the *Sturgess Queen*—my finest boat. Only the best accommodations."

"Oh, we couldn't possibly—" Hero began, but Mr. Travers interrupted.

"It's the least I can do in exchange for the immense services you'll be providing to the government of this great nation," he said with a thin smile. "I quite insist."

Houndstooth was still for a moment, his eyes on the goons' rifles. The Gate let out a ferocious squeal as the ranger pulled the lever to open it. It slid sideways, nesting neatly under the ranger's post. The wake lapped at the hippos' flanks, darkening the waxed leather of their harnesses.

"Well," Houndstooth said to the rest of the hoppers. "I suppose it doesn't change too much if we're aboard the *Sturgess Queen.* Fewer fleas than the Inn, I'm sure." His face was open, and spoke to a pleasantly surprising change in plans. His expression betrayed none of the risk he was being forced to swallow. None of the rage.

It took a full minute for the Gate to open. The five of them walked through abreast, Zahra trailing behind Stasia. As they passed below the ranger's post, Hero flung the man's hat high in the air. It spun like a discus, and the ranger leaned out to catch it. The moment Zahra's tail had passed the threshold, the squeal began again, and the Gate closed behind them.

Behind Travers, the narrow passage of the Gate opened up into the waters of the Harriet. The humid haze of the day didn't quite obscure the massive dam that dominated the horizon behind him, dwarfing the riverboats and pleasure barges that dotted the water. Here and there, a canoe-sized islet bumped up out of the surface of the Harriet. Houndstooth would have expected them to be covered with birds—but then, he supposed the ferals made this a dangerous place to be a bird.

Mr. Travers clasped his hands in front of his chest, staring at the crew with wine-black eyes. His slim, slick moustache twitched over his icy smile. "Welcome to the Harriet."

—◆—

Hero dropped their bag onto the floor of the presidential suite and took the room in. It was small as far as presidential suites went, but it was, according to Mr. Travers, the largest on the *Sturgess Queen*.

"Well," said Houndstooth. "Seems cozy enough, this. If you like red velvet." He ran a hand over the seat of the plush divan that sat under the window. Hero closed their eyes and breathed deeply. Their lips parted just a little, and Houndstooth nearly died with the effort of not noticing it.

"I do."

Houndstooth jumped. "What? You, hm, you what?"

Hero opened their eyes and considered Houndstooth, who was perched on the edge of the divan, stiff-backed, holding his hat in his lap. They cocked their head and smiled.

"I do like red velvet."

Houndstooth moved to the window and twitched the

curtain aside. "What do you make of Travers, then? I don't like that he made us check our guns. 'Standard security procedures,' indeed. I don't like it. I don't like it at all. And did you see the munitions he had stored down there? What, is he expecting a war to break out?" He cleared his throat, smoothed the front of his jacket.

"I think," Hero drawled, crossing the room to join him, "that he's the least of our problems."

Hero stared out the window. Houndstooth stared at Hero. "What's the worst of our problems?"

Hero smiled, watching the water below them. "Well, Winslow. There's only one bed in here." They turned their head, still smiling, and took in Houndstooth's rich pink blush. "And last I counted, there's two of us."

Houndstooth stammered incoherently as Hero chucked him under the chin, then strolled out of the room, easing the door shut behind them. When the latch clicked, Houndstooth collapsed onto the divan. He stared at the bed, willing the heat to dissipate from his cheeks.

—◆◆◆—

Archie and Adelia sat in the wood-paneled main lounge of the *Sturgess Queen*. Adelia's feet rested on a low, claw-footed stool. A glass of ice water sweated in her hand.

"They sure know how to treat a pregnant girl, eh?" She grinned over her glass at Archie, who sat in a wide wicker-backed armchair opposite her, turning the feral bull's tusk over and over in her hands.

"Why are you worried?" Adelia asked. "The worst thing that happens is they try to kill us."

Archie continued worrying at the tusk. She muttered something under her breath.

"Que?"

"I said," Archie replied deliberately, "that I'm not sure it's them I'm worried about."

"What do you mean?"

"I mean they knew that we would be getting to the Gate today. They knew 'ow many of us to expect. They 'ad exactly six spots in the paddock, one for each 'ippo. And they 'ad enough rooms set aside for six people, which means they knew about . . . about Neville."

"So?"

"So," Archie said, her hands going still, "I think that someone told them about us. I think that someone told them what route we would be taking. I think—"

"What's all this about?" Hero said, striding into the lounge.

"Archie thinks that we have a spy in our midst," Adelia said with a crooked grin. Hero looked sharply at Archie.

"A spy?"

"Oui," Archie replied, her brows high. "I inspected the Gate while 'Oundstooth was talking to that 'illbilly ranger. It was sturdy, intact, no recent welding that I could see. And we all know that a 'ippo isn't going to reach higher ramming speeds overland than in the water."

"What's your point, Archie?" Hero asked, not unkindly.

"My point is: if the Gate was not broken, then 'ow exactly did a single feral bull escape the Harriet and find us? Just the one? Not enough for us to notice and change course? I'll tell you how: Monsieur Travers snapped 'is fingers, and that guard let it out. I'd guess that 'appened on the same day we 'it the road. The only question is, who was gone long enough to send a telegram?"

Adelia, Archie, and Hero looked at each other. None of them wanted to be the first to speak.

The doors to the lounge swung open, and Houndstooth

strode in briskly. "Well! Why the long faces, you three? And where's Calhoun?"

Adelia rattled the ice in her glass. "I'd imagine 'e's at the blackjack tables," she said, plucking out an ice cube and pressing it to her neck. "Ay, it's too hot."

"You alright, Adelia?" Hero asked.

"Si, si, it's just—nobody ever told me that having a little girl would make me so hot all the time!"

Houndstooth, being a gentleman, said nothing; he kept his eyes averted from Adelia's ripe belly. Hero, having no such compunctions, laughed heartily. "Get used to it, ma'am. We have a saying where I'm from—boys will make you cry, but girls? Girls will make you sweat."

— ◆◆◆ —

The lamps that lit the riverboat inside and out had come on by the time Archie found Cal on the casino floor. He swayed gently on his stool, and it was readily apparent that bourbon, rather than the rocking rhythm of the boat, was what moved him. Archie pulled up a stool beside him and mentally tallied the cash that rested in stacks on his side of the felt.

" 'Ow are you doing, there, mon ami?" she asked softly. Cal swung his head around to her and grinned broadly. Blood was seeping through the bandage over his left ear. He had two toothpicks in his mouth. One was fresh; the other was chewed nearly to splinters, as though he'd forgotten to discard the old one.

"Archie! Or should I say, *Regina?*" He leered as he said her name, and she thought she could guess what pun he thought he was making.

"Actually, cherie, it's Regina. Rhymes with Pasadena."

His leer dissolved, and he became morose so quickly that Archie feared he would fall off his stool.

"You know Pasadena, oui, Calhoun? That is where you met our Adelia—on a supply trip for Mr. 'Oundstooth, was it not? A decade ago, oui?"

"I don't wanna talk about Adelia," Cal slurred. "I miss Adelia so—" He hiccupped. "—so much, and I don't wanna talk about her. She won'—she won' even talk to me about the baby, Regina. After what I did for her? She came back to me and then, and then she left, an'—I don't wanna talk about her, no, no thank you."

"Ah, of course, of course—" Cal interrupted Archie before she could finish agreeing not to talk about Adelia.

"I met 'er in Pasadena, you know," he said, having already apparently forgotten that Archie had said just that a few moments before. "I met 'er there and I loved—I loved her right away. I was so nice to her, but she just wouldn't even *lookuhme*." He slapped the table with the palm of his hand. "Wouldn't go home with a ranch hand, no sir. Too good for *that*!" His too-loud voice suddenly wobbled. "Too good for *me*. But I showed her, I did everything he asked me to do and *then some*—"

Other patrons of the *Sturgess Queen*'s bar were starting to stare. Archie put a hand on Cal's elbow. "Perhaps we should get you to bed, non? It would appear that you are winning. Best to quit while you are ahead, is it not?"

Cal shook his finger at her, squinting. "Not yet," he said in a stage whisper. "Not yet. I'm not done yet." He turned back to the dealer, who had observed this exchange with the removed patience of experience, and slapped the felt hard enough that one of his stacks of cash fell over. He left his hand where it lay, and his gaze swam up to meet the dealer's eyes. "Himme."

The dealer did as he was told, and Archie saw at once that she should not have allowed Cal to touch the table.

"Twenty-one. Again. Excellent, Mr. Hotchkiss." The dealer smiled at Cal, but his smile did not extend to his eyes. He moved his hand as though to shift more cash to Cal's side of the table, but at the last moment, he seized Cal's wrist instead.

Archie sprang from her stool, her hand going automatically to her empty holster, as the dealer gripped Cal's wrist and waved his other hand in a signal. Mr. Travers appeared as though from thin air, his hands clasped soberly behind his back.

"Well now, Mr. Hotchkiss. What have you been up to?"

The dealer lifted Cal's hand, revealing a single card underneath it.

"This is the fourth card he's swapped, Mr. Travers, sir. I wasn't sure at first, but, well." The dealer smiled at the small army of empty highball glasses that littered the table. "He got sloppy."

Cal looked from the dealer to Travers' unsmiling face, and then to Archie. His expression was that of a boy who has fallen into a well at dusk, and who has yelled himself hoarse with no answer but the rustle of wind through buzzards' wings.

"Mr. Hotchkiss," Travers said, reaching into his breast pocket and pulling out a bloody, folded pocket square. "I believe you'll be needing this back." He tucked the pocket square into Cal's shirt pocket. Cal blanched and started muttering the word "no" under his breath, over and over, like an incantation.

"Mr. Travers, sir, Cal is drunk. Might I take 'im up to his room to sleep this off? He is not 'imself." Archie's voice was dripping honey. Travers regarded her with frank interest.

"Why, Miss Archambault. It is so refreshing to see someone willing to stick up for a friend. But I'm afraid that Mr. Hotchkiss here is a cheat. Ah, ah—" He held up a finger, cutting off her interruption. "He may be drunk, but he is still a cheat. He was a cheat before he was drunk and he'll remain a cheat when he sobers up tomorrow." He took a step away from Cal. The dealer did the same.

Cal bolted for the door. The band stopped playing to watch

him pass. He was fast—but Travers' security goons were faster. They caught him under the arms midstride, hauling him into the air with the brisk efficiency and remorselessness of experience.

"No!" he cried, his legs kicking in the air but finding no purchase as he was dragged bodily across the casino floor. "No, wait, Mr. Travers, sir, please! You can't, you can't—after what I did for you? After what I did to that British bastard for you? Please, sir, I won't—I wasn't—"

Travers laid his fingertips on Archie's arm, as though to comfort her. "Watch now."

And she did. She watched as Travers' men paused at the window. Cal's eyes roamed the room, sightless with terror. He screamed. He begged.

Travers' men did not seem to hear. They swung him once— heave-ho, and his toothpicks fell to the floor—then hurled him bodily through the open window.

He screamed as he fell; the splash seemed to echo in the silent casino. Then, he screamed again. It was not a scream of terror, but a scream of pain.

After a moment, the screaming stopped—but the splashing continued.

Travers clapped his hands once in front of his chest, then addressed the now-silent patrons who filled the gambling tables of his casino. "Ladies and gentlemen, my apologies for the disruption!" He turned to the bar. "To make up for it, a round of champagne for everyone, on the house!"

Travers signaled the band, and the music started playing once again. He laid his fingertips lightly upon Archie's arm once more as the casino floor erupted in cheers.

"I hope, Miss Archambault, that you can understand. Mr. Hotchkiss was a thief, and I cannot abide thieves." His use of the past tense was not lost on Archie. "I, of course, would not even *begin* to consider allowing his shortcomings to color my opinions of the rest of your little hopper gang."

Archie managed a smile, and touched his fingertips with her own. "I . . . I am so grateful, Mr. Travers. We 'ad no idea that Cal—" But she saw his wry, knowing smile and started again. "Of course, we knew that he was a scoundrel, but we would never imagine that he would besmirch your 'ospitality so."

"Of course not, Miss Archambault. Of course not." A waiter approached holding a silver tray of glasses, and Travers handed one to Archie before taking one for himself. He touched his glass to hers, making the crystal sing.

"Cheers, Miss Archambault. May you enjoy your stay on the *Sturgess Queen,* and the very best of luck in all your endeavors."

"Santé," Archie answered, and drained her glass without looking away from Travers' twinkling eyes. Travers signaled the band to play louder, and they did—but the music couldn't mask the bellowing of the ferals fighting over their feast in the river below.

Chapter 10

"I'm not sure I understand what you mean, Archie." Houndstooth's voice was low. If Archie hadn't known better, she'd have thought he was furious. But she did know better—she'd saved the man's life somewhere between nine and a half and ten times, and she knew his moods better than her own.

So she knew that he was perched on the edge of panic.

"Dead means dead, mon ami. Nothing more to it."

Houndstooth ran his hands through his hair as he paced back and forth, staring at the carpet. Hero, seated on the divan, followed him with their eyes. "But . . . but if he's dead, then— then I can't—then I didn't—"

Archie put a quelling hand on his shoulder. "Perhaps it is best this way, non?" she whispered. "Without the revenge."

He looked up at her, his eyes flashing. "How did you know?"

She looked uncomfortable. Before she had to answer—before she had to tell him what Cal had said just before he died—the door banged open. Adelia stared in at the two of them. "Well, Archie. I suppose this means you and I each get our own suite."

"It also means we're all up to our necks in the bog without so much as a hop to ride," Houndstooth said in a clipped voice. "We can't do this without Cal." He began to pace the suite, running his hands through his hair.

Hero didn't look up from their whittling. "If you're so beside yourself about it, Winslow, I can chew on toothpicks and sling racial slurs with the best of 'em. Might need to practice some, but I'm sure I can get in fightin' shape by mornin'."

Houndstooth laughed—a genuine, easy laugh—and then sat heavily on the bed next to Archie.

"Look around the room, Hero. What's missing?"

Hero glanced around the suite. "Palpable body odor."

Houndstooth laughed again, but this time, the laugh seemed forced. Adelia and Archie exchanged a glance.

"We're missing a white boy," Adelia murmured, stroking her belly.

"So what?" Archie huffed. "If we need one so bad, I am sure I can drag one back up here for you, Winslow. There's no shortage."

Houndstooth was staring at Hero. Hero stared back at him for a long moment.

"What is it? What are we failing to understand here, Winslow? What's so tough about pulling off this hippo caper without Cal on board?"

Houndstooth dropped his head into his hands. "We need your supplies, Hero. And nobody on the Harriet is going to sell your supplies to a stranger, not even for easy money. We've been corresponding with a dealer and he's expecting Cal to come buy the goods from him, and we're working with him on the strength of Cal's reputation on the Harriet. He's expecting Cal. He's expecting a white man with a terrible mistake of a moustache." He rubbed his face with his hands, groaning. "And it's *not a caper;* it's an *operation.*"

Hero whittled faster, sending hickory shavings flying into the plush red carpet. "Right, right. All aboveboard. So, ask your federal boy. I'm sure the army can send something."

Houndstooth looked uncomfortable. "I can't ask him."

Hero's lips quirked into a half smile. "Oh, honestly. You're *embarrassed?*"

Houndstooth scowled at them. "No, I'm not *embarrassed,* it's just that—he doesn't know what we're going to do, here. He's assuming we'll net each feral, one by one, and escort them out of the swamp. That's why the contract is for a full *year.*"

Adelia swore under her breath. "That's . . . idiotic."

"That's dangerous," Archie added.

"That's why we're not doing it that way," Houndstooth said. Houndstooth slapped the edge of the map, his cheeks pink. "It was a great goddamned plan, and it's *sunk.*" Hero put a calming hand on his arm. His cheeks reddened further.

"So we need a white boy por quoi? To buy dynamite?"

Hero nodded. "Lots of it. And detonators. Fuses, timers— oh, and wax. A lot of wax."

Archie left the room without saying another word.

"Where is she going?" Adelia asked.

"Probably to go charm some poor kid into buying Hero's groceries," Houndstooth replied. "I suppose that's why she's on the team—she could talk a hippo into thinking it was a rhinoceros without breaking a sweat."

A few minutes later, the door burst open again. Adelia smirked.

"Giving up so soon, eh Ar—oh," she said.

Archie stood in the doorway, transformed. She'd slicked her hair down on either side of a part so razor sharp it put Houndstooth's to shame. Her pinstriped breeches and satin waistcoat had been exchanged for a flawlessly tailored three-piece linen suit. She spun a matching bowler hat between her hands. Her boots were half-covered by diamond-white spats. A blond moustache— one that would have kept Cal up at night with envy—bristled its way across her upper lip.

She had become an impeccably outfitted gentleman.

"You needed a white boy, oui?" she asked, her voice pitched an octave lower than usual. "Et voilà."

Houndstooth gaped at her as Hero crossed the room to examine her. "Where did you get this suit?" Hero asked. "I don't mean any offense, but I can't imagine you just grabbed it off some poor mark in the hallway just now. And that moustache— good God, Archie, it's nothing like Cal's, but it'll *do*!"

"I keep it around for special occasions," Archie replied with a grin. "Sometimes my heart calls more to suits than skirts. It is fluid, oui?" She waved her hand vaguely through the air. "It changes. The tailor, 'e was confused when I told 'im what I wanted, but for the right price, anything can be 'ad. Isn't that right, Adelia?"

Adelia's head snapped up from where she was staring at the map. "Que?"

Houndstooth seemed to come to his senses. "Archie, you . . . you brilliant woman, I could kiss you!"

Archie and Hero both scowled. "You will ruin my moustache, 'Oundstooth. Best to keep that kiss for someone who wants it, eh?" She placed the bowler hat on her head and turned to Hero, whose eyes went wide.

"Do you 'ave a list for me?"

"A list? Oh! A list. Of course, yes, let me just—" Hero scrambled for paper and scrawled out a list of supplies, handing it to Archie.

"Well, my friends, off I go. I expect all three of you to be drunk at the bar by the time I return." She tipped a wink at Hero. "We must make a good show of enjoying our stay on the *Sturgess Queen*, non?"

—◆◆◆—

Archie didn't return until the wee hours of the morning. As she and Rosa approached the dock, she looked around at the

Harriet. She hadn't really paid attention to it the day before—
she had been more focused on the guns Travers' goons were
carrying. Through the night, it had been too dark to really take
in. As the sky began to lighten, she realized that the Harriet was
precisely what she had expected: a huge, flat, muddy stretch of
water, dotted with tiny islets and bracketed by humps of dogwood-
covered land. She found herself wishing it was more beautiful,
more shaded and lush—but then, she thought, it would be good
marshland for hippos rather than a prison for ferals and riverboat
thugs.

She unloaded Rosa's saddlebags onto the floating dock that
bridged the gap between the *Sturgess Queen* and the paddock.
She brushed Rosa's teeth and put medicated drops into the albino hippo's pink eyes. Then, she sang Rosa a short lullaby and
began dragging her load aboard the boat.

She tapped on the door to Hero and Houndstooth's cabin
with one fingernail, then with two. When there was no answer,
she gave a single rap on the door with her knuckle.

Hero answered the door, breathless, still tying the belt of a
robe around their waist. Their eyes were glassy—their lips, swollen. Archie grinned wickedly.

"I'm glad to see you, too, 'Ero." She thrust the saddlebag at
Hero and turned to leave.

"Wait," Hero panted. "Wait, this isn't—this can't be enough.
I need at least four times this much dynamite."

Archie turned back, her eyes still glinting with delight.
"Ah, well, you see. They were all out of dynamite." She patted
the top of the bulging saddlebag. "This is something different.
Something . . . better. You'll see. We will discuss it further in
the morning, oui? You're busy now, and I'm so very sleepy."
She yawned theatrically. "Off to bed with both of us, is it
not?"

She sauntered away down the hallway, pulling off the false moustache. "Oh, 'Oundstooth," she murmured to herself, a smile overtaking her face as she remembered the longing look on Winslow's face when Hero had touched his arm the day before. "I can't save you this time, mon copain. You're done for."

———◆◆◆———

Archie, Hero, and Houndstooth met in the lounge at noon, each of them still blinking sleep from their eyes. Adelia was already seated in her chair, a small armory's worth of freshly whetted knives on a table by her side. The knife she was sliding along the whetstone was familiar; Archie noticed it before Houndstooth did.

"I thought that thing was lodged too deep in the bull's brain to get out? And—'ow did you get those back from Travers? I thought they were all locked away . . . ?"

Adelia grinned and continued sharpening Houndstooth's ivory-handled blade. "I'm determined, Archie. Determination is everything. Besides, I had a few years of saving Cal's pistol-ridden ass. You know how it is, in the water."

Archie watched Adelia's expert hands work. "I do know 'ow it is. Knives are a 'opper's best friend. Pistols that can't get wet, on the other 'and? A nightmare."

Adelia laughed. "Well, Cal was an idiot, wasn't he? I told him, a hopper with no knives is a dead hopper. But he didn't want to listen." She lowered her voice in a perfect imitation of Cal. " 'Well, actually, Adelia, a gun is more effective at a distance.' See how well that worked out for him, hm?"

Hero and Houndstooth walked to the dining room for coffee, their heads tilted toward each other as they walked. Archie sat across from Adelia, her elbows resting on her knees.

"Adelia, mind if I ask you a question?"

Adelia did not look up from the knife. "Yes. It's Cal's baby. No, I am not sorry that he's dead."

Archie shifted uncomfortably. "Well, that's . . . that's good to know, but it's not what I was going to ask."

That made Adelia look up. Her face was, for the first time, completely open—Archie realized she had not seen plain emotion on the woman's face before.

"What would you like to know, Archie?"

"I don't mean any offense, of course—you are incredibly skilled, obviously you are an asset. But . . . why are you 'ere?"

Adelia's face split into a wide, white smile. Archie realized that one of Adelia's canines was made of gold, and she was reminded strongly of Ruby's deadly sharp tusks.

"Why, Archie. I'm here to kill you."

Archie was startled into laughter. Adelia went back to sharpening Houndstooth's knife. She tested it against her thumbnail, then returned it to the whetstone.

"What? Me?"

"Well, not *you* precisely. But, all of you. Everyone on the team."

Archie went very still. "I think perhaps I misunderstand your joke, madame."

"Oh, it's not a joke," Adelia said, although her smile had not faltered. "I'm here to kill you all. If anyone goes rogue, if anyone tries to steal the money, if anyone sabotages the plan. I'm supposed to keep an eye on you, per the boss."

"You mean the Bureau of Land Management? Or 'Oundstooth?"

Adelia did not reply.

"Aha," Archie said. "So you're keeping an eye on us for this 'boss' of yours. But who keeps their eye on *you*, Adelia Reyes?"

Archie stood after a long, silent moment, and walked into the dining room after Houndstooth and Hero. Adelia watched her go, testing the knife on her thumbnail once more. This time, she found it more than sharp enough.

Chapter 11

They met the next day in Hero and Houndstooth's suite to assemble the bombs that would drive the ferals to the Gate.

"So," Hero said, staring into Archie's saddlebag.

"The man I bought it from, Mr. Wolffenstein? 'E said you would know what it is. 'E called it 'the Mother of Satan'?"

"Madre del Diablo?" Adelia asked. "I've heard of that before, I think. But I thought it was just a *rumor.*"

Hero took a rapid step away from the saddlebag. "No, no, it's not a rumor at all, Adelia. Triacetone triperoxide." They aimed a pointed look at Archie. "It's *extremely* volatile."

Archie shrugged. "Wolffenstein said it was so pure that it could be considered relatively stable."

Hero pulled a single tiny white crystal out of the saddlebag and threw it to the ground. It exploded with a loud pop.

"... .'e said *relatively,*" Archie said with a shrug.

"Well then *you* can be the one to handle it," Hero replied. "I hope you brought gloves."

Archie pulled a pair of long leather gloves from the back pocket of her green breeches. " 'Ero, darling, I *always* bring gloves."

For the remainder of the afternoon, Adelia sat cross-legged on the divan, massaging wax into leather pouches, rendering them effectively waterproof. Archie filled each wallet with the tiny white crystals of madre del Diablo, then handed each one to Hero, who inserted wires and bits of metal in a configuration that seemed to make sense to them and them alone. Archie asked what Hero was doing, and the response was in no way illuminating.

"Would you like to discuss the inner workings of a blasting cap, Archie? Because we can discuss the inner workings of a blasting cap, if that's what you're looking for here."

Archie had groaned and shoved Hero's shoulder. "If you don't want to tell me, then don't tell me." Hero had grinned and gone back to work, and Archie had caught Houndstooth beaming at them.

After Hero had finished doing whatever it was they were doing to make the bombs sufficiently dangerous, they wrapped each leather pouch around itself a few times. There was more room than they needed, since the crystals were so much smaller and lighter than the dynamite Hero had been expecting.

"You've worked out the equivalency, I suppose?" Houndstooth asked.

"More or less," Hero replied. "We might get a little bigger bang than we expected, but I think it'll all even out in the end. Don't worry, Houndstooth. This hippo caper will go off without a hitch."

Houndstooth opened his mouth to reply, and they all responded with him: "It's *not a caper*; it's an *operation*."

The final step was left to Houndstooth. He had a pot of melted wax, kept liquid by water boiled in his travel kettle—Adelia had rolled her eyes at him for bringing it, but there wasn't an inn north of Lafayette that could brew an acceptable pot of tea. He sealed each leather pouch, pouring wax over the seams.

After the first one was finished, he held it up. It was about the size of both his hands, and didn't look remotely dangerous.

"Are you certain that this will be enough of a bang, Hero?"

Hero looked up at him with a half smile. "I think I know how to create a *bang*, Houndstooth."

Houndstooth's ears turned violet, and he didn't speak again until they had finished making all twenty bombs.

—◆—

That evening, Hero prepared to ride into the Harriet to set up the bombs. Houndstooth accompanied them to the dock at dusk, carrying one of the two loaded saddlebags that they'd need to take out onto the water.

"Now, remember, don't place the charges too close—"

"Too close to the dam, I know. You've only told me a thousand times, Winslow." Hero smiled. "I know the dam has a crack. I know we don't want to be the ones to blow it. Trust me, why don't you?"

Abigail waited for Hero dockside, impatient. She blew bubbles in the water when she saw them approaching. Houndstooth looked at her apologetically, then whistled for Ruby, who slipped up to the dock like butter sliding across the bottom of a hot pan.

"You don't have to go alone, you know," Houndstooth said, dropping his saddlebag.

Hero regarded him with their steady gaze. "Oh, Winslow. If I didn't know better, I'd think you were worried about me."

Houndstooth rubbed the back of his neck. "Maybe I just want to go with you. Keep you company."

Hero dropped their saddlebag beside his, taking his hand. "Or maybe you don't know how to stay behind?" Houndstooth grimaced at the insight. "I'll be with Ruby. You can't come with me, not riding Abigail—she's louder in the water than a passel of fighting alligators, and if she sees ferals, she'll probably try to make friends. Besides, you need to stay here. If Travers catches wind of this . . . you can say I went rogue, that you didn't know I had this planned. You can say that the whole idea was to get the hippos out one at a time, nice and slow, like they thought. If they catch both of us, though—it would be bad for everyone,

Houndstooth. You know that." Hero kept going before Houndstooth could interrupt them. "Plus, you've got to dispose of the rest of the madre del Diablo—it only took about half of what Archie brought to get us set up, and we don't want to leave that stuff lying around."

Houndstooth was silent for a long moment, staring at Hero's face as though trying to find a constellation in a sea of stars. "I wish you weren't so damnably *brilliant,* Hero. You've thought of everything, haven't you?" He touched Hero's face with a tentative hand. "You'll be a hero, Hero. If this works. You'll be a *hero.* I just don't want you to be a *dead* hero."

"I'll be fine," Hero said, smiling. "Ruby's the best there is. She won't let anything happen to me. You can trust her, and you can trust me. You don't have to w—"

But Hero's words were stopped by Houndstooth's mouth on theirs, his hands on their waist. "I do trust you, you know," he whispered against their lips—and just like that, there was nothing left to say.

—◆◆◆—

Adelia found Houndstooth at the bar half an hour later. He was already half drunk, and well on his way to getting whole drunk, if the speed at which he gulped his whiskey meant anything.

"Mind if I join you?" she said, hoisting herself onto a bar stool.

"Of course, please do," he said politely, signaling the bartender to get her a glass of water.

"Ever the gentleman."

"Ever the Englishman, you mean," he replied, speaking into his nearly empty glass.

Adelia handed Houndstooth the ivory-handled knife. "Here—cleaned and sharpened. Sorry for, you know." She gestured to his jacket pocket, wiggling her fingers. "Reaching in there, like that. Without asking first."

Houndstooth turned the knife in his hand a few times, examining the blade. "It looks better than it has since I got it. You have a gift, Adelia."

She smiled. "I suppose you could say I have the touch." She sipped her water. "You left England to open a ranch here in the States, didn't you, Houndstooth?"

He nodded. "Left home for good when I was fifteen. It was all I wanted. I didn't know any better."

"Do you miss it?"

"What? England? Every day. And, not at all. They didn't like me there, you know," he said, swaying a little on his bar stool. "They didn't like a damn thing about me, other than my name."

Adelia laughed. "I meant being a rancher. You used to own a ranch, sì? You used to breed your very own, like Ruby." She put a hand on his arm, steadying him, then quickly withdrew her hand.

Houndstooth signaled for another drink. "I'd rather not discuss it, if you don't mind. It ended . . . badly. And I am, after all, English. We don't like to *discuss*."

"It's okay," she said, resting a hand on her belly. "I actually already know about what happened. About the fire. Cal told me." She watched Houndstooth closely. He stared into the glass of brown liquor that appeared in front of him.

"Did he now?" he murmured to the whiskey. "Did he tell you?"

Adelia waited.

"Did he tell you?" Houndstooth repeated. "Did he tell you about who burned down my ranch? Did he tell you about why he hid on the Harriet for all these years, knowing Travers wouldn't let me in? Oh, he knew," Houndstooth said, mistaking Adelia's stillness for doubt. "Travers would never let me through the Gate. I turned him down when he asked me to help introduce more vicious strains into the feral population. He spent years trying to change my mind, but I wouldn't budge. Frankly, I'm surprised he didn't burn my ranch down himself—" He glanced over at Adelia, understanding dawning across his face. She interrupted, talking fast and low.

"Don't you ever wish you could go back to it, Houndstooth? Just . . . leave this place, give up the capers, give up the vendetta? Just take the money and run?"

He stared at her, his brow knit. "Run?"

"You know." She made a shooing motion with her hands. "*Leave.*"

He shook his head, and it made him sway hard. "I can't just—"

She grabbed his face in both hands, steadying him. She looked into his eyes with urgent intensity—he feared for a moment that she was going to try to kiss him. She hissed through her teeth. "Forget what you came here to do, Houndstooth. Forget revenge. *Leave. Leave tonight.*"

"'Oundstooth, you rascal, I 'ave been looking for you everywhere!" Archie's voice filled the bar, and Adelia jumped away from Houndstooth. He looked at her as though she'd suddenly grown hippo ears, bewilderment writ plain across his normally stoic Englishman's face. Archie stood in the doorway, beaming, and walked toward them.

"Adelia, ma nénette, 'ow are you feeling? Do your feet pain you at the end of such a long day? Ah, I thought they might, so I asked the bellboy to prepare you a soak of warm water and lavender in the lounge." Ignoring Adelia's protests, Archie helped her down from the barstool and began walking her toward the lounge. "I asked 'im to bring a little glass of wine with honey in it, to settle the bébé." Her voice was as bright as the edge of a freshly sharpened knife. "I know she 'as been kicking you *right in the gut* these past few days."

They rounded the corner to the lounge, leaving Houndstooth to stare, lost, into his whiskey at the bar. The moment he was out of sight, Archie rounded on Adelia, sticking a finger into her face.

"What the hell do you think you are doing?"

Adelia's nostrils flared. She jutted her jaw toward Archie, saying, "It's called *flirting*."

Archie snorted. "I would 'ardly call it anything that advanced. What are you thinking? For the first time in the ten years I've known 'im, 'e likes someone who's worth 'is time. You stay out of it, Adelia." Archie's eyes went wide with surprise as she registered pain in her side.

"I'd gut you right here, if I didn't think he'd jump on the blade right after you," Adelia whispered. Her knife dug into Archie's side, the point of it pressed between her ribs. "If there's one thing I know about Winslow Houndstooth, it is that he cannot be tied down, no matter how much he 'likes' the latest flower he's landed on." An ugly, brittle smile crept across her face. "Just because he wouldn't have you—"

Archie cut her off with a laugh. " 'E's not my type, cherie. Put your knife away. You're embarrassing yourself, even more 'ere than you were at the bar." She took a deft step away from Adelia's blade, and turned to walk back into the bar. "Try to calm yourself down, eh?" She called over her shoulder. "I think the baby is making you crazy."

Adelia stared after her. Archie's voice drifted back to her from the bar—"Ah, Houndstooth, right where I left you! 'Ow about some water to befriend the whiskey in your belly, eh? You should be keeping your wits about you during our big caper."

"It's not a *caper*—" came the weary reply.

Adelia looked down at the knife in her hand; a drop of Archie's blood fell from the tip of the blade to the plush red carpet at her feet. It blended right in.

"Well, well, well. Miss Reyes," came a smooth, sleek voice from the shadows of the lounge. "What on earth have you been up to?"

———

Hero finished rigging the bombs in the wee hours of the morning. They were pleased by the simplicity of the setup; each one of the waxed-leather wallets was fixed to the top of an existing buoy in the Harriet, keeping them safe from accidental bumps and early detonation. The wax was a precaution—one never knew what might happen to a buoy during a stampede of ferals—but Hero felt fairly confident that the risk of immersion was low, and that the chances of success were incredibly high.

As they nudged Ruby toward the floating dock next to the hippo paddock of the *Sturgess Queen,* Hero raised one hand to their lips, and felt a smile lingering there. Houndstooth. He had a reputation—every one of the hoppers on this team had a reputation—but he had turned out to be so much more than an English snob with a taste for pretty eyes. Hero wondered what would happen when the job was over—would they go home together, to Hero's little house with its little pond? Retirement alone had been dull, and lonely, and not the respite they'd so needed. But what if Houndstooth were there? Maybe sitting on the porch and drinking sweet tea and watching the fireflies come out wouldn't be such a lonesome proposition anymore. Maybe it would be the peaceful retirement they'd been hoping for when they bought the little house with the little pond.

Maybe, Hero thought, closing the paddock gate and turning Ruby loose.

Maybe.

They walked up the dock, exhausted, and walked into the entryway of the *Sturgess Queen.* Upstairs, they knew, Houndstooth would still be awake, watching the window for their return. They could sleep beside him for a few hours, before it was time for the action to begin.

To Hero's surprise, there were voices in the lounge. The *Sturgess Queen was* supposed to be empty during the night—all the gamblers and drinkers headed to the Inn or to one of Travers' pleasure barges to recover from their losses and their headaches. The voices that Hero heard weren't shouting over a craps table, though. They were soft ones—voices that didn't want to be heard. Hero paused at the foot of the stairs when they heard a familiar accent drifting through the doorway.

"Their plan will work. And it will work quickly. It's going to happen today—the ferals will be gone by nightfall."

Adelia. The skin on the back of Hero's neck prickled.

"Oh, *Adelia.* Did you even *try* to seduce the Englishman?" The voice that answered Adelia was rich, smooth. Slick. *Travers.* Hero swore under their breath. *Archie was right.*

"I told you, I don't do seduction. Besides, the French one got in the way, and I—"

"Ah, excuses. I—that knife would be put to better use elsewhere, Miss Reyes," came Travers' reply. "In Miss Archambault's heart, for example? In Mr. Houndstooth's gullet?" Hero covered their mouth with both hands as Travers suggested ways to kill the hoppers with all the insouciance of a maître d' reading off the specials.

"The time for manipulation and the arrangement of coincidences is over, Adelia," Travers continued, his voice growing cool. "I've been willing to work with you to maintain your illusion of camaraderie, but now we do things my way." A creak and a rustle of cloth. "I have business to attend to out on the water tonight. Find me back here before noon. Bring Houndstooth's tongue with you as proof that you've done your job. No ears or toes, do you understand? That's a good girl."

Hero heard Adelia shout something that had the cadence of a vicious epithet. A door slammed—one or both of them leaving the room via a different entrance. Hero immediately turned to creep up the stairs to their room, each step cautious and silent. They moved slowly, trying to keep the boat from creaking under the weight of their footfalls.

They had to tell Houndstooth. They had to tell him, and they had to do—what? Something. Anything.

But then the door behind them swung open, and it was too late.

Adelia's face was already contorted with restrained rage from her conversation with Travers. When she saw Hero standing there, so close to the door to the lounge that it was impossible for them not to have heard everything, her expression dropped into something like relief.

"Hero," she said, a slow smile spreading across her lips. "I suppose you've finished rigging the bombs? I suppose you haven't been up to tell Houndstooth that you were successful? I suppose you just wanted a word, before you go up to bed?"

Hero took several steps backward, but they were too late to dodge Adelia's lightning-quick knives. They didn't even see her hand move before they felt the pain in their gut. Hero dropped their hands to the hilt of the knife that protruded from their belly like the stump of a silvery umbilicus.

"I—"

Before they could so much as begin making an appeal to Adelia—an appeal for what? For mercy? Surely it was too late for that—Hero felt a blow strike them in the chest, like a punch.

And there, like magic, the hilt of another knife had sprouted from their chest.

Hero fell to the plush red carpet of the entryway, at the bottom of the stairs. They looked up the stairs, away from Adelia, toward the suite where Houndstooth was waiting for them. They wanted to scream, to shout, to warn him—but it was so hard to draw breath. They hiccupped with pain, and tasted copper. They fought; they struggled, and managed to draw a single lungful of air.

"No no, dulce Hero. Sin gritando." Adelia's whisper was right next to Hero's ear. The last thing Hero saw before they passed out was Houndstooth, standing at the top of the stairs, his mouth open in a scream to answer the one for which Hero had been unable to find breath.

Chapter 12

Archie sat on the divan and watched Houndstooth pace.

"Cherie, you should 'ave a drink. Sit down. Something. You are driving me crazy with this pacing."

"I can't sit down. Not until we decide what to do with *her.*"

Adelia sat in the high-backed chair, bound by lashings of rope. Her head lolled to one side. A significant bruise marred her head where Archie had struck her with a well-flung hammer strike as she had attempted to run away from Hero's still body.

Hero lay on the bed, their breathing ragged, their wounds packed with the torn scraps of one of Houndstooth's silk shirts. The wounds had not been shallow, but Hero's sternum had stopped Adelia's knife from hitting their heart, and the blood pouring from their belly had slowed just enough to give Houndstooth a shiver of hope.

"You're certain she's been spying?" Houndstooth asked Archie for the hundredth time. Archie lifted a handful of papers she'd found in Adelia's belongings: a contract, signed in Adelia's loopy cursive and Travers' delicate calligraphy.

"'Oundstooth? 'Oundstooth. *Winslow Remington 'Oundstooth, look at me,*" Archie commanded. Houndstooth stopped and obeyed, staring at her with lost eyes, his hands limp by his sides.

"We 'ave to kill her, 'Oundstooth. We 'ave to kill her and then we 'ave to run. Now. Tonight."

"Leaving, are you?" came a low drawl from the doorway. They hadn't heard Gran Carter enter, but there he was, leaning against the doorframe: six feet three inches of coiled muscle.

His hands were nowhere near the two six-shooters that dangled from his hips, but Houndstooth and Archie both froze as though he were pointing the guns directly at them.

"I don't believe we've had the pleasure, Mr. Houndstooth." He extended his hand to Houndstooth, who shook it out of sheer reflex. "Gran Carter, U.S. marshal. You have something I've been looking for." He tipped his black hat at Archie. "Good to see you again, Archie. How've you been?"

"I 'ave been well, Gran. I 'ave been . . . busy. I'm sorry I 'aven't written." Archie sounded like she meant it.

"Oh, that's fine. I know how time gets away from you." He took a small step toward her, a smile twitching at the corners of this mouth. "I've missed you."

Archie looked at her hands, worrying at the contract that sat in her lap. "Now is not the time, Gran."

Gran cleared his throat, looking to Houndstooth. "Mr. Houndstooth. I believe you're in charge of this hippo caper?"

Houndstooth looked simultaneously pained and affronted. "It's not a caper, Mr. Carter." Behind him, Archie mouthed the words along with him. "It's an *operation,* all aboveboard. We were hired by the federal government, I'll have you know, and—"

"Oh, my apologies, Mr. Houndstooth. I misspoke. *Of course* it only makes sense that the federal government of the United States of America would hire a team of down-and-out criminals for a caper on the Harriet."

"It's not a *caper*—"

"Yes, well. At any rate." Carter grinned at Archie. "Miss Reyes is none of your concern. She's hardly a member of your crew at this point, is she?"

Houndstooth seemed uncertain as to how he should respond. Adelia had been a member of the crew until thirty minutes before; but now, with Hero's blood on her hands?

"I'll make this easy," Carter said, with the same relaxed grin. "Miss Reyes here is a fugitive, and I've been chasing her down these past five years now. She killed two good men in Arizona while she was on the run from California ten months ago—where she killed three more good men—and I'm near about fed up with her giving me the slip. I arranged with my contact at the Bureau of Land Management to get her on board for this here caper, and to make *sure* she'd be on the Harriet." Houndstooth opened his mouth to interrupt, but Carter didn't give him an opening. "I've been tracking her ever since. I was going to wait until the caper was done to pick her up, but seeing as how you've got her all trussed for me, and Travers is out of the way?" He spread his hands in a gesture of acquiescence to fate. "Seems to me the time is ripe." He gestured to Hero. "I'll even take your friend here to a doctor on my way out of town. It looks like you've done well by them, but that?" He pointed at the wound in Hero's stomach. "That's more than you can handle."

Archie and Houndstooth looked at each other. Archie spoke first. "Travers—do you know where 'e is? They were working together."

"Ah," Carter said, "last I saw, he was on a raft heading toward the dam."

"Gran, do you mind if we confer for a moment?" Archie asked seriously.

"You go right on ahead. I'll get this package all wrapped up and ready for transport," Carter responded, unhooking a pair of heavy manacles from his belt and turning to Adelia.

Houndstooth and Archie stepped into the hall. Houndstooth stared over his shoulder at Carter as the door swung shut.

"Will Adelia be . . . safe, with him?" he asked Archie, rubbing at his eyes.

" 'E will not be unkind to 'er, if you are worried. Not that she deserves kindness," Archie growled. "And if she dies, and 'Ero makes it to a doctor? I think it will 'ave been worth the risk, non?" Winslow cringed. "Winslow, you are exhausted. You should get some rest before we leave. If Travers went all the way to the dam, we 'ave at least an 'our before he returns. I will pack. You sleep."

"No, no," Houndstooth said, looking up at her with urgency. "I don't want to sleep, Archie. And I don't want to leave. I want to finish the job we came here to do."

Archie looked at Houndstooth as though he'd claimed to hear a hippo singing a French lullaby. "What? 'Oundstooth, you . . . you aren't in your right mind. I know you're worried about 'Ero, but—we can't do it. We don't 'ave any way to set off the bombs, and even if we did, we 'ave no way to know 'ow to do it, and even if we *did* know 'ow to do it, we don't know when to detonate the charges, and—"

Houndstooth shook his head. "You're wrong, Archie. For once in your life, you're completely wrong. I've never felt so clear about what we need to do. We need to do the job. I promised Hero that they'd be a *hero*—that their name would be in children's history books for decades to come, as the mastermind behind the bombs that cleared the hippos out of the Mississippi." His eyes had taken on a wild gleam. "And we're going to do it. We're going to get Hero's name in the history books, goddamn it. Whether the job is legitimate or not. When Hero wakes up, I'm going to go and tell them about how their plan worked. And as for the bombs?"

He reached into his pocket and pulled out a slim black device: Hero's detonator.

"They gave me this before they left to set up the bombs. 'Just in case.' Just in case something happened." He laughed, a lost, wild laugh, and Archie's brow furrowed further.

" 'Oundstooth," she murmured. "I 'ave to tell you something. I should 'ave told you before, but—" She took a deep breath, then rushed through her excuse. "But you 'ave spent so many years hating Calhoun, and when 'e died, it seemed like maybe you would be able to let this go. Like maybe you would be able to stop chasing revenge."

Houndstooth looked at her out of the corner of his eye. "You sounded like Adelia for a moment there."

"If you're determined to go through with this, I'll be with you. You know that I wouldn't let you do this alone. But we might not both make it out of 'ere, so I 'ave to tell you before we set out." She looked at Houndstooth as though hoping he'd interrupt, but he simply watched her with terrible patience. She took another deep breath, steeling herself. "Cal—right before 'e died, 'e said that 'e had betrayed you for Travers. I think . . . Winslow, friend. I think Travers put 'im up to it. Travers is the reason your ranch burned down."

Houndstooth stared at Archie, then looked down at the detonator in his hands. He turned it over between his fingers, his jaw working.

"I think I knew that," he finally said. "I think Adelia—I think she *told* me." He shook his head. "Well, I suppose that makes this a little sweeter."

"I'm sorry I didn't tell you sooner," Archie said.

"No, no—I understand. Really." Archie smiled, relieved; her smile faded when Houndstooth continued, "But I do hope *you* understand: I'm going to destroy Travers. I'm going to destroy everything he's built, everything he holds dear. Everything he's poured his life and his passion and his fortune into. I'm going to burn his world to the ground, and then I'm going to salt the ashes. For what he did to my ranch, and for what happened to Hero." A shadow seemed to pass across his eyes as a broad, toothsome grin spread across his face. "Oh, yes, Archie. He will *suffer*."

Archie's face was bloodless. "'Oundstooth," she whispered. "We can't—"

But what they couldn't do, she never got to say, because the door to the suite burst open. Gran Carter emerged, covered in his own blood.

Archie screamed. Houndstooth looked at her, more startled than he had been when he saw Carter himself: he had never heard Archie scream before.

"I'm fine," Carter said, placing his bloody hands on Archie's shoulders. "I'm fine. Just a lot of little cuts, Archie, just—" He clasped her close to him for a brief moment, then pushed her away, holding her shoulders at arm's length. "She's gone. Out the window, into the water. I don't think she was unconscious after all—the moment I got close enough—" He was backing away as he told them, toward the stairs. "I'm sorry, I have to go, I have to catch her before she—"

"If she's in the water, the problem is solved, right?" Houndstooth interrupted. "The ferals—"

In the distance, the sound of Zahra and Stasia bellowing cut through the insect noises of the night.

"She's at the paddock," Archie said. "The ferals must be feeding at the middle of the lake, they are not 'ere yet. Go, Gran, while it's safe in the water! Go!" She shoved her hands at him as though to push him away. Houndstooth noted that her eyes had filled with tears.

"Wait!" Houndstooth shouted. "Hero—you promised—"

Carter doubled back and raced past them, emerging with Hero in his arms.

"I'm sorry, Archie! I'll see you again! I swear it!" Carter shouted as he bounded down the stairs. "I'll see you again!"

They watched him leave; then, Archie wiped her eyes and looked down at herself. She was covered in Carter's blood from where he had held her.

"Well," she said, laughing. "I 'ave forgotten what I was going to say to you, 'Oundstooth. About your grief and your fear and about not being in your right mind." She plucked at her wet, bloody shirt. "I suppose we should get dressed, and then we should start detonating, oui?"

Houndstooth grinned at her. "Let's blow up the Harriet."

Chapter 13

Archie and Houndstooth made their way to the hippo paddock in silence as the stars began to wink out. When they arrived at the paddock, Ruby, Rosa, Abigail, and Betsy were already nosing at each other, competing for attention at the dock.

Archie pulled up short.

"'Oundstooth?" She said. "What—ah, what should we do about Abigail and Betsy?"

"We can't leave them," he replied. "Hero will want to see Abigail when they wake up."

"Do you think they'll follow us, like Stasia and Zahra?"

"If they do, they'll make a decent rear guard, if any ferals try to sneak up on us. I suppose there's only one way to find out." He shrugged. Archie looked at him strangely. "What?"

"Nothing," she replied. "I've just never seen you *shrug* before. It does not look right on you, 'Oundstooth."

Fortunately, Abigail and Betsy did indeed trail behind Ruby and Rosa as they made their way to the Gate—following the trail of apples that Houndstooth dropped into the water every few minutes. Archie stifled a laugh when she noticed him doing it.

"Where did you get those?" she asked.

"I like to be *prepared*, Archie," he replied, his voice dripping with condescension.

". . . Did you steal them from my saddlebag?"

Houndstooth took his time before answering. "Hero ate all my pears," he said in an even tone. Then he snapped the side of

Ruby's harness, and the two of them sped ahead toward the Gate.

❧

"So: we open the Gate, we hit the detonator. The ferals flood the Gate while we watch from a safe distance. We close the Gate. Très facile." Archie had repeated the plan six or seven times on the way over. Every time, she proclaimed how easy it would be to execute.

"Très," Houndstooth replied, having heard hardly a word of what she'd said. He watched the water as they travelled, but it was still and silent save for the occasional grumbles of the four hippos and their two riders.

And it *was* très facile. No ferals bothered them as they made their way from the *Sturgess Queen* to the Gate, though their bellows floated through the still night air like thunder from where they were gathered in the muddy center of the lake.

Archie and Houndstooth reached the Gate without incident. The ranger's familiar, broad-brimmed hat was silhouetted in the grey light of the early morning. Houndstooth called up to the tower.

"Hello up there! Can you open the Gate? Official government business."

The ranger didn't respond. Houndstooth repeated his request. When he received no response, he looked at Archie. She shrugged.

"Perhaps 'e is asleep? Surely we could go up and wake 'im."

Ruby, however, refused to approach the ranger's tower. She balked and danced, avoiding the place where the tower ladder met the water.

"What's gotten into you, Ruby-roo?" Houndstooth asked, tugging on the reins of her harness. She ducked her head below the water and blew a rude series of bubbles, turning her back to the Gate once again.

"Ruby, what are you—Ruby!" Houndstooth cried out indignantly as Ruby dipped into the water once more, soaking him to the waist. "Ruby, you damned impertinent cow, stop this behavior immediately!"

Houndstooth yanked on Ruby's harness, and she reluctantly nudged closer to the ladder. Houndstooth jumped off of her, catching himself on the ladder, then looked back at where the sleek black hippo was fidgeting in the water.

"We'll have words later, you and I," he muttered to her. She flapped her ears at him, and he was struck with a sudden sense of unease. "Archie, do you mind staying down here to keep an eye on her? Lord only knows what's gotten into her this time."

Archie saluted from her perch atop Rosa's back. Houndstooth returned the salute, and began to climb.

He reached the top of the ladder and shouted another greeting to the ranger, not wanting to startle the man with the rifle.

"Hello up here? I'm coming up, but I'm unarmed!"

He crested the top of the ladder and found himself inside the little box of a sentry tower. His eyes adjusted to the dimly lit outpost, and he realized that there were two men in the tower with him. The ranger, in his wide hat, was silent. It was the other man who spoke.

"Oh, good," came the second man's smooth, soft reply. "I was worried you'd bring weapons with you, and then I'd have to kill you myself."

With that, Travers shoved the ranger over the edge of the tower. The utter lack of resistance the man showed to being pushed told Houndstooth that he had already been dead when they'd arrived. Travers turned to face Houndstooth, a thin smile on his face and a revolver in his hand.

"Well," Houndstooth said, raising his hands slowly into the air. "I know when I'm outmatched. Are you going to kill me, Travers?"

"No, no, certainly not," Travers drawled, advancing a few steps. "The ferals will take care of that for me. They take care of most of my problems for me, you know. Cheaters, thieves, nosy inspectors. Mercenary hoppers who don't know when to go home with their tails between their legs." He took another step toward Houndstooth. "I'll have that detonator in your pocket, if you don't mind."

Houndstooth kept his hands in the air. His voice was cold as he watched Travers advance. "I don't know what you mean, Travers. Hero had the detonator."

Travers laughed—a sound like molasses dripping into the bottom of a barrel. "Oh, don't play games with me, Mr. Houndstooth. The house *always* wins." He pointed his gun to Houndstooth's bulging breast pocket. "Right there. Quickly now—before my men have to motivate you." He gestured down to the water, and Houndstooth leaned as far toward the ledge as he dared. Travers' goons held Archie at gunpoint. She looked up at Houndstooth, disgruntled.

"Four on one, eh, Travers? None too sporting of you."

"Oh, Miss Archambault could easily take on two of them— perhaps even three, I wouldn't put it past her. I play to win, Mr. Houndstooth. Now, let's not waste any more time. Give me the detonator, and I'll let you go down to her. You two can try to escape! Or at the very least, you can die together." He cocked back the hammer on the revolver. "Come now. I don't have all day."

Houndstooth held up the detonator, and before he could say a word, Travers had taken it from him.

"Thank you, Houndstooth. You know, I'd been expecting

someone sly? Not you, though," Travers said, flipping the detonator in his hand. "This really does make my life *so* much easier."

"Fat lot of good it'll do you," Houndstooth laughed despite himself. "That's one detonator. You do realize who hired us, don't you? The federal government won't be deterred by one little weasel of a man with a revolver. They *will* get these hippos out of the Harriet, Travers. Your tiny kingdom will crumble."

Travers grinned, a dark joy spreading across his face. "Oh, Mr. Houndstooth. I want the hippos out of the Harriet, too! Just, not quite the same way." He began to pace. "My little kingdom will become an *empire*. Just me, my riverboats, and the ferals, from Minnesota to the Harriet."

Houndstooth watched Travers like a mouse watching a snake. "And how exactly are you going to get your riverboats over the dam, Travers?"

Travers held up the detonator. "Your little crew of hoppers helped with that, Mr. Houndstooth." Houndstooth frowned, not following Travers' logic. "Oh, yes! Yes, you see, Adelia told me all about the bombs you planted in the river. How handy! A whole passel of bombs, already rigged for my convenience." He paused in his pacing, his face shining with excitement. "Last night, while you were crying over your poor departed little lover, I was out on the water, moving the buoys they set up. All sixteen! Oh, it wasn't easy," he hastened to add, mistaking Houndstooth's dawning horror for unbelief. "But I've always been a determined man, Mr. Houndstooth. Determination is everything."

"You're . . . you're going to blow the dam," Houndstooth breathed, his head swimming with implications.

"Oh, yes, Mr. Houndstooth," Travers replied fervently. "I'm going to blow the dam. I'm going to send a flood of ferals up the Mississippi, along with all their little hops. I'm going to seed the water with teeth and reap my reward." His voice descended to a harsh growl. "I'm going to *own this river.*"

He raised the detonator high, and Houndstooth knew that he was going to press the button, destroying the dam. Destroying Hero's legacy. Destroying his chance at vengeance.

Houndstooth launched himself at Travers, knocking the man off his feet. They landed at the very edge of the ranger's platform. The revolver spun off, splashing into the water thirty feet below. The detonator clattered to the floor just out of reach. Houndstooth pressed his arm against Travers' throat.

"Do you remember when I said I was unarmed, Travers?" Houndstooth pulled the ivory-handled knife from his belt; Adelia had sharpened it so finely that the edge was very nearly invisible. "I lied."

Travers grinned savagely. "Do you remember when I said I wouldn't kill you, Houndstooth?" Houndstooth felt a pain in his side. "I lied, too."

Houndstooth's vision went briefly red. He slashed wildly, and when his vision had cleared, Travers' face had been slit from brow to lip. Blood flowed into his eye and mouth and ran hideously down the side of his face.

"That," he spat with grim satisfaction, "was for killing Cal before I had the chance." He slashed again, leaving another gash across Travers' face, marking him with a bold bleeding *X*. "And *that* was for my ranch—the ranch you couldn't burn down yourself, you fucking *coward.*"

He went to step forward, to deliver a killing blow, but he found that something was tugging at his side. He reached a hand down to free himself. All the wind seemed to leave Houndstooth's lungs as his fingers found the hilt of the tiny knife that protruded from his side. *Just like Hero,* he thought.

Travers took Houndstooth's moment of distraction as an

opportunity. He hit the hilt of the knife with the heel of his hand, shoving it farther into Houndstooth's side. As Houndstooth roared in pain, Travers scrambled for the detonator. Houndstooth tried to reach for him—tried to stop him—slipped in Travers' blood, and fell hard.

Travers had the detonator.

He raised it over his head, and pressed the button.

Houndstooth half expected to die right then and there. He half expected the entire Harriet to blow up. What he didn't expect, not even for a moment, was for the detonator to fail, because Hero had made the detonator, and Hero was the smartest person Houndstooth had ever met.

And he had been right. The bombs didn't fail.

A rumble like thunder sounded in the distance. Houndstooth looked out of the ranger's outpost, and saw a cloud rising through the pink morning light in the distance. He yanked the blade out of his side—it was a short one, too short to have done serious damage, but it hurt like hell. He threw the knife over the side of the tower as Travers laughed. When he looked, Travers was clutching his face, holding the flap of his lip in place with one bloody hand.

"You've done it," Houndstooth whispered. "You crazy bastard, you've done it."

"I've done it, and there's not a damn thing you can do to stop those hippos from filling the Mississippi."

Houndstooth looked over the edge of the ranger's tower and into the rippling water. His heart stopped for a moment.

"Travers, open the Gate."

Travers remained on the floor, laughing hysterically.

"Open the Gate, damn you, open it!" Houndstooth made for the large lever that would start the Gate opening, but Travers grabbed his leg.

"Don't bother," Travers gasped through his laughter. "I've disabled it. Cut the cable. It won't open. The hippos can only go North, now."

"Look outside, Travers," Houndstooth urged the bleeding, cackling man. "Look at the water."

Travers rolled to one side. He was close enough to the edge of the platform to look over. His laughter stopped abruptly.

"Do you see that?" Houndstooth asked, pointing down at the debris that was rapidly collecting against the Gate, battering Archie and the hippos. "That's the front of the wave. You blew the dam, Travers. All the water that was behind that dam is headed our way, and it's going to carry *everything* with it."

Travers grinned, pulling himself to his feet. He needed both hands to do it; when he dropped his hand from his face, his skin fell open in a ghastly gash. "Well," he said, "good thing I'm up here, isn't it? The waters won't be rising above thirty feet. Looks like all those ferals will be trapped against the Gate, hmm? And I'm sure they'll be hungry." He placed a hand firmly on Houndstooth's back. "Enjoy the flood, Houndstooth."

He pushed hard, and Houndstooth flipped over the railing, falling into the rising waters of the Harriet.

Chapter 14

Archie watched the cloud of dust billow across the horizon as the dam blew. A wave emerged out of the spray falling detritus, a huge ripple that didn't crest but instead grew as it approached. Even at a distance, it was big enough that she could see the shadows it pushed ahead: boats, buoys, ferals.

She watched as Travers shoved Houndstooth over the edge of the ranger's outpost. She watched as he fell.

In the moment before Houndstooth hit the water, the wave hit the Gate. Archie, Rosa, Betsy, Abigail, and Ruby all rode the swell, slamming into the Gate as the wave broke against it. Betsy let out a pained roar before the water crested over her head.

Houndstooth slammed into the Gate next to Ruby. Archie suspected that this was no accident—the Cambridge Black had watched her hopper closely as he fell. A moment later, he was on Ruby's back, looking dazed and sodden but whole. Archie breathed a sigh of relief at the sight of Houndstooth, safe.

Then she realized that none of them were safe at all.

Behind her, two of Travers' goons screamed. Archie turned to see their mangled bodies, trapped between the Gate and a weather-beaten canoe. The current—fast, now, and relentless—kept the canoe pressed against them, and the water rose intermittently over their heads. They struggled in vain to free themselves.

Archie urged Rosa forward with only a moment of hesitation, but before she could reach the men, a shadow loomed overhead. She wheeled Rosa around and saw Houndstooth, already fleeing along the length of the Gate. Archie followed him, pressing Rosa forward, trying to get out of the path of the fast-approaching Sturgess Queen.

Travers' other riverboats were tethered, docked, anchored hard; they would have flipped over and sunk under the wave. But the Sturgess Queen was designed to tool around the Harriet, providing gamblers with a constantly changing view of the scenery. The huge wave had swept it to the Gate, and it nearly filled the narrow passage. Archie looked over her shoulder and could see nothing but the planks of the boat as it rushed toward her.

Rosa slammed into the sentry tower with all the force of her three thousand pounds. Archie pressed herself against the hippo's back as the boat barrelled toward her. In front of her, Houndstooth did the same, pressing one hand against the stone of the tower as if it could steady him.

And then the boat was passing them. Not missing them—the leg of Archie's breeches tore open and she felt half of her skin go with the fabric—but not striking them. Not killing them.

The boat slammed into the Gate with a deafening crash.

The current was strong, and the Sturgess Queen was massive—but the Gate was bigger. The Gate was stronger. It groaned under the impact of the riverboat, but it held. The water at the base of the boat flushed pink with the pulp of the two men who had been crushed against the grate. The debris that the current pushed toward it gathered against the hull of the Sturgess Queen: sticks and leaves and a half-rotted rowboat. As Archie watched, a tiny, squirming hop poked its head out of the water, scrabbling against the side of the boat.

Travers' two remaining goons eased around the corner of the sentry tower. They didn't seem to notice Archie and Houndstooth as they splashed in the water, arguing over who would be first up the ladder and into the ranger's tower, to safety. One of them managed to dunk the other, and clambered over him toward the ladder. The man in the water reached up an arm to grab his colleague's leg.

With a jerk and a splash, the man disappeared under the water. He came back up again, sputtering. Then he was airborne, flipped by the nose of the first adult feral to reach the Gate.

Archie and Houndstooth watched as the man flailed between the feral's jaws. The man screamed in ear-splitting agony as his blood ran down the hippo's jowls and into the water. His colleague scrambled up the ladder to safety, not looking back even as the screams died with a wet crunch.

"Archie," Houndstooth said, his voice thick. "I think this might be it."

"You may be right, 'Oundstooth," Archie replied grimly. "But I am determined to live. And determination is everything, is it not?"

She swung her meteor hammer in a wide circle over her head and watched the water as the ferals surged toward them, borne on the swell of the current. The heavy metal head whipped through the air as it gained speed.

At first, the ferals didn't notice Houndstooth and Archie. They were smacking into each other, into the *Sturgess Queen*. They bellowed and bit as the water shoved them into each other. One of the bulls let out a roar that rattled Houndstooth's very bones.

The first feral to notice them was a small female with a long crack running through one of her fangs. She whipped toward them, fury in her wild eyes, and charged.

Rosa fled left, carrying Archie out of the path of danger and far from Houndstooth—but Ruby did not follow. She let out a roar that put the raging feral bulls to shame. She turned her wide mouth toward the attacker and opened it, ready to fight. Her golden tusks glinted in the sun. Houndstooth unsheathed his knives, bracing his knees in the saddle, and bared his teeth, echoing Ruby's stance.

Water fanned in front of the feral as she bore down on Ruby and Houndstooth, her own jaw yawning wide—but then a brown blur slammed into her from one side, knocking her into the water. Betsy—sweet, small, battle-scarred Betsy—bowled the feral over, sinking her fangs into its flank before it had a chance to recover from the impact.

"Betsy!" Houndstooth cried as the little brown hippo disappeared into the roil of ferals. He looked around for Archie, but she, too, seemed to have vanished in the fray. A grey-backed hippo brushed up against Ruby, and Houndstooth jumped, prepared to fight—but it was Abigail, cowardly Abigail, *Hero's* Abigail, trying desperately to hide between Ruby and the tower.

A roar drew Houndstooth's attention back to the roiling mass of ferals, who were savagely fighting each other as the water buffeted them into the Gate. Houndstooth's safe shelter against the tower was keeping him and Ruby out of the worst of the current—but it was too much to hope that they would completely escape notice, and Abigail's flight had drawn the attention of a huge, one-eyed bull.

It was that bull whose roar had shaken Houndstooth's bones— a roar that was directed at cowering Abigail. The bull began to move toward them, parting a path through the seething mass of grey that was the feral melee. Houndstooth went cold with fear. The bull was easily half again as large as Ruby. His massive head swung to and fro as he snapped at other, smaller ferals. He was coming for them, and they wouldn't stand a chance.

Houndstooth tried to steer Ruby out of the way—tried to maneuver her out of the path of certain death—but she wouldn't budge. Houndstooth cast his gaze frantically around for Archie, but he couldn't see her, and there was no *time* because the bull was free of the tangle of ferals and he was charging at Ruby with all the fury of a freight train.

Ruby did not bellow at the bull. She stared at him dead on, and Houndstooth could have sworn he felt her tremble. Time seemed to Houndstooth to have slowed to a crawl. He patted Ruby's flank with an unsteady hand. He closed his eyes for a brief moment, trying to accept that there was no way out of the path of the bull—but he realized that closing his eyes did not make it easier to face his death. He would never see Hero again, and he couldn't swallow that with his eyes closed.

His eyes flew open just in time for him to see Rosa. She galloped around from the other side of the ranger's tower, water shearing before her, a white blur with Archie standing atop her back. Archie yelled, a thundering cry that made even the feral bull hesitate for a moment in his charge. Archie, magnificent Archie—she swung her meteor hammer hard and released it, and it flew true and straight, and it hit the bull hard between the eyes with a crack like lightning. Blood stained the water. The bull stood in the water and swayed like a drunk, his eyes still locked on Ruby. He made a single, unsteady movement forward. Houndstooth threw a knife and it sunk deep into the hippo's remaining eye—a surreal echo of Adelia's strike back at the islet where Neville had died.

The beast fell.

Archie crowed as Rosa crowded beside Abigail and Ruby. "That makes ten times I 'ave saved your life, 'oundstooth! No more of this nine-and-a-half nonsense, eh?"

"Where's Betsy?" Houndstooth asked her. Archie pointed to a small brown smudge on the other side of the water—Betsy had gotten herself out of the fray. Houndstooth blew an exasperated sigh. The hippo would have to be retrieved. As he watched, the smudge made its way onto the bank across the water from the sentry tower.

"Archie," he said slowly, "I think she's got the right idea. Getting onto land."

As he spoke, a small bull with gleaming tusks just a few meters in front of them tore into its neighbor, then cast its head around, hungry for a fight.

"You are both right," Archie replied. "We 'ave to get to 'igh land."

The bull seemed to hear her voice. With incredible speed, it detached itself from the frenzy of fighting, roaring hippos and turned on them. Houndstooth felt at his pocket—the only knife he had left was his ivory-handled switchblade. Archie's hammer hung at her waist, useless in the melee. They looked to each other, exhausted, out of options—but then, in a final, miraculous rescue, four bobbing shapes slapped into the furious little bull and toppled it.

The buoys.

Archie and Houndstooth stared at the buoys as they bobbed by, knocking the feral bull under the water each time he attempted to surface. Archie turned to Houndstooth.

"I thought they all blew? I thought . . . I thought Travers moved all of them to the dam?"

Houndstooth gaped. "Oh, my God, Archie. No. He found *sixteen* of them." A smile began to spread across his face. "But Hero made *twenty*. 'Always have a backup plan.' I told them we didn't need a backup plan, but . . . they knew better. And they made twenty, and they put four of them on a separate . . . thing. Frequency. So they wouldn't go off right away." He was a little out of breath from pain and the explanation. "They made twenty. And those are the last four."

Archie let out a whoop. "Twenty! Twenty, goddamn it, 'Ero,

twenty!" She laughed, full-throated and gleeful. "Come on, 'Oundstooth, while the ferals are still fighting each other! If you ever want to thank 'Ero in person we'll 'ave to follow our Betsy and get out of this mess!"

Together, with Abigail tucked between them, Archie and Winslow struggled across the narrow, feral-infested passage. They dodged teeth and pushed past battling pairs of grey, bloodied hippos. Pressing forward, always forward, they finally scrambled up onto the land alongside the Gate.

"Inland?" Archie shouted over the rushing water and the bellowing ferals.

"No," Houndstooth yelled back, wheeling Ruby around by her harness and pointing to where Betsy was waiting for them. "Upstream!"

They rode alongside the water, watching as more and more ferals swept past, carried by the current. They rode until they weren't deafened by the ferals' fighting anymore. Archie immediately dismounted and helped Houndstooth to slide off of Ruby. He sat on the ground, his hand pressed to his still-bleeding side.

"'Oundstooth, you're so pale—how much blood 'ave you lost?" Archie said.

"Never mind, now, Archie. I'll be fine. Where's—" He gasped as a fresh wave of pain overtook him. "—where's Abigail?"

Archie looked around. Betsy stood a ways off, farther inland, panting; there were a few new cuts marring her flank, fresh battle scars to join the old ones.

"Je suis désolé, 'Oundstooth, I don't know, she was right there between us, I don't know 'ow she could 'ave slipped away." She scanned the water, but it was a froth of feral hippos, and she knew there was no use—but then, there she was. Abigail, surging her way *up* the current toward them. She scrabbled up the slope toward them, slipped; Archie grabbed her harness and gave a mighty heave. Between the two of them, Abigail made it onto the bank. Ruby nosed at her, and the two hippos wandered toward Betsy, who had sprawled, exhausted, on the ground.

Archie gave Rosa a nudge. "Go on," she said. The hippo snorted at her, unmoving; Archie rubbed her bristly nose and murmured to her. "You 'ave done so well, my Rosa. Go on. Go and rest. You 'ave earned it."

Rosa lumbered off to join the other three hippos where they lay in the shade, exhausted from the battle. Archie settled herself next to Houndstooth on the muddy riverbank.

"Well," she said. "We are trapped, mon ami. We cannot get overland with the ladies over there—the Gate extends too far inland for Rosa and Abigail to cover the distance, and I think Ruby might not be in good enough shape right now for the journey anyway. We cannot take them through the ruins of the dam, not safely—and we certainly cannot take them into *that,*" she said, gesturing to the roiling mass of furious ferals. "So. What do we do now? Smoke a cigar and call it quits?"

Houndstooth was still out of breath, his face very pale; but when Archie eased his shirt away from his side, she saw that he had nearly stopped bleeding. He gave a little laugh and considered her.

"Hero was too smart for me, you know. They had so many plans; so many contingencies. 'Just in case,' they kept saying; and I kept asking 'in case of what?' "

Archie watched Houndstooth, frowning. "Are you alright, friend? You seem—"

"Ah, I'm fine," he said, waving her off. "I'm telling you what we do *next.*" He patted at his vest, then reached to an inside pocket. He pulled out a little leather pouch, sealed with wax; then, he handed her his ivory-handled knife.

"Miracle I managed to hang on to both of these after that fall. But then, it's a bit of a day for miracles. Be a love and open this, won't you, Archie? My hands aren't too steady."

Archie slit open the wax and tipped the contents of the pouch into Houndstooth's waiting hand.

" 'Just in case,' they said. 'Just in case.' " He held up the little black detonator. "Just in case the charges don't blow, let's have a backup, they said. Just a few buoys that could start the chain, in case things go wrong. But of course the first round of bombs worked perfectly," he laughed thinly.

Archie looked from the detonator to the Gate; to the swarm of ferals that frothed against the *Sturgess Queen,* pressing the buoys right up against the riverboat. She looked up at the tower, where Travers leaned against the railing, watching the chaos below, still laughing with his hand pressed to his mangled face.

"Four buoys left undetonated, Archie," he said with a weak smile. "How many sticks of dynamite is that equivalent to?"

Archie grinned. "I 'ave no idea, 'Oundstooth."

"Shall we find out?"

Archie put her hand over his. They pressed the button together, and sat back, side by side, as the four backup buoys exploded in a glorious display of fire and fury.

A few moments later, the flames from the buoys reached the half-saddlebag of madre del Diablo that had been left unused. The *Sturgess Queen* cracked open in a thunderous explosion of fire and splinters. Archie and Houndstooth toppled over under the force of the shockwave. The Gate blew back in a gust of shrapnel. The blast sent feral hippos flying—several of them bowled into the ranger's tower. The tower gave a mighty groan.

It creaked.

It tipped.

It *fell.*

Archie and Houndstooth watched as Travers, tiny at such a distance, clung to the railing of the sentry post for a long moment before dropping into the water. They watched as the ferals that had survived the explosion, recovering but shaken, swarmed him.

They were too far distant to hear his screams, but they could see his body flying through the air as the furious feral hippos tossed him between each other.

"I told you," Houndstooth gasped. "I told you that he would suffer."

"That you did," Archie replied. They couldn't hear his screams over the sounds of the ferals, but it was enough for both of them to simply watch as the ferals destroyed him in the water next to the wreckage of the Harriet Gate.

"Well, 'Oundstooth. I would say this caper was a raging success, no?" Archie asked.

"It wasn't a *caper*," Houndstooth mumbled just before he blacked out.

Archie patted his chest as he lay on the ground beside her. "I know," she murmured. "It was an operation."

She sat next to him as the water calmed. When he woke, she knew, he would want to go after Adelia. He would want to beat Gran Carter to her. He would want to go find Hero, and together with them, he would want to see justice served. But for now—just for a few hours—she decided to let him rest. He would need it.

The sun rose higher in the sky overhead, and the day grew hot. Houndstooth and the hippos slept; and Archie watched as the ferals, unconstrained by dam or Gate or raging current, took the Mississippi.

Epilogue

Gran Carter rode up to the dock of a little clapboard house a mile outside the Harriet Gate astride a borrowed Arnesian Brown hippo named Pauline. Hero was in front of him, tied at the waist to keep them upright.

He dismounted and hauled Hero up to the back door of the house, leaving Pauline beside the other hippos at the gated dock. Carter's nostrils flared. He smelled the air and shook his head—by some miracle, Hero was not putting out the familiar septic battlefield stench of a gut wound. There was only the clean, hot smell of blood in the air.

A miracle.

Or was it? Carter rapped hard on the door and waited for the doctor to answer, hoping he'd be at home. While he waited, Carter reflected on the facts.

Fact number one: Adelia Reyes was, without question, the deadliest, most ruthless contract killer of the day—possibly of all time.

Fact number two: Adelia Reyes had hit Hero with two knives. The first had been aimed at Hero's heart, but had struck their sternum just softly enough to lodge there.

Fact number three: The second knife had been aimed at Hero's gut, but had managed to avoid nicking their bowel, their liver, their gallbladder. Carter touched Hero's forehead lightly—it was only slightly warm. Feverish, sure, but not frightening. Infection hadn't even begun to set in yet.

It didn't add up. Either Adelia was losing her touch—

impossible—or she had let Hero live on *purpose*—even more impossible.

Before he could try to resolve the matter, the door swung open. A tall, dark-haired man stood in the doorway, wiping blood from his bare hands.

"What's this?" he asked, looking at Hero's limp form. "What's happened here?"

"Stabbed. Twice. Gut and chest." Carter watched the doctor's face begin to set into a practiced bad-news expression, and hurried on. "But the woman who stabbed them missed. She missed . . . everything, doc. Please, can you help them?"

The doctor leaned inside and called for help. A young white woman, stout and muscle-bound, appeared in the doorway to carry Hero inside.

"One more thing, doctor, please—" Carter pulled a photo out of his pocket. "Have you seen this woman? She may have come through with minor wounds from a feral fight?"

The doctor smiled broadly, revealing carved-ivory teeth, straight and white and shining. He did not look at the photo. Carter sighed, and pulled a small bag out of the same pocket, handing it to the doctor. The doctor weighed it in his hand before looking at the photo.

"No, can't say as I've ever seen her. I'd remember that tattoo, I reckon."

Gran tucked the photograph away. "Worth a try. I'd best be going, but your patient will have people coming along for them shortly." He tipped his hat and sprinted back down the dock to Pauline.

The doctor watched Gran go, then eased inside, shutting the door behind him and turning the dead bolt. He rested his back against the door for a moment, his eyes closed. When he opened them, she was standing there, waiting for him. Her eyes glittered in the half dark of the room.

"You'd best tend to your patient, Doctor," Adelia Reyes said with a small smile. "It's as Agent Carter said: they'll have people coming along shortly."

TASTE OF
MARROW

Chapter 1

Ysabel would not stop crying. She spasmed with grating, earsplitting screams every few seconds. Her face, knotted and purple, jerked every time Adelia tried to maneuver her nipple toward the baby's mouth.

"Maybe she doesn't like you," Hero said mildly.

"Babies don't have opinions," Adelia replied through gritted teeth.

"Nobody told *her* that," Hero muttered. They turned their attention back to the kneeling saddle on the ground in front of them, and continued working grease into the leather of the pommel.

"Ysa," Adelia murmured in a pained singsong. "Ysa, mija, please just—*there*." She winced, triumphant, as the screaming stopped and the baby latched at last. "You see? All she needed was—ah!" She cried out in pain as the baby startled at nothing in particular and pulled away from her breast without letting go of the nipple. Her cry made Ysabel startle again, and the baby's face began to scrunch in preparation for another piercing wail.

"Good luck with that," Hero said. They eased themself upright, grimacing, and braced their hands on their lower back for a cautious stretch. They walked into the trees, away from Adelia and the screaming baby, without waiting to hear a response.

Hero knew that they'd need to start a fire soon, before dusk turned to dark. They'd wait until Ysabel had stopped eating—the sound of wood splintering was sure to startle the baby again. In the meantime, they made their way through the scrubby, moss-hung trees to the murky little pocket of the Catahoula where Adelia's hippos, Zahra and Stasia, were dozing. Hero squatted to wash their grease-smeared hands in the warm water, watching the surface of the pond for ripples more out of habit than worry. They watched the scum that floated away from their skin in the water and an idea drifted through their mind: a system to send rafts of nitroglycerin floating to waterlocked targets— but how to prevent a trailing wick from getting waterlogged? A remote detonator, or a system of watertight tubes that could protect a lit fuse, or perhaps a flaming dart shot across water, or perhaps . . .

They let their hands trail in the water for a while as they mentally troubleshot the concept. Hero couldn't remember the last time they'd allowed their attention to wander so close to the water's edge. But this was a safe place for them to let the ideas blossom. It was a pleasant, secluded little spot off the banks of the lake that Hero and Adelia had chosen to set up camp, well away from the Mississippi and the marshes and far from the reach of the ferals in the Gulf. Hero missed their Abigail—they'd been borrowing Stasia, and it just wasn't the same. But otherwise, it was a fine camp. They were surrounded by scrubby brush and gangly trees; it was out-of-the-way enough that no one was drawn to them by the sound of the baby crying. Hero wondered how far Ysabel's wails carried, and they allowed themself a moment of satisfaction at Adelia's struggle. *Serves her right,* they thought, ripping up a fistful of marsh grass to scrub their palms. Still, they couldn't help wishing that the baby was a little less of a squaller.

But not for Adelia's sake. It was just because Hero had to be stuck in the company of the little creature all day and all night, and their sanity was suffering from the constant barrage of noise.

Hero started to stand, but a flash of pain above their navel knocked them back and they sat hard. They yanked the hem of their shirt up and pressed a wet hand to the fat rope of scar tissue there, feeling for the unbroken skin. *There*—there was the scar, and they looked down at their hand and confirmed that no blood filled the creases in their palm. "It's okay," they whispered to themself. "It's okay. It's just a phantom pain. You're fine."

They sat there on the pebbly sand with their palm braced against their belly. They *were* fine. But the "fine" was so *new*—this was the first day that Hero could truly say they felt healed, and even that was tentative, raw. The wound was relatively fresh, in more ways than one. It was the wound that Adelia had given to Hero just a few weeks before Ysabel's birth.

Hero took a slow, deep breath and took their hand away from their stomach, letting their hem fall back into place. In the distance, the baby had stopped screaming. A clutch of ducks drifted silently by on the water—a welcome signal that the ferals, who would have eaten anything that moved too slowly back on the Harriet, hadn't made it to the Catahoula yet. The night was almost peaceful now. Hero closed their eyes and tried to remember their last time they'd felt almost-peaceful—the day that a handsome man rode up to their door astride a pitch-black hippo and asked if they'd like to join him for one last job.

They'd said yes at the time. They would have said yes again in a heartbeat.

But Hero hadn't seen Winslow Houndstooth since the night before Adelia's knife had made that scar on their belly. Since her knife had nearly killed them.

Hero fidgeted with the third button down on their shirt. They wouldn't unbutton it to feel the scar there—the twin of the one on their stomach. *It hasn't disappeared since the last time you looked at it,* they told themself irritably. But it bothered them, and they fidgeted in earnest as they went over the questions they'd been asking every day since they'd woken up.

It didn't make any sense.

Hero liked things that made sense. They liked diagrams and switches and sensible arrangements of wires. They liked dosages and measurements and titrations. Adelia was ... a thicket. A tangle of intentions and motivations that Hero really could have done without.

But they had to figure it out. Adelia could have killed Hero so easily—but instead, her knives had struck the only places on Hero's body that could look mortal without actually killing them. Hero knew the exact amount of coral snake venom required to make a person quietly suffocate due to paralysis, and Adelia knew exactly where to aim her weapons. Both of them had too much experience to make stupid mistakes that would let a target walk away.

Hero knew that they'd been allowed to live intentionally. They just didn't know *why*.

Hero had woken up with no idea where they were, and there was Adelia, changing the bandage on their abdomen with steady hands and intent focus. Hero had tried to startle away from the woman who had stabbed them, but a white-hot stripe of pain had flattened them before they could move. It took them weeks to recover—weeks of Adelia's focused attention and care. Whenever Hero tried to ask why Adelia hadn't killed them, she pursed her lips and changed the subject.

And then Ysabel had come, and there hadn't been room to keep asking. And Hero had kept on healing, had kept on slowly recovering. They'd helped with the baby here and there, although they didn't know much of anything about babies and didn't care to learn. And the pain in their belly had faded.

Hero dug their hands into the coarse sand and watched the still surface of the water. The pain in their belly had faded, and Adelia had recovered from Ysabel's birth. It was time to leave.

They knew it—had been thinking about it all day. They would tell Adelia that night, after the baby was asleep. It was settled. Hero would be gone by daybreak.

But where? Home? Back to their little house with its little pond, to be alone for the rest of their lives?

Because, if Hero was honest with themself, that was why they'd stayed with Adelia for so long. It was easy to focus on the wound in their belly and Ysabel's birth and the work of finding food and starting fires and staying two steps ahead of the law. It was easier for Hero to do all of that than it was for them to think about going home, sitting alone on the front porch, and looking at the empty rocking chair that Houndstooth should have been in. It was easier for Hero to do that than it was for them to wonder why it was that they'd survived the collapse of the Harriet dam, while Houndstooth—

No. *No,* they thought, slamming a door in their mind. *Don't think about that.* They turned their mind back to the problem of why Adelia hadn't killed them, and then realized how closely that question fit with the question they weren't going to think about. *Something else, anything else.*

They looked at the water, and gripped fistfuls of sand, and thought about how to keep a lit fuse dry. A sense of calm washed over them as they considered waxes and weights, how to keep the fuse from attracting fish, the problem of seepage, the problem of oxygen. And what if the fuse itself was on fire? Could they make it burn so hot that the water wouldn't matter?

They were drawing equations in the sand, calculating how many grams of gunpowder an inch of cotton wick could support—but then a scream cut through the muggy night air. Hero was used to screams cutting through all manner of night air at this point; sleeping a few feet away from a newborn baby will have that effect on a person. But this scream didn't sound at all like Ysabel.

It almost sounded like . . . *Adelia*.

Hero scrambled to their feet and pelted back toward the campsite. They slipped on a patch of loose scree, their leg shooting out behind them, but they caught themself and continued without breaking stride. Another scream—this one from Ysabel—and shouts, more than one person. "Shitshitshitshitshit," Hero chanted under their breath as they ran. They held one arm in front of their face to guard their eyes from twigs; with the other hand, they reached down to unstrap their fat-bladed kukri—usually reserved for utility, but it would do the job that needed to be done, whatever that job might be.

Except that it wasn't there. They groped at their hip even as they had a vision of the knife, sheathed, on the ground next to the kneeling saddle they'd been polishing. They would have sworn, but they were already swearing. "*Shitshitshit.*"

Hero burst into the little clearing where they'd left Adelia and Ysabel not fifteen minutes before. There was a resonant *thunk* next to their head—they looked, and saw the handle of a knife sticking out of a tree trunk less than a foot from their face. They pulled up short, their breath frozen in their throat.

Five men surrounded Adelia in a wide circle. Kerchiefs were tied over their faces, and their hats were pulled low, leaving only their eyes exposed. Adelia's outstretched right hand gripped the butt of Hero's kukri, and she turned in a slow circle, keeping the men at a distance and stepping around the empty sheath at her feet. In her left arm, a swaddled Ysabel whimpered steadily.

Hero's heart pounded in their chest so hard that it hurt. The odds in this situation were decidedly *not* in their favor. They weren't a fighter. They did poisons and explosives, the weapons of a thinking person. They had tolerable skill with a knife, theoretically, but against five people? They didn't stand a chance.

"Alright now, that's enough," one of the men said. "We ain't gonna hurtcha none, just—" Adelia swiped at him with Hero's kukri and he jumped back with a shout.

You don't have to fight, a small, reasonable voice whispered inside of Hero's mind. *You could just walk away from this.* Hero had been with Adelia for nearly two months. Adelia was more than recovered from Ysabel's birth. *You don't owe her anything,* the reasonable voice said. *You don't have to get involved in this at all.*

"I don't see why we can't hurt her a little bit," another of the men said. Blood seeped from a cut on his thigh. "Just knock her out, boss."

Hero took a slow, quiet step backward. They were good at being quiet—they could melt into the brush and no one would ever have to know that they'd been there at all.

"You knock her out, if you're so damn smart."

"Fuck that, she already cut me. You do it."

Hero took another step back. *You don't owe her anything,* the small voice whispered again.

"Jesus Christ, you two," a third man growled. "It's a woman and a baby." He shook his head at his colleagues, then lunged.

"No!" Hero heard the shout before they realized it was their own voice, and then they were running. They yanked the knife from the tree trunk with a back-wrenching tug, and then they were fighting.

It was exactly as awful as they'd feared. The men all looked the same, and even though Hero was certain they'd counted five before, it seemed like they were everywhere at once. Hero punched one of them in the gut, and another took his place right away. A fist connected with Hero's eye and everything went white, and then hot blood was getting into their eyes and they couldn't see anything. Hands grabbed at Hero's arms, and their pulse pounded in their ears, and they were being dragged away from Adelia. Ysabel was screaming. Adelia was cursing. Hero lashed out blindly behind themself with the knife and felt it catch on fabric and a man's voice near their ear said *agh hey watch it*. They lashed out again, and the knife caught on fabric again, and then they *pushed*.

The blade sank in with almost no resistance at all. The man who had said *watch it* made a sound like he was confused, or maybe startled. The grip on Hero's arms slackened, and they yanked themself free, wiping blood from their eyes with one sleeve. There was a meaty *thud* behind them, but they didn't stop to look, couldn't stop to look, because Adelia was shouting and the men were grabbing at Ysabel and the trees were shaking—

Wait, what? But before Hero could fully register their own confusion, the treeline exploded in a shower of leaves and loose moss, and three thousand pounds of damp, grey, furious hippopotamus thundered into the clearing. Zahra scattered the bedrolls under her close-set feet, barreling toward Adelia with all the momentum of a coal train. She knocked two of the masked men aside with a brutal shoulder check—one of them landed next to Hero with a splintering thud and didn't get up again.

Zahra's jaws gaped wide, revealing her cruelly sharp teeth, and she snapped at the remaining two men. The one farthest from the hippo turned to bolt and knocked hard into Adelia. The two of them fell in a tangle of limbs. The man's companion yanked him up by the arm and they both ran. One of the men Zahra had knocked over scrambled to his feet and followed them. Zahra started to charge after them, kicking up dry grass, but Adelia whistled sharply and the hippo trotted to a reluctant stop. She stood snorting at the place in the treeline where the men had disappeared, the vast grey expanse of her trunk heaving like a bellows.

"Adelia," Hero shouted, running to where she sat in the

patchy grass of the clearing. "Adelia, are you alright? Where did he get you?" Adelia's breath was ragged, and she was clutching at the grass by her thighs with both fists. When she looked up at Hero, her face was clenched in naked agony. "Show me," Hero said, kneeling next to Adelia, not touching her but holding their hands a few inches from her shoulders as if they could shake the injury away.

But Adelia was shaking her head and tears were brimming in her eyes.

"Show me," Hero whispered. "I can help."

And then Hero realized that they could hear Zahra's huffing breaths, and they could hear the singing insects that were starting to come out as the sun went down. They could hear the groans of the man they'd stabbed. They could hear the crackle of dry grass under their own knees.

They could hear things they hadn't heard since Ysabel was born. For the first time in six weeks, it was quiet.

Hero stood up and scanned the entire clearing. "Adelia," they said, trying to keep their voice calm. "Where's Ysabel?"

Even as they said it—even before Adelia's anguished, furious scream split the night open—Hero knew the answer.

Ysabel was gone.

Chapter 2

"No one ever suspects the fat lady, hmmm?"

Regina Archambault whipped around to see who had whispered in her ear—but no one was there.

"Archie? Wassamatt'r?" The man Archie had been talking to a moment ago swayed toward her, his bourbon breath scalding her nostrils.

"Not a thing, chérie, not a thing." Archie placed a steadying hand on his shoulder, making the movement seem like a caress. The man—forty-something, white, all his teeth but none of his hair—looked down at her hand as though he were going to lick it.

"D'y'know," he said, casting a half-squinted eye at Archie's satin-swagged bosom, "that I'm the riches' man on the Pochnaroon?"

Archie pressed a hand to her chest, feigning surprise while tugging the neckline of her gown an inch lower. "Well, now, Mr. 'Aberdine, I never would 'ave guessed such a thing!" She gave Haberdine's bolo tie a tug, aimed a plump-lipped smile his way. "The richest man on the Ponchartrain, and so 'andsome as well? 'Ow could you keep this secret from me?" She pouted in the way a man like this would expect a Frenchwoman to pout. "I thought we were friends."

"It's not going to work."

That voice again, but this time Archie didn't turn to look at who it was. Whoever they were, they'd find her eventually. She wasn't going to play their game.

"I own"—Haberdine stifled a belch—"well, I *used't'own* all

the boats on the Ponchatrawn and half th'ns on the Missississip, an' I tell you what, I—" He stopped midsentence, his eyes on Archie's leg. She'd reached into an inner pocket of her gown while he was talking, and she'd tugged on a strategically loosened string. A significant slit had opened up in the fabric, running from her calf to the top of her thigh.

"Tell me what," she whispered into Haberdine's ear, letting her leg edge toward him so that he could see the sheen of her stocking. His fingers trailed along the rent in the fabric. *Her* fingers trailed along the lining of his inner waistcoat pocket.

"Well, now, Ms. Archie—I was gonna say that if I thought I was rich before . . ." Haberdine licked his lips as his thumb traced the clasp of her garter where it met the top of her stocking. "T'ain't nothin' to how I'm set up now I've sold my boats."

"Sold them?" Archie murmured, tracing a fingertip along his earlobe while feeling in his trousers for a billfold.

"Sol'm to Whelan Parrish, m'dear," Haberdine said. "Why, that boy's buying up all the property he can get a *handful* of—"

Archie jumped prettily, and Haberdine chuckled. "Oh, mon dieu, Mr. 'Aberdine, I—"

"Who's your friend, Marcus?"

Haberdine snatched his hand out from under her skirt. Archie's lightning reflexes, honed over a lifetime of grift, were the only thing that saved her from dropping his wallet on the ground between them. She slipped the wallet into a pocket in her bustle as she turned to see who Marcus was sweatily eyeing.

"Marcus, my love, I've been looking for you everywhere." There was no mistake to be made—it was the same voice as the one that had been taunting Archie all night, from the moment she'd "bumped into" Haberdine on the dance floor to the first drink he'd bought for her. The young woman belonging to the voice was, in many ways, Archie's opposite. Where Archie was pale, she was dark; where Archie was broad as a pistol's grip, she was thin as a knife's edge; where Archie's hair was piled in a tower of blond ringlets, this woman's was close-cropped and glossy, set in immaculate waves. But there was something more there. Where Archie was tired, this woman's skin seemed to glow.

Where Archie was enjoying playing with Haberdine, this woman's eyes spoke to hunger. This wasn't a game to her.

"Cayja," Haberdine slurred, grinning at this new woman. "I was jus' talkin' business with this'r upstanding lady. Meet Ms. Archie—er, Archie . . ."

"Just Archie is fine," Regina said, extending a hand.

"Acadia," the other woman drawled, ignoring it. "Marcus, dear heart, we had probably better get back to our boat."

"But th'party's just getting started!" he said, gesturing expansively to the crowd that surrounded them. He was right— their party boat, just like every other one that floated on the surface of the Ponchartrain, was packed with shouting, dancing, drunk people, and the crowd was growing livelier by the minute. "In fact, I could use a refill—" And with that, Haberdine gracelessly excused himself from the company of both women.

"I am sorry," Archie said, "I didn't know that 'e was spoken for—"

"Git," Acadia said through gritted teeth. Her fists were clenched in the full pink skirt of her gown, and Archie could see her holding back a formidable anger.

"Pardonnez-moi?"

"I said *git*," Acadia spat, something like fear glinting in her eyes, and Archie revised her earlier assessment. This wasn't a woman. This was a girl *dressed up* as a woman.

"Are you alright?" Archie asked softly, remembering other times she'd met desperate young women wearing pearls that older women had loaned them. "Is 'e—are you safe 'ere?"

Acadia stepped closer to Archie, glancing around them before she answered. "Well . . . I suppose maybe I can trust you . . ."

Archie bent her head to listen. "Of course, chérie."

Acadia's lips brushed Archie's ear at the same time as a needle-sharp knife pricked her hip. "This is my grift, Regina Archambault." Her voice was low, husky, a shade above a whisper but more intimate for it. Her breath was hot on Archie's throat. "That man just sold his empire, and I've been working on him for a fucking month, and the fortune he's sittin' on is *mine*. So *git*."

Archie nodded. "I see. Thank you for letting me know." She put a fingertip on the girl's knife and pushed it away from her abdomen. "It is as I said: I did not realize 'e was spoken for. I'll take my work elsewhere."

"To another boat," Acadia said. "There are plenty here. This one's mine."

Archie nodded. She couldn't help respecting the girl's work—after a few hours in Haberdine's company, she'd been tempted to pitch him overboard. A full month . . . the girl would be earning her fortune. " 'Ave a pleasant evening," Archie said. The girl gave her a curt nod, and with that, they parted ways.

Archie smiled to herself as she paid one of the Ponchartrain gondoliers a penny to ferry her back to the *Marianna Fair*. It had been a good night, even if she'd been called away. She reached into one of the pockets of her skirt, the one where she'd slipped Haberdine's wallet before being so rudely interrupted. The wallet was fat, ripe with bills—likely his advance on the sale of his empire.

She felt in the pocket again.

There was a rustle of paper there. Thick, heavy stock, debossed or imprinted with something. She pulled the paper out, held it up to the gondolier's lantern, and laughed.

It was a calling card. The girl had left a card in Archie's

pocket—nervy as hell, that one. She felt around in the pocket again, and realized that, while the wallet was still there, the two watches she'd lifted from other marks that night were gone.

"Well earned, Acadia," she laughed to herself, studying the calling card. "I'll 'ave to be in touch with you, eh?"

For the rest of the trip between the party boats and the *Marianna Fair*, Archie watched the water. Strictly speaking, she shouldn't be worried—the ferals hadn't made it as far as the Ponchartrain yet, at least according to all the latest accounts. They wouldn't like the brackish, choppy waters of the lake. It was why there were so many people on the water even this late in the season—everyone was congregating in places they thought the ferals were avoiding.

Still, Archie watched the water. She flinched every time a ripple crossed the surface.

— ✺ —

Archie eased open the door of the suite she was sharing with her old friend, tiptoeing so as not to wake him. But when she got inside, she found him standing at the little desk that took up half their room, working by the light of a single gas lantern.

"I'm just—hang on," Houndstooth said distractedly, waving a hand at Archie without looking up.

Archie sighed, unclipping her skirt and tossing it on the bed before pulling on a pair of well-worn breeches. She didn't bother trying to tuck herself behind a screen—Houndstooth was too wrapped up in his work to notice her partial nudity. She needled him, even though she knew he wouldn't listen. "You should go to sleep, Winslow. It must be two o'clock in the morning, my friend."

The only response she got was the sound of his grease pencil smudging across the map, and the lapping of water against their boat. She frowned at Houndstooth. He was bent over the tiny desk, a long parenthesis in the flickering light of the gas lantern. Archie tutted. She didn't care to be ignored. She turned away from Houndstooth, bumping into furniture on her way to the washbasin. She loosened her corset, washed her face, took out her false curls, began putting her hair up into the crown of braids she'd be sleeping in. She could see the entirety of the little room in the palm-sized mirror that hung on a nail over the washbasin: the narrow bed, the narrower chair, the postage stamp of a desk. The little window that wouldn't open to let in the salty breeze coming off the lake.

Houndstooth was muttering something under his breath. Archie pursed her lips, tying a silk scarf over her braids. She set her hands on her hips and turned to stare at him.

"Houndstooth," she said.

"If they followed the currents," Houndstooth muttered. "But—no, that wouldn't be—no, no, damn it." His elbows arrowed out as he pushed his hands through his hair. For a moment, Archie thought he'd turn around and acknowledge her, but he just bent back over the map. She put a hand on his shoulder and he startled.

"Archie—what are you doing up?" He finally looked at her. "Where have you been in that dress?"

"I've been obtaining us travel funds," she said. " 'Oundstooth, you look terrible. You need to rest."

He laughed. "Well, thanks, Archie, that's very sweet of you."

Archie laid a palm against Houndstooth's cheek. He felt warmer than he should have. "I think you are not well, perhaps. Please, my friend. Get some sleep. I'll take the chair for the rest of the night. You take the bed." It was a generous offer—the chair was narrow enough for Houndstooth to sleep in, but it was far too small for Archie. She knew that if he took the bed, she would spend half the night trying to find a way to squeeze herself comfortably between the carved wooden arms—but that didn't matter. Not with Houndstooth blinking back at her as if he barely recognized her. *Maybe he'd talk to me more if I was a gull-damned* map, she thought bitterly.

"I can't sleep, Archie," Houndstooth said. His eyes were bright, but they were rimmed with shadows. Archie frowned at him, and his shoulders drooped. He whispered, "I can't sleep while Hero is missing."

Archie rubbed her forehead so that Houndstooth would not see her rolling her eyes. *So melodramatic.* "You can't find them if you're exhausted," Archie replied, shaking her head. "Please. Just . . . rest until sunrise. I'll wake you up then." She patted his cheek a little harder than necessary. "I promise."

Houndstooth glanced at the bed, and Archie could see the battle between the physical need for rest and the pull of his—she mentally elided the word "obsession." She nudged him toward the bed. "I swear on Rosa's head, mon amie. I'll wake you at sunup."

"Alright," he muttered, "but only because I know you won't let me concentrate anyway." He stretched out on top of the covers, his bloodred hippo-leather boots hanging off the end of the bed. Archie turned the gaslamp down until it was dark in the little cabin.

She tried to settle into the chair and sighed. It dug painfully into the sides of her thighs. She shifted, but she knew that it wasn't an issue of her position—the chair was just too damned small. Damn if her thighs wouldn't be bruised later. She folded her hands over her stomach and closed her eyes, determined to try to sleep in spite of the nagging discomfort of the chair. She listened to Houndstooth's breathing slow down, and she listened to the gentle lapping of the waters of Lake Ponchartrain against the side of the boat, and she tried hard to doze off—but it was no good. She was too worried about Houndstooth.

When did it happen? Archie asked herself. She couldn't pinpoint the exact moment when her old friend had gone from *determined* to *fixated*. He'd always been stubborn, always a little . . . performative. But it seemed like he'd crossed a line somewhere.

When the Harriet Gate fell and the Harriet Dam blew, they hadn't known that Hero was missing. Hurt, yes—but not *missing*. They hadn't known Hero was *missing* for nearly a day—the amount of time it took them to escape the Harriet, dodge the ferals that had been released into the river, and find the doctor that Hero had been taken to.

The doctor they had been taken to by U.S. Marshal Gran Carter.

Archie's hand crept to the inside pocket of her shirt, where she'd tucked Carter's latest letter. It was too dark to read it, and if she unfolded it Houndstooth would wake up, thinking that she was interfering with his map. But that was okay—she didn't need to look at it. She'd memorized it.

I miss you. I want to see you again. I miss the way you smell. I miss the way you taste. I'll be on Ponchartrain in a fortnight, aboard the Marianna Fair. *Meet me there, and we can—*

Archie's eyes snapped open. Was that—no. She'd thought for a moment that she'd heard a splash, but it had probably just been the water lapping against the side of the boat. She reminded herself for the hundredth time that the lake was safe. Houndstooth made a soft sound in his sleep, a bad-dream sound, and Archie closed her eyes again. She tried to slow her breathing. She would need to sleep so that she could get Houndstooth through the next day of searching for Hero. She had never seen him like this before—she had to remind him to eat, to drink water, to comb his hair . . .

This time, Archie stood from the chair before she knew what she was doing. There had *definitely* been a splash, and a scream. She pressed her face to the window, trying to see through the streaky glass, but she couldn't make out what was happening on the lake. There was another scream, closer, and then a sound that made the bottom drop out of Archie's gut: the grating bellow of a feral's roar.

"Putain," she whispered. "Son of a bitching *fuck*. Houndstooth—!"

"Let's go," he said. She turned around and he was already standing behind her, one hand gripping the waxed leather saddlebag that held the majority of their possessions. He reached past Archie to grab the map he'd been scribbling on. Archie grabbed her jacket from the back of the chair and whipped it on as they left their room. The hall was strangely silent.

"Where's everyone else?" Archie asked Houndstooth's back.

"They probably haven't woken up yet. Or they don't know," he called over his shoulder. "I don't think there are any other hoppers on board."

Archie hesitated. "Couillon," she muttered again. She banged on the door closest to them with the flat of her hand and didn't stop until the door swung open. A grey-faced man answered, and Archie grasped him by the lapels of his nightshirt. "Listen," she said, her nose a half-inch from his. "There are ferals in the water. They'll kill everyone here, and this boat is small enough for them to flip over. Everyone on board needs to get to shore immediately and then run inland. Do you understand?"

"But—how—" the man sputtered. "Who are you?"

She slapped him. Not as hard as she could, but as hard as he needed to be slapped. "Wake up the others," she said, gesturing to the two other doors in the hall. "Get their help waking the crew downstairs, and then get to shore before the ferals get here. If you want to live, it's what you'll do. Do you understand?" The man hesitated, and Archie lifted her hand again.

"I understand!" he cried, holding his hands up in front of his reddening cheeks. "But—where are you going?"

But Archie was already gone, tearing down the stairs after Houndstooth. Behind her, she could hear the man starting to knock on doors. *Good.*

By the time she and Houndstooth reached the main deck, the screams were constant. The moon provided just enough light to see shadows in the water—some moving, some not. There was a fire, and Archie thought it was probably the wreckage of a houseboat or maybe a skiff that had anchored for the night. The grunting of the ferals was everywhere.

Houndstooth dug around in the saddlebag and hauled out Archie's meteor hammer. She gave it a couple of practice swings as Houndstooth strapped a knife to each of his arms.

"Winslow," she said urgently, staring across the water at the silhouettes of the ferals. "The harpoon. If there's ever been a time—"

He shook his head. "I haven't practiced with it. I'll row, you just . . . try not to hit me with the hammer, eh?"

"Then *I'll* use it," she snapped, and then took matters into her own hands. She reached into the saddlebag, pulled out four lengths of cylindrical brass, and started latching them together.

"Archie, we don't have time to—"

"If you die trying to get off the water, we'll never find Hero," Archie said. "And my hammer might hit the raft, it's no good out here. Where's the head? Never mind," she said, digging into the saddlebag again. "I've got it." She pulled out a notched spearhead the size of her forearm and attached it to the end of the long pole. She fumbled—she wasn't used to putting the damn thing together, and she kept startling as people screamed and ferals bellowed and wood splintered—but then she felt a satisfying *snick* and she knew that the head was secure. "Alright," she said, "let's go. You steer."

Houndstooth stepped over the railing of the *Marianna Fair* onto the raft that was tethered there—the raft on which he and Archie had arrived just a few nights before. He held it steady as she lowered herself slowly onto it. The roaring of the ferals came closer, and the process of shifting ballast to the center of the raft was taking too long, but if Archie was going to be on the back of the raft with the harpoon and Houndstooth was going to be on the front of the raft with the pole—they couldn't capsize. Of this, Archie was certain: falling into the water meant death.

Finally, *finally*, they were ready, and Houndstooth lowered a long pole into the water and pushed off. They were moving slowly, trying not to attract the attention of the ferals. Ripples spread across the water in front of them and behind, and Archie watched the black surface of the lake, waiting for a single ripple that moved in the wrong direction.

She looked up at the shore. It seemed so far. Houndstooth let out a grunt of effort, and Archie felt a pang of sympathy—his wounds from their battle on the Harriet probably hadn't fully healed yet. She glanced over her shoulder at him, and she thought she saw his silhouette tremble.

She almost didn't hear the splash next to the raft. Almost.

She looked down and saw a ripple in the water, the front of a wake that started a hundred yards away. Archie yelled and pulled back the harpoon. An instant later, a feral's head burst out of the water, teeth bared, nostrils flared and blowing water. The feral bellowed, a bone-rattling roar, its mouth gaping like a bear trap. It snapped at the raft, its jaws closing inches from the place on the platform's edge where Archie's foot was braced. Archie lunged with the harpoon. The hippo roared again, and

Archie put all of her considerable weight behind her weapon as she drove it through the roof of the beast's mouth. The sharp head of the harpoon drove through the feral's skull like a pitchfork sinking into a rotted log, and Archie yanked back hard before it pierced the other side of the animal's head. The harpoon jumped back into her hand, slippery with blood and saliva; lakewater and gore filled the feral's mouth, black in the moonlight.

Archie's momentum nearly knocked her flat—but then Houndstooth gave a mighty shove with his pole, and the raft jumped forward. The feral—dead, surely it was dead—started to sink beneath the surface of the lake; but then, as Archie watched, it bobbed back up to the surface. Archie swore under her breath— she must not have gored it deeply enough in the brain. She wiped one hand at a time on her breeches, trying to get a good grip on the blood-slick shaft of the harpoon, ready for another attack.

The feral twitched in the water.

Then, as she watched, it jerked beneath the surface.

Archie swore again and looked past the feral—it was hard to see in the water, and they were moving away from the beast as quickly as Houndstooth could row. But she was sure that she could see more ripples. She glanced up at the sky, which was just starting to lighten, and cursed the sun for taking so long to rise. She looked back down at the water and—yes, there, ripples, those were *definitely* ripples.

Her suspicion was confirmed a moment later as two more ferals burst up out of the water. They roared at each other as they fought over the carcass of their late fellow.

Archie nearly fell off the raft as it shuddered. She shouted, raised the harpoon, certain that a feral had gotten under the raft and was about to tip them over—

"Archie, we're here! It's the shore!" Houndstooth was yelling behind her. "You get off first, I have to brace us!"

Archie started to argue, but then she saw one of the ferals near the carcass of the one she'd killed raise its head. She was certain it was looking toward the sound of Houndstooth's shouting—and then it disappeared beneath the surface of the water.

"Fils de pute," she said, then jumped off the raft and into the shallows. Houndstooth's side of the raft dipped into the water, threatening to capsize. He tossed Archie the saddlebag as she waded to shore before jumping off the raft himself. They ran to shore, their legs frothing the water, and kept running. They didn't stop, not even at the sound of the *Marianna Fair* splintering. Not at the sounds of screams in the water. Not at the sound of their raft shattering under the jaws of the feral that had chased them to shore. They kept running inland toward the freshwater paddock, toward Ruby and Rosa. They kept running until it was light out and they could be sure that they were too far for the ferals to chase them overland.

They kept running until they were far enough from the carnage that they could no longer smell the blood in the water.

Chapter 3

The unconscious man looked small and soft without the bandana tied over his face.

Adelia squatted beside the man and studied him. He was a stubbly, tan, nose-broken type. His mouth hung slack, and Adelia could see his little pink tongue in there, flopped over to one side.

She had always been struck by how soft people were. They could throw punches, sure, but at the end of the day, they were a mess of vulnerabilities. This man's face had been covered in an attempt to protect himself from Adelia's inevitable retribution— and yet he'd yielded to Hero's clumsy jab. Hero was bad at fighting; Adelia had been astonished that they had managed to land a blow.

But then, Adelia reminded herself, people could be surprising.

Ysabel had been surprising. Adelia had expected to love the baby, to cherish and nurture her—but she could never have anticipated how much she *liked* Ysabel. It usually took Adelia months to warm up to people, and yet the moment that Ysabel was born, Adelia had felt as if they'd been best friends for years.

Go figure.

Adelia felt a faint smile shade her lips at the thought of her daughter's eyes staring up at her, wide and dark and just like her own. She smiled that little smile in spite of the gut-clenching terror: *Those men have Ysabel.* She smiled because she knew what to do with this man, this man who had helped to steal her baby.

She drew back her hand, and she slapped the unmasked man

across the face, with approximately one-tenth of the force that her rage demanded.

He came to, spitting blood. He coughed, gagged, started to choke. Hero shoved him upright and slapped him on the back, and he coughed again, then spat something white. Adelia picked it up.

"You lost this," she said, showing the man his tooth. He breathed hard through his nose as he poked at his gum with his tongue. He spat blood again, then looked from Hero to Adelia with wide, spooked eyes.

"What's your name?" Adelia asked softly. Hero stood behind the man, fidgeting with their shirttails. Adelia smiled at them. They winced. Adelia supposed that her smile was not very reassuring at the moment—not while she was holding a bleeding man's tooth.

Oh, well. If he had wanted to keep all of his teeth, he would not have helped those men steal Ysabel.

"You—you *bitch*, my *tooth*, you—"

Adelia dropped the man's tooth on the ground and grabbed him by the chin. In one hand, she gripped his lower jaw, prying it open. With the other, she reached into his mouth and grasped the tooth just behind his right canine—the companion to the one he'd already lost. She gripped it between her thumb and forefinger and gave an experimental tug. The man made a throaty howling sound, and she extracted her hand from his mouth.

"Qué?" she asked pleasantly. "I didn't catch that."

"My name's Feeney," the man panted. "Doug Feeney."

"Ah, excellent! It is nice to make your acquaintance, Doug Feeney," Adelia said. Then, before he could sag with relief, she grabbed his jaw again. He choked in surprise, his eyes popping. Adelia felt that ghost of a smile again, a kind of comfort warming her fingertips. Yes. She knew exactly what to do with this man.

Having a child hadn't made her forget her craft, and it certainly hadn't taken the edge off her speed.

She reached into his mouth and found the tooth she'd tugged on before. As Doug Feeney let loose a gargling screech, she gave a sharp twist of her wrist. She wrenched her elbow back, and with a rich, wet crack, Doug's tooth ripped free of his jaw.

Adelia rocked back onto her heels as Doug spat blood and whimpered. She picked up the tooth that she had dropped onto the ground, and rattled the pair in her cupped palm like dice. "There," she said. "Now you match."

Near the treeline, Hero was retching. Adelia held in a *tch*. She had known that Hero was thin-skinned, but this was ridiculous. It was only a tooth, after all. He had plenty more.

"So, Doug Feeney," Adelia said. "Who sent you?" He opened his mouth to answer, and Adelia held up a warning finger. "Don't lie to me." She tossed one of his teeth into the air and caught it on her fingertip. It was easy—like catching the blade of a knife point side down—but the man gaped anyway, blood and drool running out of his open mouth. "If you lie to me, things will not be pleasant for you."

"Adelia," Hero said. "I don't know if—"

Adelia looked at Hero patiently. Hero swallowed, then looked away. "What is it, Hero?" Adelia said, careful to keep her voice kind. She wanted to hear what Hero had to say. She really did.

"I just don't know if we can believe what he says," Hero said. "What's to keep him from steering us wrong?"

Adelia looked from Hero to the man on the ground. "Are you going to lie to me, Doug Feeney?" she asked. "Are you going to 'steer me wrong'?"

He shook his head vehemently, then spat blood onto the ground. It wasn't that much blood—he was being dramatic. Adelia tutted. "In my pocket," Feeney said. "Just look in my pocket, it's right—no, not that one—" Adelia had already shoved him hard, forcing him to lie down. She began to turn his pockets inside out with the quick efficiency of a woman who had searched more than her fair share of unconscious men for information. A folding knife fell to the ground, and she placed it in the center of Feeney's chest along with a pocket watch, a handful of peanut shells, and a smooth rock. Oh, and Feeney's teeth. Those went on his chest too, right where he could see them. Finally, she found a crumpled paper, limp with the humid sweat of the man's pockets.

She handed the paper off to Hero for safekeeping, then picked up the smooth rock. "What's this for?" she asked.

Feeney stammered and tried to sit up. Adelia pressed the tip of her index finger to his forehead, keeping him supine. She liked him better that way. "I, uh, I—it's a souvenir." The tip of his tongue poked out to wet his lower lip where it had split under Adelia's slap. "I'm not from around here, and whenever I travel I try to bring a little something home for my boy."

"How old is your boy?" Adelia asked. Her eyes were locked on the man's dilated pupils. He seemed unable to look away from her, even at the sound of Hero tearing open the letter. His breath came fast and shallow. *They sent a lamb,* Adelia thought. *They sent prey to hunt me down.* She returned the rock to Feeney's chest and picked up the pocket knife. She opened it, examined the blade.

"He's five," Feeney whispered. "Please don't kill me. He's five."

Please don't kill me. How many times had Adelia heard those words? She had always been very good at ignoring them, but something was different now.

It wasn't Ysabel. Ysabel was . . . "symptom" wasn't the right word. She was a by-product of this softening, a piece of the emerging puzzle that was life after retirement. The desire to have Ysabel had come after Adelia had decided that she was done killing, after her last job in California had gone so wrong, nearly a year before.

Not wrong. Right. It had gone perfectly, and five men had been dead before she'd so much as blinked. Five men dead, and her heartbeat hadn't so much as stuttered. That had begun the shift—a feeling that she needed to stop the work she'd spent a lifetime perfecting. A certainty that it was time for a change.

She still wasn't sure that she liked the change.

"I wasn't going to kill you," she murmured, still examining the man's knife. "But thank you for asking so nicely."

Feeney started to sob as Adelia took up Hero's kukri—a fat, heavy knife, better suited to hacking through underbrush or dislocating joints than to the fine grade of work Adelia preferred—and began honing the blade of the folding knife against it. She used short, quick strokes. The Adelia of a year ago would have used long strokes, theatrically long ones, slow and grating. She would have watched with detached satisfaction as Feeney grew hypnotized with terrified anticipation. But it wasn't a year ago, and Adelia wasn't interested in Feeney's terror. The adrenal hunger of knowing that this man had helped steal Ysabel hadn't worn off, but its edge was gone, and now Adelia just felt tired. It was the same fatigue she'd felt throughout the hippo caper on the Harriet, as Travers had endlessly wheedled her and blackmailed her and threatened her.

She was so tired.

"Adelia, you should read this," Hero was saying, but Adelia shook her head.

"Momento," she said. "I'm almost finished." She sheathed

her fat knife and picked up the smooth stone from Feeney's chest, then rose from her crouch to face Hero. "Qué onda?"

"This is a letter for you," Hero said. They held out the paper, but Adelia didn't take it. Her hands were occupied; she scratched at the smooth stone with the folding knife, not looking up.

"And?"

"It, um." Hero faltered. "It's a ransom letter, sort of. It says that if you want Ysabel back you have to go to Baton Rouge and get her."

Adelia glanced at Feeney, whose face had taken on the glazed look of a man who couldn't process any more fear. She nudged him with her foot. "Feeney. If I go to this place, will I be ambushed and killed?"

"No," he breathed. "Not that they told me, anyway. They just said to get the baby and leave the letter, though, so . . . maybe."

"Hmph." Adelia turned back to her etching on the smooth stone. "Alright, so, we'll go there." She paused. "*I'll* go there. My apologies, Hero. I did not mean to presume."

Hero remained silent, and Adelia allowed herself a small internal sigh as she dropped the stone into her shirt pocket. She had no right to expect Hero's forgiveness. Even if it had been a coup to make the injuries seem grave while avoiding any mortal wounds, she'd still stabbed Hero. She'd still made them feel pain and fear and the terrible loneliness that comes with waking up in a strange place with strange injuries.

It had been nice to have company, though. While it had lasted.

Adelia crouched beside Feeney and held the blade of his folding knife where he could see it, very close to his eyes. The glazed look on his face gave way to renewed fear, and he began to blubber again. Adelia tapped the flat of the blade against his lips.

"Shhh," she said. "Listen." He went silent as she held the blade up in front of his eyes again. "You need to take better care of your knives. Whet the blade every so often, especially if you're going to leave it folded up all the time in your sweaty pocket. And oil this hinge, sí?" She turned the knife so he could see the little flakes of rust building on the place where the knife folded. "This is a good blade and it could last you a long time. You could pass it down to your son someday, if you take good care of it."

Feeney didn't nod—smart of him, with the tip of the knife so very close to his eyes. But he licked his lips and whispered, "I will. I'll take better care of it."

"Good," Adelia said. She folded the blade and tucked it back into the pocket it had fallen out of. Then she did the same with the other detritus on Feeney's chest—even the peanut shells. She held up his teeth, examining them, and then put one into his shirt pocket. The other she dropped into her own shirt pocket, winking at the horrified man as it clicked against the stone that was in there. "Just in case," she said. "If that letter is a trick, I'll come back to get the matching one."

Finally, Adelia untied the rope from Feeney's wrists and coiled it, hanging it on her belt. She could have simply cut him loose, but it wouldn't do to waste good rope.

Don't kill me, he'd said. It kept echoing in Adelia's mind. *Please don't kill me.*

Feeney scrambled to his feet, and Adelia grabbed his arm, preventing him from running away. He so clearly wanted to run away.

"Here," she said, pulling the smooth stone from her shirt pocket and putting it in Feeney's hand. "This will be a better souvenir for your son than a plain stone. Now, he'll always know where it came from. He'll prefer that, don't you think?"

The man turned the stone over in his hand to see Adelia's etching of a hippopotamus. Its mouth gaped to show fearsome fangs, and a little bird was perched on its nose. Adelia thought it was quite good.

Feeney didn't say anything. He closed his fist around the stone, looked between Hero and Adelia, and then bolted into the trees.

Adelia sighed. The boy would like the stone, especially if his father told him the story of its provenance. He would probably carry it around in his pocket until the day he died.

She nodded at Hero, then took the letter from them and studied it. Hero hadn't left out anything but the signature line—Whelan Parrish, a name Adelia had hoped she'd never have to hear again. She quickly committed his words to memory before folding the paper and tucking it into the sheath of the knife on her thigh for safekeeping. She rested a hand on Hero's shoulder as she passed them.

"Thank you," she said.

"For what?" Hero asked, glancing down at Adelia's hand.

"For trying to help," Adelia said. "You could have run, but you didn't. I know you're not a fighter—I'm sure that it was very frightening to run into the middle of that fight. I . . ." Adelia realized that she'd started journeying through her thanks without a destination in mind. "Thank you for trying," she finished clumsily. She walked away before Hero could answer.

As Adelia headed to the pond to begin preparing Zahra for the trip to Baton Rouge, she took a mental inventory. It would be a one-week ride at the minimum. She had her bedroll and supplies, and a bag of Ysabel's swaddling cloths, but only enough food to ride for a few days without stopping for provisions. She considered her options: the food might last just long enough if she cut herself down to half rations, but she had been ravenous since Ysabel was born. She made a mental note to buy more food at the earliest opportunity, although it would mean spending the last of her money. She cursed herself for not stealing anything from Houndstooth or Travers before fleeing the Harriet. She had her weapons—mostly small blades, since those had been easiest to wield during her pregnancy, but she'd hung on to her best machete just in case. She wondered if perhaps she should sell it, just to give herself a bigger financial cushion for the journey.

Some distant part of Adelia's mind raised concerns about her priorities. She should be wailing and tearing her hair out and then lying on the floor for weeks, refusing food and water, mute with unspeakable grief. She should be nurturing the beginnings of a lifetime of wounded rage—not mentally cataloguing which of her knives was the most valuable. *Mama would be so disappointed in me,* Adelia thought, remembering the many times that her mother had slapped her tearless face.

And yet, as she waded into the water up to her waist and began checking Zahra's teeth and feet and underbelly, making sure that she was prepared for the long journey ahead, Adelia could not find anger within herself. She had never been able to find anger—not the kind of anger her mother had specialized in, anyway. Adelia could be angry at a distance; she could feel the nagging discomfort of *wrongness,* and the desire to fix it. She could be angry in the moment, when a flush of adrenaline drove her at her opponent. But she could not find within herself the sustained outrage that she was certain she ought to feel. She was not angry that Ysabel had been taken; it was simply a problem.

A problem that she was going to fix.

When she was satisfied that Zahra was in good shape for a long ride, Adelia sprinkled the hippo's broad grey back and sides with white resin, to keep the padded underside of the saddle from slipping around and giving Zahra blisters. She heaved her kneeling saddle up onto Zahra's back with a grunt—she had always been strong, but something had slipped out of place during her long labor, and lifting the heavy saddle wasn't as easy as it used to be. She secured the saddle over Zahra's back and patted her girl on the flank. "I'll be right back, Zita." Zahra grumbled a little, and Adelia rolled her eyes as the hippo presented her broad, flat nose insistently. "I have spoiled you," she said, scratching under Zahra's chin. The hippo grumbled again and pushed at Adelia with her nose until Adelia planted a kiss on the tip of it. This finally satisfied the beast, and Adelia was allowed to leave the pond without comment.

She dripped her way back through the trees to the camp. When she emerged from the treeline, she saw immediately that Hero's bedroll and saddlebags were gone. *That was fast,* she thought with dismay. She found Stasia settled under a tree, eyes half lidded. She wondered how Hero was planning to haul the saddlebags without a hippo to ride. She had known, from a few comments that Hero had made and from the way their eyes watched the horizon, that they had been planning to leave her soon. Still . . . it stung her. *I would have given them Stasia,* she thought. *If they had just asked.*

Adelia pulled up short as she walked farther into the little clearing and saw that her own bedroll was gone as well. And her saddlebags—everything. All of it was gone.

She reached for the knife at her side and turned in a slow circle, shifting her weight onto the balls of her feet and bending her knees into a familiar defensive stance. There was a rustle at the treeline a few feet from her, and she twisted, pulling her arm back to throw her knife at the figure that was emerging there—

"I think I've got everything packed up," Hero said, wiping their hands on their trousers, "but you'll probably want to take one last look around before we—" They looked up, and their eyes went round as they took in Adelia, who had frozen in the instant before releasing her knife. They looked over their shoulder, then back at Adelia. "What are you doing?" they asked slowly.

As she lowered her throwing arm, all Adelia could think to say in reply was, "What are *you* doing?"

"Breaking camp," Hero said. "I . . . I assumed that you were saddling up Zahra and Stasia, right? I thought that if I packed for both of us, we could head out sooner, maybe make it to Larto by nightfall." Their eyes were on Adelia's knife, which was still unsheathed. "Would you mind putting that away? You're making me kind of nervous here." They lifted one hand toward their belly in an abrupt, abortive movement, and Adelia was sure that they were remembering the last time they'd watched her throw a knife in their direction.

Adelia sheathed the knife without taking her eyes off Hero. "You're—you said *we* as if—are you coming with me?" She felt very small, asking that. She didn't know how to do this. She didn't know how to be a person who would ask that question.

"Yes," Hero replied levelly, and Adelia respected that they hadn't said "of course" or something equally dishonest. "I was going to leave. I was actually . . . even before this all happened, I was going to tell you that it was time for me to go."

"I know," Adelia said.

Hero rubbed the back of their neck and appeared to find something important to study in the treeline. "But you were right, before. When you said that I tried to stop those men. I tried. But I failed. I didn't keep them from taking Ysabel. And it wouldn't be right for me to leave you on your own to get her back. Where I'm from, we . . . we don't leave people alone like that." They looked at Adelia, clenching their jaw. Their voice went stern. "I'll help you find her. And then I'm gone, understand? We get Ysabel back, and then that's the end of the line."

They didn't say more, and Adelia didn't press them. But as she led Stasia back to the pond to be saddled, she found herself swallowing around a peach pit of unspeakable words that had appeared in her throat. She pressed her face to Stasia's flank and breathed in the hippo's musty clay-smell, and gave herself permission to be relieved. She'd be alone again soon—Hero was leaving her. But not yet. Not while her baby was missing.

This, at least, she would not have to face alone.

Chapter 4

Houndstooth stared down at his map, twirling his grease pencil between two fingers. His left hand was smudged with black, and he was sure that he had similar marks on his face. Even as he thought it, he reached up with his smeary hand and rubbed his forehead.

"Damn it," he muttered, "where are you, Hero?"

"Houndstooth?" Archie's contralto fluted through the trees. He looked up—he didn't think he'd been gone long enough yet for her to notice and come looking for him. She'd been watching him like a hawk all day, and now—just when he'd been getting somewhere, she was interrupting him again.

His mouth twisted into a grimace as Archie's voice reached him once more. "Houndstooth! Dinner is ready. Come eat it before I give your share to Ruby!"

"Dinner?" Houndstooth looked around, blinking. Surely it wasn't time for dinner yet—he'd only told Archie that he needed to stretch his legs a few minutes after breakfast. He would surely be hungry if he'd missed lunch—but, no. The thought of food only made his stomach clench.

His legs ached and tingled painfully as he stood up and stretched. He'd been hunched over his maps for—well, for however long it had been. Hours, evidently. Archie would be worried—she'd try to convince him to eat and sleep and bathe, as if those things mattered when Hero was missing. As if they hadn't already wasted enough time.

Walking back through the trees, Houndstooth allowed

himself to think for just an instant the thought he'd been fighting to keep at bay: *Archie is slowing you down.* He knew it wasn't true—knew that Archie was probably the only thing keeping him alive—but some small sinister part of him insisted on bringing up the idea of leaving Archie behind to focus on finding Hero.

As always, he pushed the thought away as soon as it arose—but this time, it didn't leave him easily. It was insistent: *Archie is in the way. She's a distraction.*

Houndstooth pushed his hands through his hair as he reached the sandbar where they'd made camp. It sloped down into a long, shallow bank of clear, ankle-deep water. The deeper waters that Houndstooth's inky Ruby and Archie's bone-white Rosa preferred were less than a quarter mile away, flush with the water hyacinth the hippos adored. Even now, Houndstooth could hear Ruby's pleased grunting as she grazed. He'd be fishing purple flower petals from between her teeth for days.

Archie sat on a long, weathered log that stuck out over the water on one end. It was a huge fallen tree, complete with a tangle of roots that propped it up above the water. Tadpoles and tiny fish hid in the shadows of the old, dead roots in the water, and Houndstooth couldn't help smiling at them. Between the little fish and the pristine water hyacinth, he and Archie both knew that they'd found an oasis: this place was untouched by the ravenous, terrifying scourge of the ferals.

"There you are," Archie said with a too-bright smile. "I've been thinking about where we should go next. Are you 'ungry?" She was an excellent con artist—a liar for a living—and yet when she looked at Houndstooth, she failed to conceal the worry in her eyes. Houndstooth wondered if it was because he knew her so well that he could see the lie behind her smile, or if that was simply an indicator of the depth of her concern.

Distraction, the little voice in the back of his mind whispered. *How long has it been since you've looked at the map?*

He pushed the thought away and sat next to Archie. "Here I am," he said, trying to match her smile. He thought he did a good job, but Archie's smile faltered as she looked at him. She handed him a tin cup full of campfire-hot stew—dried beans and hippo-belly jerky, a raft of fat and starch and salt—and a hunk of crusty bread. He made appreciative noises as he forced himself to eat. It was a good stew, he could tell that much just from looking at it, but he could barely taste it. Still, he exclaimed when he found a little fish in the bottom of his cup, cooked through, flaky and tender but small enough to eat whole. He glanced at Archie as an actor glances past the footlights, wondering if his performance was being received well.

She wasn't even looking at him.

Archie was staring into the water, watching the little fish that darted in and out of the tree roots.

"I suppose the water here is shallow enough to keep them safe from bigger fish," Houndstooth ventured. Archie made a noncommittal noise and stirred her stew halfheartedly. Houndstooth watched the fish alongside her in a comfortable—if odd—silence. The two of them had spent many evenings in each other's company over the years, on one job or another, and silence between the two of them was rare at best. Both of them were natural storytellers, and whenever their conversations grew dull or seemed to be petering out, Archie would break into bawdy songs about French girls and their various flexibilities. But Houndstooth realized as he watched the fish that Archie hadn't sung once since they'd left the Harriet. In fact—he thought back over the last two months of traveling alongside his old friend—she had been silent much of the time. He hadn't noticed, since he'd been busy poring over maps and plotting routes and writing letters to contacts throughout the bayous, but Archie had been keeping her counsel. Unless, that is, she was imploring him to take better care of himself.

Houndstooth chewed on this particularly stringy bit of guilt. Something was bothering his friend, and he'd been so busy trying to avoid her care that he hadn't noticed until just now. And even now, he'd only noticed because she suddenly *wasn't* trying to take care of him.

"Are you alright, Archie?" he said after a moment's hesitation. The little voice in his head murmured that there was no time for this kind of distraction.

"Hm?" She didn't look away from the fish. "I'm fine. I'm just—fine." Houndstooth's brow creased. She'd stopped herself from saying something. It wasn't like her. Something was wrong, but— *Let it go,* the little voice hissed. *Get back to the maps. Hero could be dying right now.*

"Alright," Houndstooth said, pushing away the guilt that nagged at him again. "Well, thank you for making supper. Delightful, as always." He took his cup to the water and rinsed it, then stood and watched for a few seconds as the little fish darted out from the tree roots to gulp down the fragments of bean and gristle that floated near the shore. *Aha,* Houndstooth thought. *Maybe—if I can draw Adelia out from wherever she's hiding, then I can make her tell me where Hero is—* He stopped himself from thinking *if Hero's still alive,* because there was no other option. Hero had to be alive.

They had to be.

He started to wander toward his bedroll and lantern, knowing that he would need some light. Night was falling fast, and he couldn't afford to wait. But what kind of trap should he set? Something to do with Cal, maybe? Or, no—Adelia already knew that

Cal was dead, he kept forgetting. Something to do with the baby? What about—

"I think we should go to Baton Rouge," Archie said behind him.

Houndstooth turned around, cocking his head. Baton Rouge was at least three days' hard riding away, and it was practically dry. "Why on earth would you want to go there?" he asked.

Archie was looking at him with grim determination. "I think we need to regroup. I think that we should board Ruby and Rosa for a week or two while you rest and eat. And"—her eyes flicked away from his for an instant, just an instant—"I will be able to send a letter there, to Carter. I will be able to tell him where to find us. If we stayed put for a change—"

Distractions. Houndstooth trembled with sudden fury. He felt his lip twist into a sneer and before he could stop himself, he was laughing. It was not a kind laugh, and Archie flinched at the sound of it. "I see," he said in a low, smooth voice. "Of course— I should have realized that you were *pining.*"

Archie's brows shot up, then drew down in confusion and hurt. Her accent was thick with shock. "Now, see 'ere, 'Oundstooth—"

"No, no, please, Archie, I insist," Houndstooth said, and even to his own ears his voice sounded cold and sharp. It was practically his father's voice. "You're absolutely right. We simply *must* spend the last of our money to board Ruby *and* Rosa *and* Abigail, so that we can go spend another two weeks wasting time while you write love letters to someone who doesn't even want you badly enough to come meet you where you are. Or do you think he'll come all the way to Baton Rouge to spend a night in your *company?*"

Archie's face darkened. She took three slow, deliberate steps toward Houndstooth. "I think," she said quietly, "you should take a walk, oui? Clear your head for a few minutes. You are not thinking straight, 'Oundstooth, my old friend."

"I'm not?" he spat. "I'm not thinking straight? Au contraire, *Regina*." Archie shook her head at him warningly, but even as he knew that he should stop he continued. "I'm the only one of us who's been thinking straight this whole time. I'm the one who's been focused on finding Hero and Adelia, while *you've* been getting distracted by—what?" He walked to her bedroll and flipped up her rough blanket with one foot, revealing a packet of letters bound with a dark green ribbon. "Love notes?" He kicked at the packet of letters, knocking it into the dirt. "Fantasies? Of a future with a *U.S. marshal*?" He kicked at the letters again furiously. His feet felt almost numb. "What, are you going to settle down with Carter, *Regina*? Are you going to have a parlor where you host fine ladies for tea and discuss the weather? Are you going to birth a litter of brats and spend your time chasing them away from the fine china? Are you going to tell stories about the days when you *used* to be a legendary hopper who was worth a *damn* to her crew, who had an ounce of loyalty, who was planning to make something of herself? Is that the life you want?" He wheeled around and pointed a shaking finger at the water. "Then go! Go get your *beau,* if you really think he'll have you."

Archie was standing very still. She was staring, Houndstooth realized, at his feet. He looked down and saw that his left boot heel was crushing one end of the packet of letters. The green ribbon had come partially undone, and was dusky with dirt. Houndstooth wiped his mouth with the heel of his hand, feeling oddly empty and almost drunk. He swayed on his feet, once, then steadied himself.

Archie walked over to him and put her hand on his arm. She pressed it down until it rested by his side, then raised her hand to his face. She brought her fingers in front of his eyes and he could see, in the dying light of the day, that they were wet.

He reached up to feel his own face. When had he begun to cry? But there, among the stubble of his patchy beard—when had he let himself grow a beard?—was wetness.

"I think you need to go for a walk, chérie," Archie said. Her voice shook, and Houndstooth could not tell from her face what emotion caused the tremor. "Do not come back until the moon is up," she added, pressing a loving hand to his wet cheek, "or I think I will kill you."

Houndstooth nodded, then stooped to pick up the packet of letters. He pressed it into Archie's hands. She stared at the space near his right ear. "Go now," she whispered. "Go see to yourself."

Houndstooth walked into the darkening trees. As the buzz of nocturnal insects began to rise, he let himself get lost on the little islet. He let himself get lost in the dark, and he let himself cry, although he couldn't have said what exactly the tears were for any more than he could have said who it was that he had truly been shouting at back at the camp. He wandered until it was too dark to see the trees in front of him, and then he sat on the ground and put his face in his hands and wondered if he could ever find his way back.

Chapter 5

Hero dismounted at Port Rouge with an aching spine and half-numb legs. A week of hard riding along the Black River, the Red River, and a series of marshes and tributaries that dodged the Mississippi had left them feeling threadbare and ready for a week's worth of sleep. Stasia, Hero's borrowed steed, had served Hero well enough, and they patted her flank, torn between gratitude for her speed and a yearning for their old friend Abigail. Nearly all of the waters they'd ridden through had been shockingly docile, a surprise for which Hero had been infinitely thankful. They'd asked a flint-eyed dockworker at Alligator Bayou about it on their way to Thompson Creek.

"Oh, hell," he'd said, chewing on a long strip of what Hero guessed to be salt cod. "It's been a strange couple of months, what with the dam collapse and all. River's fucked. Bayou's alright, for the most part—only been a couple attacks, and them just people being stupid and all." He paused to swab sweat from his brow with his forearm, an exercise in futility as far as Hero was concerned.

"When you say 'people being stupid' . . . ?" Hero was deeply skeptical that the ferals hadn't been an issue.

"Just don't go out at night, and watch for wakes 'thout a boat attached to 'em, and I'm sure you know the rest." He appraised Zahra and Stasia, eyeing the scars that marred the hippos' flanks, but before he could ask about where Hero and Adelia were riding from—or where they were headed—they were already gone, riding toward Port Rouge.

Port Rouge was a puddle of a marsh tucked into an elbow of the Mississippi near the top of Baton Rouge proper. It was man-made and clumsy the way most hopper wallows were—wood and stone and sandbags from a generation before walled off the shallow half mile of brown water to form a wet pit for hippos to wade in. But there was vegetation growing there, and water-birds, and a high enough divide keeping the river out, so Hero and Adelia paid the fee to board Zahra and Stasia there with only a cursory amount of grumbling over the cost.

"Will they be alright in there?" Hero asked, looking over their shoulder as Zahra and Stasia waded over to investigate a heron.

"They'll be fine," Adelia replied distractedly as she adjusted her shirt.

"Do you really buy that the ferals are laying low?"

"I'd wager—*hnf.*" Adelia adjusted her shirt again, wincing. "I'd wager that they've mostly been causing troubles farther south. That's the way the river flows, sí?"

"Still," Hero started to say.

"Still, sure, fine. Hop-blighted *damn,* this hurts." Adelia made a little pained growling noise, then abruptly stepped off the road into the thin brush beside the river.

Hero felt inexpressibly awkward. They didn't say anything, but they turned away so that Adelia could do whatever it was that she did when her breasts hurt. They tried to ignore the steady stream of curses in both English and Spanish that drifted to them from the brush, and wished that they'd known some solution to her pain. That was their whole job, and they knew it—on every team they'd ever worked with, they'd been the one who people would turn to when every idea had proven to be a bust. But this was a whole different swamp to navigate, and the best they could offer Adelia was a useless, sympathetic wince every time her swearing started to heat up. Their brain spun, trying to think of something, anything—a device, or a chemical—but they were at a total loss.

When Adelia emerged from the brush, Hero clapped their hands to their mouth to stop themselves from laughing or asking questions. The entire front of Adelia's shirt was soaked—no, Hero realized. Adelia's *entire* shirt. And her hair. It looked as though she'd dunked herself into the river.

Adelia glowered. "I spilled," she said tersely.

"Okay," Hero said—but they couldn't help themselves. "Did you jump into the water to get it back?"

Adelia started to stalk ahead, but then, to Hero's shock, she stopped and waited for them. When they caught up to her, she muttered, "I'm hot. The water makes me feel better."

Hero glanced sidelong at Adelia. Twin flags of pink rode high on her cheeks, and they allowed themselves a small smile at the notion that Adelia—stone-faced, ice-cold Adelia—might be a little embarrassed.

They reached Baton Rouge just before nightfall. Adelia kicked open the swinging doors of the Hop's Tusk with one booted foot. Her hair and shirt were dry, but she'd been swearing a steady blue streak for the past hour, and Hero pitied the poor soul that got between her and her bedroom. Sure enough, Adelia stormed the bar and slapped money down on the scarred wood with a flat palm. Hero slipped into the shadows beside the door and watched as the garter-armed innkeeper behind the bar handed Adelia a key and snatched his hand back as though he were afraid to lose it. Adelia made for the stairs, pushing her way through the crowd with a stiff shoulder, and then she was gone.

Hero eased their way to the bar and sat, groaning at the relief their legs felt. They doubted that they'd be able to get up again any time soon, and debated asking the innkeeper for a pillow, a blanket, and twenty-four hours to sit on the stool without moving.

They scrubbed their face with their hands, trying not to let their eyes close for too long. When they lowered their hands, there was a drink sweating on the bar in front of them.

"Excuse me?" they called, and the innkeeper slid over to them. He was a sallow-faced white man with drooping, hound-dog eyes and a few fine wisps of hair stretched across a freckled scalp. Hero reflected that the poor wilted fellow looked like he'd rather have been on a burning raft in the middle of a lake of hippo shit than standing behind that bar. His eyes darted continuously along the nearly empty stretch of the bar, watching for someone else who might possibly need his attention.

"Yes?" he said, still not looking directly at Hero. "Is there a problem?"

"I didn't order this drink," Hero said.

The innkeeper unfolded a handkerchief and dabbed sweat from his top lip. "It's on the house. Courtesy of, hm. The lady." Hero thought for a mad instant that he meant Adelia, but then he gestured at a woman who was perched at the far end of the bar, nursing her own drink. She didn't look up, and Hero quickly looked away, their face and neck burning in a rising flush.

They couldn't remember the last time that someone had sent them a drink at a bar. They couldn't remember the last time they'd *been* in a bar without being on a job.

The drink looked very good. But . . . *Houndstooth.*

Hero took a deep breath. *Don't think about it.* They grabbed their drink and took a long, deep slug of the brown liquor. It went down oily and hot, and burned in their belly like a live coal. They tried to pay attention to the heat, to the vile taste of the alcohol. They didn't admit to themself that they were hoping it would scald away the thought of what had happened on the Harriet after they'd left.

Hero took another drink, even though it made their eyes water. They wondered if that was what other people thought poison was like going down. So undeniable. They traced a finger through the ring of condensation on the wood in front of them, smudging it into a long oval. Remembering when a long, slim finger had traced that oval onto the inky hide of a hippo named Ruby.

They finished the drink too fast and their head was swimming. But it was better than thinking about other people swimming. Or failing to swim.

All the papers, all the songs, all the stories. They had all said the same thing: *no survivors.* And now all the booze was gone, and Hero felt a crack forming in the dam that held back all the things they had been trying not to think about.

"Well, that's one way to tell a gal you'd like her company."

Hero jumped, looked at the stool next to them. The woman—no, Hero corrected themself, the *girl,* for she couldn't have been older than seventeen or eighteen—the *girl* from the end of the bar had settled herself next to Hero. Her dark hair was barely longer than a razor would allow, and her warm brown skin was just a few shades lighter than Hero's own. She looked almost familiar, but something about the way she carried herself told Hero that it was probably this girl's job to look familiar.

Hero coughed. "Sorry, I—uh. I sort of—I'm tired," they finished weakly. "It's been a long day."

"A long week, I should think," the girl said, taking a sip of her drink. Hero did a double-take, and the girl laughed. She flagged down the innkeeper and signaled for another round before Hero could stop her.

"How did—who are you?" Hero asked, suddenly acutely aware that they were alone. Adelia, with all her weaponry and her sure aim and her expertise, was gone. They were on their own, and if this girl turned out to be trouble . . . they would have to do a better job of defending themself than they had back on the Catahoula.

"Call me Acadia," the girl drawled. "It's not my real name, but you don't need to know that and I'm not going to tell it to you. Thanks, handsome," she said, tipping a wink at the innkeeper as he dropped off two more drinks. He looked at Hero, and his eyes seemed to flash a warning. *Too late,* Hero thought, and raised their glass to Acadia.

"Are you going to kill me?" Hero asked, their throat tight. It wasn't as hard to ask as they'd thought it would be. Out of habit, they slid their free hand into their pocket. A vial of powder was there, always at the ready. One puff of air across the cork would blow more than enough of the poison into this "Acadia's" eyes. She'd be foaming from every orifice within seconds, dead within minutes. Hero let their thumbnail sink into the wax seal around the cork, but not all the way. Not yet.

Acadia glanced at them out of the corner of her eye. She didn't laugh, a small mercy for which Hero was profoundly thankful. "Not tonight," she said mildly. "Maybe another time, if you need killing."

"Well. Alright," Hero said, slipping their hand back out of their pocket, leaving the tiny vial unopened. It was a reasonable enough answer, all things considered. They sipped at the drink the innkeeper had brought, knowing that they'd end up drunk if they kept it up, but not able to will themself to care. "What can I do for you, then, *Acadia*?"

"I think we're from the same place, you and I," Acadia said. "Your accent is a little faded, but I can hear it."

Hero cocked a half smile at the girl. "I don't think we are, but that's a very nice try."

Acadia shrugged. "I would swear I've seen you before."

"Maybe on a wanted poster," Hero muttered into their glass.

"You gave up that life a long time ago, though," the girl said, and again Hero found themself staring at her, incredulous. "Oh, I know all about you, Hero Shackleby. You had quite a storied career. Although I've always wondered—I mean, everyone wonders—"

"What do you want?" Hero snapped. They didn't have the time or the energy to dance that old, familiar dance. The whelp was going to ask Hero why they'd retired, it was as obvious as a hop's hunger for milk, and Hero just . . . couldn't have that conversation. Not now.

The girl put her palms up in surrender. "Okay, alright, I'm sorry." She poked Hero in the shoulder with a nail-bitten finger. "Sensitive. The drinks were supposed to ease you up a little, you know."

Hero snorted into their glass.

"Well, fine. I've got something I'm supposed to give you." She pulled a limp piece of paper out from between her breasts. She laid it on the bar between them and added, "But I'd appreciate if you didn't read it until I was gone."

"Who's it from?"

"Read it and find out."

"That's fair," Hero said. If the girl was a messenger, she'd just finished doing her duty. Hero could respect that. Messengers weren't paid enough to keep information on their employers a secret, but they also weren't paid enough to get tangled up in the interpersonal dramas that trailed between people they didn't know.

The girl sipped her drink again, and Hero noticed that she was barely swallowing any of it. *Clever.* "So," she asked, her voice a shade too casual. "Is it true that you're here with Adelia Reyes?"

Hero didn't answer.

"I'm sure you don't want to tell me," the girl continued. "It's just that, I've been wanting to meet her ever since I was a little girl."

Hero snorted again. "You're still a little girl," they said.

The girl's eyes flashed. "I've killed men," she said in a low voice. "I think that qualifies me for something more than 'little girl.'"

"We've all killed men," Hero said—but then they gentled their voice and tried to remember a time when having killed a man had meant something significant to them, too. "I'm sure Adelia'd love to meet you." The girl rolled her eyes at the polite lie. "Or . . . she'd find it acceptable, at least. Are you staying here?"

The girl shook her head. "When she wants to meet me, just have her tell the innkeeper. He'll make sure I get the message." She looked at Hero with an entrepreneurial gleam in her eye. "And, hey. If you ever need anyone for a job, you know how to find me. My fees are very reasonable."

"So you don't work for my secret admirer?" Hero said, waving the note.

"I don't work for anybody," Acadia drawled. "I work for money. If you've got some you're looking to offload, you just let me know. Don't forget what I said about Adelia, either."

Hero took a last long drink from their glass, swallowing hard. They could feel the liquor winding its way around their arms and legs and throat, pulling them down toward drunken sleep. It was a delicious sensation.

"I'll tell her," they started to say. But they heard the swinging doors at the front of the inn creak and thump open, and by the time they looked up, Acadia already had one foot out the door.

———✦———

"Adelia?" Hero rapped one knuckle hard on the warped wood of the door at the end of the upstairs hallway.

"Momento," Adelia called from inside. Hero leaned against the cracked plaster wall to wait until Adelia was done with whatever ministrations her swollen breasts still required. They nudged the straw and sawdust that littered the floor with their foot, sweeping a clean arc of wood planks.

Don't think about it, they told themself, firmly shoving aside the memory of the last time they'd shared accommodations with someone. *Not now.*

"Okay, come in," Adelia said behind them. She'd opened the door and walked away, leaving Hero standing in the open doorway with their hands in their pockets. One hand crushed the already rumpled note from Acadia. Or, from whoever Acadia worked for.

Adelia leaned out of the sole window, emptying a small washbasin into the alley below. A smell filled the small room—buttermilk and sweat and earth, suspended in the humidity of the night. Adelia's thin linen shirt, unencumbered by her usual leather engirdment of sheaths, stuck to her back, and her loosely tied hair had sprung into damp curls around her face and at the nape of her neck. A flush colored the back of her neck, and Hero frowned.

It wasn't that warm in the room.

It was warm, sure, and humid as a hop's armpit, but it was no worse than it had been during their long ride. And they couldn't ever remember seeing Adelia sweat before.

"Are you alright?" they asked, unthinking. They flinched—Adelia wasn't the kind of person who liked to be worried about.

"I'm fine," Adelia snapped. "Why?"

She turned and Hero's frown deepened. Two bright, high spots of color had risen in her cheeks, and her eyes were bright.

"Do you have a fever, Adelia?" Hero stepped forward, putting their hand out to feel Adelia's forehead before they had time to think better of it. There was a flash of movement, a shout—and then Hero was on the floor, their face pressed into unfresh sawdust and grime, their arm twisted painfully high behind their back above an acute weight that they could only assume was—yes, it had to be a knee pressing into their spine.

A moment later, the weight was gone, and their arm was free. They scrambled up and saw Adelia standing a few feet away, one hand pressed to her forehead.

"Oh, Hero—I'm, hm." She cleared her throat awkwardly. "I'm sorry. I didn't—I didn't mean to, ah. To . . ."

"To flatten me?" Hero asked wryly, rolling their shoulder until it popped.

"I don't like to be touched without permission," Adelia said in a quiet voice that carried what Hero thought to be a shadow of regret. "I'm very sorry."

"It's alright," Hero said. "I should have asked. Can we call it even?"

Adelia nodded, then looked awkwardly away. The tension of unfulfilled violence hung in the air, and Hero wondered what would have happened if Adelia's weapons hadn't been safely stowed by the time they came in. They were willing to bet that there would be blood on the floor of the little bedroom.

Best to not think about that, either, they told themself, even as their hand drifted up to the scar on their belly.

"Well," Hero said in an overjovial voice, forcing themself to sound calm. "At any rate. I have something you should see."

Adelia raised her eyebrows. "Oh?"

"Here," Hero said. They pulled the folded paper out of their hip pocket, unfolding it before they handed it over. "A message."

"From who?" Adelia demanded, eyes flashing.

"The one and only; Whelan Parrish," Hero answered. "Via a girl named Acadia. Does the name ring a bell?"

"No," Adelia said absently as she scanned the note. "Should it?"

"I don't think so," Hero said. "But she'd like it to."

"Maldito." Adelia tugged at her shirt, fanning herself. "This is—me cago en la madre que te parió! We have to go. Parrish—we have to go and meet him—"

Hero held up a hand and sat hard on the bed. "Not tonight."

"Not tonight?" Adelia's chin snapped up and she glared at Hero with a ferocity that made Hero long for the ferals on the Harriet. "*Not tonight*?! I'm sorry, Hero, did you have somewhere else to be? This man has *Ysabel* and he's probably going to—"

"Here," Hero said simply. "I have to be *here*. And so do you, Adelia. We need to rest. We need to bathe. We need to regroup. He isn't going to hurt the baby tonight, but if we go see him and try to take her back in the state we're in right now? We'll both wind up dead, and then there'll be no one left to kill the sorry son of a bitch." *And besides,* they didn't say, *you're not thinking straight, you fever-brained loon.*

Adelia fumed for a moment, but Hero knew that she'd see the truth in what they had said.

"Fine," she finally snapped. "But we go first thing in the morning, after we eat and . . . and wash, and make a plan. Dawn. We leave at dawn."

"That sounds perfect," Hero said. "Now, how about some sleep?" They tried out a smile, but Adelia just snarled at them. They shrugged mildly, then leaned back against the headboard and lowered their hat over their eyes.

Adelia would sleep eventually. If those fever flags flying on her cheeks were any indication, she'd probably sleep even better than Hero intended to. She'd have to, or else they'd need to wait another day before going to find Ysabel.

It'll be fine, Hero thought, peeking out from under their hat at Adelia's pacing, watching her eyes glitter with rage and fever and murder. *She can wait. Vengeance is a slow game.*

Hero had always been good at slow games.

Chapter 6

The ride to Baton Rouge had been a silent one. The intervening week, on the other hand, hadn't been silent—it had been something much worse.

It had been polite.

"I will be back in an hour," Archie said, settling a brushed felt bowler over her slicked-back hair. She'd borrowed Houndstooth's straight razor to hone her crisp part; her hair looked better than his had in months. "Please do not feel the need to wait for me to 'ave supper."

Houndstooth didn't look up from the letter he was writing. "Thank you for letting me know."

Archie pursed her lips for a moment, then shot her cuffs and walked out the door without another word. The tension between her and Houndstooth had been thick as hop fat for the past eight days, and she didn't know how to cut through it. They'd fought before, more than enough times—but never like this.

She walked down out of the townhouse where she and Houndstooth were staying and onto the street. Her gold-tipped cane flashed in the late-morning sun, and she felt a weight slip from her shoulders as she brushed the brim of her hat at two young ladies, who giggled back from under their shared parasol.

Not her type, but it was nice to see them blush.

She knew she was handsome. Her pinstriped linen suit was painful to keep free of wrinkles while she was traveling, but it fit her like a dream and was better tailored than the suits of most of the men she tipped her hat to on the street. The last time she'd worn it, she'd been riding through the night to get her hands on enough explosives to ruin a dam.

She preferred the way the fabric looked in the sunlight.

Oh yes—she knew she was handsome. Even Houndstooth's eyes had flashed with envy the first time he saw her waistcoat—dove-grey paisley with the slightest sheen of lilac. She smiled to herself, remembering how she'd salted the wound by telling him that her Parisian tailor would only accept clients in person. She always enjoyed dressing herself more when she could share her flashes of sartorial brilliance with her friend.

"Pardonnez-moi, sir?" Archie looked down to find a hunched girl tugging at her coattail. The girl was young, too thin, and had grease smeared across the dark brown skin of her face. She smiled tentatively up at Archie. "Sir, could you spare a coin for a poor, hungry girl?"

"For you, girl?" Archie reached into her coat as though she were pulling out a pocketbook. "Of course I could spare a coin. Although not if you're going to *steal* it from me." She pulled a slim Châtellerault blade from the inside pocket of her jacket, flicking it open under the girl's chin. Her other hand gripped the girl's wrist as she pulled the girl's hand from the pocket of her vest. Her watch dangled from between the girl's fingers.

The girl's face split into a wide grin. "Damn," she whispered, careful not to bump her jaw against Archie's knife. "I should have gone for the knife instead of the watch."

"Oui, so you should 'ave," Archie agreed. "The mother-of-pearl on the grip would've kept you fed for a week. That is, if I didn't find you first, and slit your belly open like a lake trout."

Keeping a grip on the girl's wrist so her pocket watch couldn't vanish, Archie ducked into one of the narrow alleys that scored the street. She extracted her watch from the girl's grip and tucked it into her interior jacket pocket, along with the closed knife. The girl withdrew a handkerchief from her blouse and wiped the grease from her face with an effort.

"You should smudge it more around your mouth," Archie advised. "When you just do the cheekbones and the jaw, it makes you look too pretty to be an urchin. And per'aps grow out your hair? This fuzz," she said, gesturing to the too-short-to-curl cut, "it is very recognizable in this city."

The girl pursed her lips. "Thanks," she muttered, looking put out.

"You're welcome for the free advice," Archie said dryly, tugging her waistcoat straight. "You'll 'ave your coin if you've brought me news." The girl's eyes flicked toward the mouth of the alley, and Archie clicked her tongue. "Do not play games with me, Acadia. Have you seen him, or no?"

"No," Acadia finally admitted.

"You're sure?" Archie deflated a little, resisting the urge to lean against the wall of the alley. Despair or no, that grime wouldn't scrub out of her linen pinstripes easily.

"I'm sure," Acadia said tartly. "I would know if I'd seen a six-foot-four black man wearing a marshal's star around here. You're not the only person who would pay for that kind of information, you know."

Archie sighed. "Fine. I'll see you tomorrow, oui? I'll come downtown around . . . noon, I think. It will be my last day 'ere— even if you don't see 'im, you'll 'ave coin for your trouble."

Acadia seemed to soften. "Hey, he'll show up," she said. "I know for sure that your letters posted—I gave them to my best rider. I'm sure he'll be here." She patted Archie's arm awkwardly, then gave the collar of her jacket a tug. "And if you keep dressing up this nice, you'll look damned fine when you meet him."

She winked and turned on her heel, walking out of the alley and leaving Archie behind. Archie took a deep breath, telling herself that the girl was right. Carter would show up.

He always did. Even if it took a year. He always showed up.

Archie straightened her jacket where Acadia had tugged it out of line. She reached into the breast pocket for her watch to check the time as she walked out of the alley, then swore. She looked up and down the street, whipping her bowler off in frustration—but there was no sign of the girl who had just stolen both her pocket watch *and* her Châtellerault.

—◆◆◆—

By the time Archie got back to the townhouse, Houndstooth was gone. She breathed a sigh of relief as she walked in and shucked off her jacket, which was clinging to her arms despite the light weight of the fabric. She had been hoping to talk to him about the next part of their journey—but she'd also been dreading it.

She walked into the dining room, of a mind to investigate any breakfast leftovers Houndstooth had abandoned. If there were any good pastries left over, she would go and visit Rosa down at Port Rouge. She'd been there at least every other day. She didn't like boarding Rosa—the albino hippo's skin inevitably dried out at the neglectful hands of the half-drunk hoppers who ran the port. A pastry now and then felt like the very least she could do.

When she opened the French doors to the dining room, all thoughts of Rosa fled her mind as she stifled a scream.

The white jacquard wallpaper was marred with wicked holes and slashes. Letters were pinned to the wall with a collection of tiny throwing knives. Phrases and words in the letters were circled with grease pencil; some of the letters had thick, smudgy black lines drawn between them, stretching across paper and wallpaper alike. Question marks, crosses, and overlapping circles were drawn at irregular intervals.

In the center of the wall, Houndstooth's map hung askew like a head on a pike. A fat oval was drawn around Baton Rouge.

"'E's lost 'is mind," Archie breathed, staring at the ruined wall. She swore under her breath; then, dissatisfied, she swore over her breath. She threw her jacket onto the table as she stalked across the room to stare at the wall.

They were letters, she realized, from all of Houndstooth's contacts across the country. There were letters from old enemies in New York, people whose names he couldn't say without spitting. There was a letter from the lover who had abandoned him. There were letters from people he'd worked with and people he'd swindled and people who had left tooth marks on his fists.

He'd circled key phrases in each—"I haven't even heard of that person" was circled in one letter, with the word "LIE" scribbled above it. "Near Houston" was circled in another, with "HERO WOULD NEVER" scrawled across the words. The map was covered with notes and references to letters and dates, with arrows pointing to cities.

But Baton Rouge was the place he'd circled. And now he was gone.

Archie swore again. A really good swear—a streak that would have curled the hair on Cal Hotchkiss' toes, the devil rest him. How had she failed to notice? How had he carried out all of this correspondence right under her nose? She thought back to her nights out avoiding him, her trips to rendezvous with her own messengers—and she realized that it had probably been child's play for Houndstooth to work around her all this time.

Then she rolled up her sleeves and started removing letters from the wall, laying them out on the dining room table. Once she'd re-created Houndstooth's tableau, she hitched up her pants and sat in one of the plush, high-backed chairs that circled the table.

She picked up the nub of grease pencil that Houndstooth had left behind, and then she got to work trying to figure out where it was that he had gone.

Six hours later, Archie was slapping open the swinging wooden doors of the Hop's Tusk with both hands. She stood in the doorway, letting her eyes adjust to the low light inside the bar. The heat of the gaslamp just outside the doors warmed her back. She tilted back the brim of her bowler and used her cane to hold the door open beside her.

She saw him at the bar before her eyes finished adjusting. His hat was on the stool next to him, and he was slumped over the scarred wood of the bar, his eyes fixed on a glass of brown liquor.

Archie sat next to him, picking up his hat. She tugged the bottom of her vest down more sharply than was strictly necessary to make the fabric lie smooth. She tried to decide whether she should kill Houndstooth. She tried to decide if it would be a mercy to do so.

"I'm not drunk," he said after a long time.

"Fine," Archie replied. She could hear how taut her voice was, and tried to take a slow, deep breath.

"I've been staring at this same damned glass for three hours," he said. "Waiting."

"For me?" Archie said, knowing that wasn't the answer.

"For them," he whispered. He looked up at Archie, and fervor burned in his eyes. "They're here, Archie. Both of them. Hero and Adelia—they're *here,* I know it."

"Chérie—"

"No, Archie, *no!*" He shook his head hard. "They're *here,* they're *staying here,* and I'm going to find them and I'm going to *find Hero* and—"

"I don't think they're 'ere," Archie murmured. "You misunderstood, 'Oundstooth. I think Hero is dead."

Houndstooth shot up from his stool, and before Archie's eyes could track the movement he was holding a knife to her cheek.

"Don't you dare—" He nudged his cheek with a rolled-up sleeve, his eyes fierce and glassy. "Don't you say that. They're not dead. I would know."

"If they're not dead," Archie said softly, feeling the burn of Houndstooth's blade as it scored her cheek, "why haven't they written to you?"

Houndstooth's arm drifted down, then snapped back up. "Adelia probably isn't letting them," he said.

"Why would Adelia keep them alive?" Archie asked, and Houndstooth's lips pursed. He swallowed hard around his total lack of an answer.

His eyes slid away from hers. Archie eased the knife from his hand too easily. She laid a hand on his shoulder and pressed down until he was slumped on his barstool again.

"They can't be dead," he said to the glass of whiskey. "We . . . we deserve better than that. Hero deserves *better* than that."

"It might not be about 'deserves,'" Archie said. She tried to keep her voice soft, gentle. Kind. She picked up Houndstooth's glass and pressed it into his grease-smudged hand. "It's time to stop looking, mon frère. You are killing yourself."

Houndstooth looked hollow on the barstool next to her. He'd always been thin, but now Archie realized that he looked desiccated—like a crumbling leaf. He looked ready to disintegrate at a touch. Rather than test his strength, Archie pressed two fingers to the bottom of his glass and nudged it up toward his face.

He drained it, then slammed the glass down on the bar, gasping. Archie raised an arm to signal to the pinch-faced innkeeper for two more drinks. He nodded from across the bar, then continued wiping out the same glass he'd been drying since Archie walked in. He eyed them from under furrowed brows. Then, his eyes darted to the door an instant before it banged open.

"Archie!" A dark blur rushed across the bar, stopping just far enough away from Archie to avoid being grabbed. The girl was breathless, bone-thin, and swimming in layers of royal blue satin. She looked like she'd run from a dance hall ten miles away. But then the girl whipped off the hat—and the hair with it—and propped a leg on the barstool next to Archie.

"Acadia?" Archie gaped at the girl. "Where did you get that dress?"

"From the none of your goddamned business surplus store," Acadia snapped, pulling a letter out of her boot. "Here," she said, and thrust the rolled-up paper at Archie. Archie took it, and before she could unfurl it, Acadia had replaced her wig and hat and was on her way out the door, and then was turning on her heel to snatch the letter back.

"You can read it after you pay me," she said, holding out her other hand.

"And will you be returning my watch in exchange? And my knife?" Archie held out a hand, and after her Châtellerault and timepiece had been deposited into it, pulled out a billfold from her breast pocket. She traded the girl more than she'd agreed to pay in order to get the letter back, more than the letter should have been worth. As she started to unroll it again, Acadia disappeared through the swinging doors, running as fast as her feet would carry her.

Archie read the letter. She read it again. And she read it half-way through again before the still-swinging doors were stilled by a large pair of calloused hands. A shadow filled the doorway. One of those hands reached up to remove a battered black leather hat with a glinting silver star on the brim.

Archie looked up as Gran Carter entered the Hop's Tusk. Behind her, Houndstooth was still staring into his empty glass—but he looked up as Carter's booming voice filled the room.

"Archie?"

Archie stared at him with wide eyes, the letter dangling from her fingers. He crossed the room in a few long strides, cupped her face in his hands, and kissed her with all the desperation of a drowning man pushing his way into a pocket of air. He knocked her bowler hat off, tangling one hand in the lapel of her waist-coat, and pressed the full length of his body to hers. She grabbed the front of his duster in two fists, crumpling his own letter against his chest—but after a long moment, she pushed him away.

"Archie," he breathed again, pressing his forehead to hers. His voice was a bonfire. "I missed you so goddamn much."

"Carter—"

"Did you get my letter?"

"Just now," she said. She squeezed her fist against his chest, and the paper crinkled against him.

"Just now? But—if you didn't read it before, then why are you here?" He looked toward the bar, where Houndstooth had braced his elbows on the counter and was holding his head in his hands.

"We didn't know," Archie started—then she corrected herself. "I didn't know."

Carter kissed Archie again, more briefly this time, and then started for the stairs. Archie followed fast on his heels, unsheath-ing a long, wicked length of steel from within her cane.

Houndstooth looked up at both of them, then stood from his barstool. "Where are you two going?" He stooped to pick up the paper that Archie had dropped to the floor. He scanned it, then looked up to where Carter and Archie were running up the staircase. "Hey!"

Archie paused, gripping the banister in one hand and her blade in the other. "I was wrong," she said, "you 'ad it right. 'Oundstooth"—Houndstooth was already halfway to the foot of the stairs by the time Archie finished—"they're *here*."

Chapter 7

Bang.

Adelia's fingers were slipping.

"Let go!" Hero called up. The words echoed faintly. Adelia's fingers reflexively clenched around the wood of the windowsill as another *bang* echoed from within the room. He was breaking down the door.

"Adelia," Hero hissed again, "let go, I'll catch you! It's not that far!"

The next *bang* was accompanied by a *crunch* and then a shout. Adelia felt one of her fingernails split as she dug it into the wood of the windowsill—she flinched as a splinter slid into her nail bed, and then the world spun, and then she was falling.

"*Oof—ghhuuuuh—*" Hero was staggering under her, and then she was on her feet, although she still felt like she was falling. A firm hand on her back, and normally she would flinch away but the hand was cold even through her damp, clinging, too-hot shirt. It felt nice, like cool water—and then the cool hand was pushing her, and then they were running as shouts drifted down from the open window like blossoms falling from a magnolia tree.

A hat settled onto Adelia's head, and the cool hand was pushing her into an alley, and then Hero was beside her, breathing hard with their back pressed to wall and their face turned to the street.

"Fuck," Hero panted, wiping their forehead and throat with their kerchief. "Fuck, that was close."

"What happened?" Adelia's voice was raspy, shaking, and she realized belatedly that she was shivering. Hero noticed and shucked off their coat. As they reached across her to pull it over her shoulders, their forearm brushed her left breast, and pain erupted all through her chest. Her vision tunneled.

"Whoa, there," Hero said, catching Adelia before she could fall. "Whoa, now—"

And then Adelia was the one falling like a magnolia blossom; she watched the ground float up toward her, watched Hero's hands flutter into her field of vision, watched a hat—her hat?—land in front of her. The world slid sideways, and then she was looking at the saddlebag that rested on the ground between Hero's boots, and then she closed her eyes and slid into blessedly still darkness.

Adelia woke up drowning.

She sputtered, her arms spasming. She reached out and grasped at the first soft thing she found. Her fingers were weak, sore as hell from gripping the window, but she tightened her grip with a will when the subject of her grasp let out a high-pitched noise. With her other hand, she pushed her hair out of her stinging eyes, blinking away water mixed with what must have been either her own sweat or her own blood. She sat up as she did it, ignoring how the movement made her head spin.

"Let—*go*—"

Adelia blinked a few more times and a dark face came into focus, barely visible by the thin light of the clouded-over moon.

"Hero?" she asked, and then she realized with horror that her weak fingers were clutching at Hero's throat. She pulled her hand away—god, no, for the second time in a day she'd almost—

"Lo siento," she rasped, her voice hoarse. She felt as though she'd swallowed a bolt of burlap. Hero was coughing, tears streaming down their face, and Adelia felt a flush of shame fighting her urge to shiver. "Why am I wet? What happened?"

Hero was too busy gasping to answer, so Adelia looked around. She was sitting in reddish clay, in a puddle. There was an ewer knocked over next to Hero, and a puddle.

Not drowning, then. Revived.

Adelia pressed her hands to her face, ignoring the feeling of cool clay slipping between her fingers and her cheeks. She was exhausted, felt as though she'd just ridden Zahra a thousand miles overland while carrying Stasia on her shoulders. She took a deep, slow breath, and realized that she could smell her own sweat over the rich decomposition smell of clay.

A groan and a splash sounded from behind her, not close but not far either. She startled, looked—and there, nosing at the edge of the paddock, was Hero's old hippo, Abigail.

"Hero," Adelia breathed. "Hero—*Hero*!" She slapped at Hero's arm, and they glared at her, rubbing their throat.

"Yeah, welcome back to life," they snapped. "Carried your ass all the damn way here, and I don't mind telling you that you haven't hardly lost that baby weight enough for my scrawny self to—"

"*Shut up,*" Adelia said, grabbing Hero by the chin before they could flinch away. "Tell me later. *Look.*"

She directed Hero's chin, and their features clenched with the unmistakable air of patience about to reach a breaking point—but then they saw Abigail, and their face went slack.

"It can't be," Hero breathed. They scrambled up, slipping in the wet clay, and ran to the edge of the paddock. They reached right through the half-rotted wood at the edge of the water and pressed both hands to the nose of the little Standard Grey hippo that was huffing bubbles into the water there.

"It had better be," Adelia said, "or else you just grabbed a strange hippo by the face."

But Hero didn't hear her. They were weeping, their face pressed between Abigail's nostrils. They hadn't seen her since the night the Harriet fell, the night they had nearly died, two months before—a night that suddenly felt so, so far away.

While Hero sobbed all over Abigail, Adelia rested her head in her hands and tried to piece the night together. Her thoughts were disjointed and slow, and her left breast throbbed with a steady pain, as though a hot coal had been inserted behind her nipple by someone with a steady hand and an eye for detail.

It hadn't hurt this badly when she'd expressed her milk back at the inn, while Hero was downstairs at the bar—but her breast had been hot and red, swollen-looking. *Infection,* she thought, remembering the sickly smell of the milk she'd washed out of her shirt when they'd first arrived at Port Rouge. It had hurt then, and the pain was even worse now.

She remembered going to sleep at Hero's behest.

She remembered waking up to a pounding on the door, and the sound of Hero talking to the mousy little innkeeper. She remembered the murmured exchange, catching the words "U.S. marshal" in the instant before Hero tore the blankets from her and pulled her out of bed.

She remembered Hero urging her out the window as footsteps hammered down the hall outside their door. She remembered the sounds of the door being broken down.

So, Adelia thought. This was it. He'd found her. Gran Carter had tracked her down—and he wasn't alone.

"Hero," she said abruptly. "Hero, we need to talk."

"In a minute," Hero said.

"It's important."

Hero didn't answer. Adelia looked up and saw that they were

staring across the water at a patch of reeds that swayed gently in the cool night air. They were saying something that almost sounded like "Ruby."

"Hero?" Adelia hauled herself upright and walked over to the paddock to stand next to Hero as they held up a hand for silence. Abigail huffed warm air over Adelia's fingers, then dismissed her as having nothing to offer and returned her attention to Hero, who patted her nose absently. "What is it?" Adelia asked.

"I thought I saw something," Hero murmured. Their eyes were fixed on the reeds, which had gone still. Across the water, a hippo muttered to itself or someone else, then let out a long bleating groan. Hero shook their head, then looked at Adelia. "You look better," they said. "We should ride while your fever is down. I think it broke while I was carrying you here. At least, you were sweating like it had broken." They grimaced, and Adelia gave them a sympathetic frown.

"Thank you," Adelia finally managed, feeling awkward as she said it. "For saving me."

Hero shrugged uncomfortably and began performing an unnecessarily thorough inspection of Abigail's ears. "Wasn't anything you wouldn't have done for me," they muttered, and Adelia felt tears spring to her eyes. That wasn't something anyone had ever said about her before.

"Hero," she began—but then Hero straightened, wiping their hands on their pants, and shook their head.

"We'll talk about it later," they said. "For now, we need to go. We can't stay here." They started walking toward the locked tack shed next to the paddock, and Abigail began hauling herself out of the water, following her hopper. The hippo lumbered over to Adelia, water streaming from her belly, and nosed at her shoulder.

"Hola, Abi," Adelia whispered, wiping at her eyes. She gave the hippo's shoulder a pat as Hero swore at the lock on the tack shed. They had their eyes right up next to it, straining to manipulate their lockpicks by moonlight. "Your Hero over there is something else, eh? What do you think—would you trust them?" Abigail gave no reply, but continued to drip as Adelia rubbed her side. "I thought so," Adelia murmured. "I thought you would say that."

Hero returned a few minutes later, carrying Abigail's riding saddle in their arms.

"I don't know who found her," they said, "but they've been taking good care of her. I thought this whole time that maybe— when the Harriet—" Their voice broke, and they didn't continue. After a moment, they shook their head and made a noise like they were swallowing a piece of glass. "Never mind," they muttered, and they saddled Abigail in silence.

The hippo entered the water with no great urgency, pausing frequently to flip her ears and duck her head. "No point rushing her," Hero shrugged after Adelia's third sidelong glance at them. "She likes to move at her own pace, Abigail does. Meantime, we should figure out where it is you want to go. Somewhere Carter won't be able to find us, I should think."

"Where I *want* to go is to a house in the country with a bathtub and a soft bed," Adelia said. Abigail finished blowing bubbles in the water, and presented herself at the water's edge. "Where I'm *going* to go? That should be obvious."

"Where *we're* going to go. Enlighten me," Hero drawled, swinging themself into the saddle and holding out a hand to Adelia. There was just enough room on the saddle for both of them. Adelia gripped the webbing on Abigail's harness and adjusted the grip of her thighs on the sides of the saddle.

"We're going to visit Whelan Parrish," Adelia replied. "We're going to find out what the hell it is that he wants. And then we're going to get Ysabel back."

As Abigail set off, a splash sounded from behind them. Hero, who was bent forward and cooing into Abigail's ear, didn't seem to notice. Adelia looked over her shoulder and saw that the reeds were moving again. A bone-white nose stuck up out of the water for a moment before disappearing again below the surface.

"Did you say something?" Hero asked.

"No," Adelia replied. "I thought I saw—no, never mind," she said, shaking her head. "It was nothing."

It had been nothing. A trick of the moonlight on the water. As they rode out of Port Rouge, Adelia began to shiver again. She told herself that it was just her fever, returning in earnest and making her see things. *It's only the fever,* she told herself. *Don't tell Hero about your hallucinations. You'll only reopen the wound.* Her conscience twitched. *Haven't you hurt them enough?*

—◆◆◆—

"Adelia?"

Adelia startled awake. She couldn't remember the last time she'd woken naturally. Whether she was startling awake because the baby was crying or because someone was trying to catch her or because she was dreaming about blood and death—it didn't matter. She was always stuttering into consciousness, her breath in her throat and her heart pounding.

"What is—what?" she said, her voice rasping in her throat. Her mouth tasted like a dead thing. A canteen appeared before her, and she drained it before she could think to turn it away. *You're getting complacent,* she scolded herself.

"Thought you might want to wake up," Hero said mildly over their shoulder. "We're getting into an iffy part of the water."

Adelia blinked, took in her surroundings. It was bright out, startlingly bright, and the air over the surface of the water teemed with dragonflies. Abigail was pushing forward through a thicket of water hyacinth quickly enough that Adelia guessed the hippo had eaten her fill a ways back. But she could see what Hero was worried about: a few hundred feet ahead of them, the hyacinth started to thin, exposing the muddy waters of Thompson Creek.

"I'm awake," Adelia said, and she reached instinctively for a weapon, any weapon. Her throwing knives were still strapped to her left arm, and the long, curved knife she kept strapped to her thigh was still there—but the rest of her weapons, she realized belatedly, were still back at the Hop's Tusk.

Adelia suddenly felt very naked.

"Don't be too nervous," Hero said. "I don't think any ferals will have made it this far up the creek. And if they did, they've probably been gorging themselves on whatever was living in here. So they shouldn't be too hungry, I don't think."

"I'm not nervous," Adelia snapped, scanning the surface of the water. It was still, save for the water bugs that skimmed back and forth, waiting to be eaten by enterprising fish.

"Sure," Hero said. "Anyway, I'd say we're just a few more hours away from the place Parrish told us to meet him. We're not making bad time at all. Wondered if you might want to talk about what it is that we're going to do when we get there?"

Adelia wanted so badly to growl that they'd kill Parrish on sight—but she knew that wouldn't be the case, and she suspected that Hero would see right through her. "I don't know," she finally admitted. "I suppose we will have to wait and see."

"He won't have Ysabel anywhere we can get to her," Hero said. "You know that, right?"

"I know," Adelia murmured, hating that Hero was right. "We will have to figure it out when we arrive. I . . ." She faltered.

"You don't want to guess," Hero filled in. "You don't want to try to make a plan that will inevitably turn out to be wrong."

"Aren't you the smart one? Why don't you have a plan?" Adelia snapped.

"I was too busy saving your life to come up with one in the last hour," Hero replied tartly.

Adelia didn't say anything—Hero was right, and they knew that they were right, and they didn't need her to tell them so. She bent slowly toward the water, pushing the thinning hyacinth aside to scoop up a hatful of relatively clear water. She poured it over herself, sluicing away fever-sweat. Abigail's tail flicked behind her, and for a few minutes, the only sound was the splash of Adelia's hat dipping into the water and tipping over her head.

Hero coughed. "Do you mind?" they said, and at first Adelia didn't know what they meant—but then she realized that they were close enough together on the saddle that Hero's back was soaked.

"Sorry, sorry." Adelia laughed, combing her wet hair back from her face with her fingers before putting her hat back on. "I—I didn't think—"

"It's fine," Hero grumbled, and the set of their shoulders was so offended that Adelia burst out laughing again.

"I really am very sorry, Hero," she said. "I think the fever cooked my brain."

"It's alright," Hero said with a glance over their shoulder. "It's kind of nice. My back was getting mighty hot what with your feverish self trying hard to be a furnace back there. How are you feeling?"

"Like a trough of hop shit," Adelia said.

Hero chuckled to themself. "So, a bit better, then?"

"A bit," Adelia said, smiling. She tilted her head back and let the sun warm her damp face for a few minutes before returning her attention to the water. A ripple broke the surface and she tensed, reaching for a blade to throw—but it was just a fish, reducing the number of water bugs on the creek by one.

"What about after?" Hero murmured, softly enough that Adelia wouldn't have heard it if Abigail hadn't stopped to investigate a toad in her path.

"What about it?" Adelia replied.

"What will you do, after we get Ysabel back?" Hero tugged on Abigail's harness, and the hippo waded forward again, leaving the relieved toad behind. "Will you go back into the wilderness and hide?"

Adelia shifted in the saddle. "No," she said, "I don't think so."

"Will you go back to work? What's going to happen?" Hero sounded oddly agitated. Adelia felt a heat rise in her scalp, and took off her hat to fan herself with it.

"No," she said, forcing her voice to be cold and flat so that she wouldn't yell. "I will not be going 'back to work.' That—that will never happen." Hero didn't say anything, and Adelia found herself wanting to continue in spite of—because of?—the sudden flush of anger. "I have not 'worked' in nearly a year now, Hero, did you know that? Did you know that it's been that long since I've taken a life?" She spat into the water. "A year. That's the longest I've gone since the first time. A year."

"I didn't know that," Hero murmured, their shoulders tense.

"I didn't even kill Travers," Adelia said, her pulse pounding in her ears. "I didn't even kill *you*, Dios ayúdame. I am—do you understand me? I am finished with it." Her fists were clenched tightly in her lap, and she could feel her fingernails driving crescents into her palms. "I am done with that."

"Sure," Hero said. "I hear you. You've retired." They got quiet, spoke in the slow cadence of someone finally coming to understand. "You didn't kill me."

"I've retired," Adelia repeated, flexing her fingers. "I am *retired*."

"Give you some advice?" Hero asked, then continued without waiting for Adelia's reply. "Find yourself something to do. Find a hobby. Otherwise . . . you get restless. Lonesome."

"Lonesome?" Adelia asked, holding back a sharp, bitter laugh. "I have been alone all my life, Hero. I don't think loneliness would be a problem for me."

"Alone and lonely ain't the same thing at all," Hero said, shaking their head. Adelia couldn't see their face, but it sounded as though the words hurt them. "You of all people should know that. And even if they were the same—you would think that being alone and retired would be no different from feeling alone in your job. But you'd be wrong."

"You wouldn't know a goddamn thing about it, Hero," Adelia snapped. "You may not be as infamous as Archie, but you have your own reputation, sí? You always worked in a team. It's why your hands have stayed so *soft*." She regretted it the instant she said it, but they both knew it was true—Hero was a behind-the-scenes type, a tinkerer, a poisoner. They had fingers made for capping vials and twisting wires together. They didn't have the knife scars ubiquitous to most hoppers, with one notable exception.

"Exactly," Hero murmured. "I've been hearing that my whole life. It's lonesome being a killer, Adelia. But it's lonesome staying behind while the killers pour your poison into someone's drink, too. It's lonesome to be back at the ranch while someone else sets up the bombs you rigged. Don't tell me I don't know lonesome." Their voice was soft, but not sad. Not even angry. Just . . . resigned.

Adelia chewed on it—the idea of Hero being lonely. The idea of their bright mind—always working—growing bored in their retirement. She chewed on it, and perhaps it was her fever making her bold, but she finally asked the question that she had known all along she was not supposed to ask.

"Why did you retire?" she said. "Why not just ... roughen your hands a bit?"

"Same reason as you," Hero said. "I got tired of killing people." Adelia started to protest, but Hero held up a hand. "Don't try to deny it. I heard you a minute ago—you're finished with it. You're done. I know how that is too."

"Oh?"

Hero spat into the water, then reached down to run a hand across Abigail's flank. "You kill the first one, and it's not as bad as you thought it would be. You kill the second one, and it's not better, not exactly. But it's more not-so-bad. You kill the third one and you realize that you're good at it." They scooped up a handful of water and splashed it across the hippo's shoulders, darkening her grey hide. "You start to get a reputation, and you realize that people think you're *great* at it. You start to take real pride in your work. You start to make real damn money." Another handful of water, this one across Abigail's neck. The hippo grunted appreciatively, flapping her ears. "You dream about contracts and you start tasting your own poisons to get a feel for how they land in the gut, and you love it. And then you're doing it *because* you love it, and you think you've really found your calling. You're so fucking *good* at this." They poured another handful of water between Abigail's ears, rubbing it across her skin with a long-fingered hand. "So you keep on mixing poisons and blasting vault doors open until you could do it in your sleep. And then one day, some kid shows up at your door and says that they've heard you're the best in the business, and you think—am I?"

Adelia didn't say anything, even as Hero's pause thickened.

"You realize," Hero finally said softly, "that you're only doing the job because you're good at it. That you only love it because you're good at it. You realize that somewhere along the way, you forgot that you're killing people. You don't feel a goddamn ounce of the remorse that your mother's preacher said you'd feel if you ever took another life—you just feel bored." Their voice dropped to a whisper. "You feel bored by the murders. And you wonder who you are, that you can say that about yourself—that you're bored by the murders."

Adelia swallowed hard, brushing away a mosquito that had come to investigate the tears that had traced trails to the hollow of her throat. She watched the sandy banks of Thompson Creek drift by—she spotted only a single feral sunning itself on the shore, so still that not even Abigail noticed it there. She lifted a fistful of muddy water to her face to wash away the salt and sweat that had accumulated. By the time her face was dry, Abigail was climbing up out of the creek and starting down the man-made stream that led to Whelan Parrish's barge.

Chapter 8

Houndstooth's hands were steady for the first time in nearly three months. He finally understood how the ferals must have felt when they slid up the Mississippi and found themselves free of the Harriet.

He felt good.

He twirled his favorite ivory-handled knife between his fingers like a baton, sober as mountain air, and strode in a slow circle around the ladder-backed chair. The chair was resting on its side on the sawdust-strewn floor. It was a well-made chair, Houndstooth mused. It had stood up to the impact of his boot when he'd kicked it over.

He couldn't say as much for the innkeeper tied to the chair, of course. No—that man's nose had taken the brunt of the impact when his face had hit the floor, and he was bleeding all over the place. The sawdust could only manage so much.

It would need to manage quite a lot more if the innkeeper didn't start answering questions soon.

"I can do this all night, Percival," Houndstooth said, letting his already-low voice drop to an even deeper baritone than usual. "You, on the other hand? I don't know if you'll be able to keep up with me." He crouched in front of the innkeeper, grabbing a fistful of the man's thinning, oiled hair. He pulled hard enough to lift Percival's head from the floor. Blood had pasted a good deal of sawdust to the man's cheek. "You're a mess," Houndstooth said, shaking his head slowly. He lifted his knife and used the edge to scrape Percival's cheek clean. "Oh, dear," he said. "My mistake. I seem to have taken some whiskers off of you." He wiped his knife on the innkeeper's shirtfront, then lifted it again. "I'll just even you up, shall I?" He scraped the blade against the man's other cheek, letting him feel just how sharp it was.

"I don't know where they went," Percival whimpered. Houndstooth dropped his head, and it bounced off the wooden floor with a crack.

"The problem here," Houndstooth said, twirling his knife again, "is that I don't believe you. I don't believe you because you do this . . . this *thing*." He tapped the tip of the blade against Percival's front teeth. "You bite your lip, see? Right before you tell me that lie."

"It's not a—what are you doing?" Percival's voice rose to a high quaver as Houndstooth grabbed the top of the ladder-backed chair with one hand, hauling it upright.

"Well, it's tricky, trying to look at you when you're all sideways down there, eh? That's no way to have a conversation," Houndstooth said. He brushed sawdust from his palms, then stooped to pick up his knife. He tossed it a few times, watching it flash as it spun through the air, savoring the clarity of purpose that had entered his mind at last.

"I don't enjoy being lied to," he said, pulling a second chair in front of Percival's. He rested one elbow on his knee and started paring his fingernails with the blade of the ivory-handled knife.

"Where's the marshal? And the other gentleman, your—um, your friend, from before?" The innkeeper kept glancing toward the stairs as though anyone could come walking down them who might save him.

"They're conferring." As he said it, a *thump* sounded from just above their heads, near the room that Hero and Adelia had been occupying until just a half hour before. "They have some catching up to do. It's none of my business, and it's *certainly* none of yours." He tapped the innkeeper's forehead. "Eyes on me, eh, Percival? Let's not try to eavesdrop, now. S'downright rude."

Percival reluctantly looked from the ceiling to the stairs, then to Houndstooth. The side of his face that had struck the floor was swelling; blood trickled from a cut over his eye, from his nose, from the corner of his mouth. *Disgraceful,* Houndstooth thought a bit giddily.

"What do you want?" Percival whispered. "I—I'll give you— there's not much in the till, but it's yours. Please." His teeth found his lower lip again. "I don't know where they are."

Houndstooth's hand shot out. Before the innkeeper could so much as flinch, Houndstooth had the man's lip gripped between his thumb and index finger. He held tightly to it even as Percival thrashed like a fresh-caught catfish. It only took a few seconds for Percival's higher functions to cut off his instincts—when he was finally still, Houndstooth leaned in close enough that he could have kissed the little weasel on the nose. He smiled, not relinquishing his grip on the innkeeper's lower lip, and whispered to him as softly as a lover.

"You're a fucking liar, little man. You're trying to play a game to which you've never learned the rules. You're making mistakes." He tapped Percival on the teeth with the tip of his knife again. "You keep biting your fucking lip and then lying to me. So here's what's going to happen. Look at me, Percival," he said, and the innkeeper tore his eyes away from the stairs behind Houndstooth. His saliva was starting to drip down Houndstooth's wrist, but Houndstooth hardly noticed. He watched the other man's eyes like a bobcat watching a hare. "Here's what's going to happen. I'm going to cut off your lip—ah, ah, no no, hold still, now—" Percival had tried to yell, a wet, half-strangled noise. Houndstooth waited for the man to quiet down again; until his breaths started to come in short, shallow pants. "I'm going," Houndstooth began again, "to cut off your lip. That way, you'll have nothing to bite, and you'll have to tell the truth. How does that sound? Good?"

He lifted his knife and held it to the corner of Percival's lower lip. A sense of serenity—as deep and thorough as sleeping under the stars with Hero's hand resting on his chest—washed over him as he applied the faintest bit of pressure to the blade. After a few seconds, blood was running freely down his wrist, staining his shirtsleeve.

The tenor of the innkeeper's screaming changed abruptly, and he seemed to be attempting words. Houndstooth paused.

"What was that?" he asked, not looking up from the man's lip, which was still three-quarters attached. "If you keep interrupting, this will take forever, you know." Percival's response was unintelligible, since he couldn't move his lip or jaw. "That sounded a bit like 'I'll tell you everything,'" Houndstooth said. "Was that what you were saying, Percival, old friend?"

Percival nodded, then screamed as the motion of his head drove Houndstooth's knife farther into his lip.

"Excellent!" Houndstooth released the innkeeper's lip and drew the knife back in one fluid movement, eliciting another scream. "I knew we could come to an understanding." He smiled, wiped his blade on Percival's sleeve, and set it aside.

"I don't—don't hurt me, please, I'll tell you everything I know. But I don't know exactly where they went." He spoke in a rush. *Motivated at last,* Houndstooth thought, and he felt his smile grow wider. "I just know who sent for them. But you have to swear you won't tell him that I'm the one who told you—he'll kill me, or he'll have someone else kill me, please, you have to promise me—"

Houndstooth propped his foot on the edge of Percival's

chair, leaning back in his chair and folding his arms. "And who, pray tell," he asked softly, "might that have been?"

" 'Oundstooth? What are you—mon dieu. 'Oundstooth!"

Houndstooth rolled his neck, letting out an involuntary sigh. "Just a minute, Archie," he called over his shoulder—but it was too late. Archie was already rushing up behind him. He braced himself for the warm weight of her hand on his shoulder, half longing for the contact and half dreading it.

"Help, please, he's lost his mind," Percival began to whimper, slurring the words over his mangled lip. Archie stood beside Houndstooth, not touching him, and took in the scene.

"I most certainly *have* lost my mind," Houndstooth said, his eyes fixed on the innkeeper. "Who knows what I'm liable to do next, if you don't give me that name?"

" 'Oundstooth." Houndstooth held up a hand. Archie grabbed his arm and yanked until he faced her. "You've gone too far, 'Oundstooth. *No*—" She held up a finger, hissing so quietly that the man in the chair leaned forward to hear, dripping blood onto Houndstooth's boot. "Is this what you think they would want from you? Is this what you think they would ask you to do for them? Is this what you think they want you to be, when they're not around to tether you to your humanity? Mon dieu, 'Oundstooth," she whispered, shaking her head. "You 'ave become a *demon*."

Houndstooth wiped sweat from his top lip with a shirtsleeve. His hand had the slightest of tremors. He eyed it with suspicion. "We can ask them in person, Archie, my friend. Percival here was just about to tell me who's housing Adelia. And Hero."

Out of the corner of his eye, Houndstooth could tell that Archie was watching him, evaluating. He knew that she was weighing his behavior over the last two months against all that she knew about him. He gritted his teeth and turned to meet her eyes, schooling the fury from his face. He smoothed himself to a semblance of his usual wry calm, raising an eyebrow at his flushed friend. She studied his face for a few long seconds, then nodded. "Don't let me interrupt, then, by all means," she said, waving a decorous hand at Percival.

Houndstooth gave her a smile, which she didn't answer. Then he returned his attention to the limp, bleeding man in the ladder-backed chair. He tapped Percival's lower lip with the nail of his pinky finger. "Well?"

Behind him, footsteps pounded down the stairs. He ignored them—ignored the sound of Archie explaining things to Carter in a low murmur, ignored the sound of them whispering about him. None of it mattered, because Percival was finally gathering his courage.

"Alright—okay. The girl who delivered the message. She works for a lot of folks—steals from a lot of folks too, knocks over taverns from time to time. It's why I let her work out of my bar, see? I figured, if this was her base of operations . . ."

Houndstooth shifted in his chair, raising an eyebrow and making a rolling "get on with it" motion with one hand. Percival took a shuddering breath.

"The man she's been running for most often lately is named Whelan Parrish. He's a federal—"

Houndstooth didn't realize he'd risen to his feet until he heard his chair hit the floor. "A federal agent with the Bureau of Land Management," he finished, and Percival gaped at him for a moment before nodding.

"Yes, he's a—he's with the Bureau of Land Management, how did you . . . ?"

Houndstooth snatched his hat from his head and threw it to the ground. It landed in the pasty puddle of sawdust and blood near Percival's feet. "Son of a whoring hop-shitted *fuck*," Hounds-tooth spat.

"Did he say Parrish?"

Houndstooth turned on his heel and stalked toward the foot of the stairs where Carter stood. "Yes, *Carter*, yes, he said *Parrish*. I believe you're acquainted?"

Carter didn't flinch, even as Houndstooth came close enough to him that their noses nearly touched. He placed a firm but gentle hand on Houndstooth's chest, applying just enough pressure to put a few inches between them.

"I corresponded with him several months ago about the Harriet job," he said, his voice low and even. Houndstooth's pulse pounded in his ears—he wanted Carter to hit him, wanted to fight him, wanted anything but this calm, cool response.

And then, of course, it got worse.

"From what I understand," Carter continued in that unbearably soothing tone, "you know him better than anyone else in this room, Houndstooth."

"Who the 'ell are you two going on about?" Archie demanded.

Houndstooth closed his eyes and took a deep, slow breath. He answered Archie with his eyes closed. He could handle Hero's disappearance—could handle the weeks of searching, and the sleepless nights, and the wondering if they were even alive. But somehow, the idea of looking at Archie in that moment was nearly enough to break him.

"We're talking about Whelan fucking Parrish," Houndstooth said, failing to keep his voice level. "The federal agent who hired us for the Harriet job."

Archie didn't quite succeed in holding back a gasp. " 'Oundstooth—do you mean—"

"Yes, Archie."

"But isn't he—"

"*Yes,* Archie."

"But didn't you two—"

Behind them, there was a clatter as Percival finally fainted, knocking his ladder-backed chair to the floor and crushing Houndstooth's best grey hat. Houndstooth gritted his teeth hard enough to make his jaw ache. "Yes, Archie," he said. "The man who's got Hero and Adelia right now is Whelan Parrish, federal agent for the Bureau of Land Management. My blue-eyed boy."

Chapter 9

Hero watched from under the brim of their hat as a bead of sweat traced its way down Adelia's temple. They wondered how much longer she'd last.

They shifted their weight against the white-painted wainscoting in Whelan Parrish's parlor and scanned the room again, letting their eyes skip over the white-blond man seated across from Adelia.

"You're an idiot, Mister Parrish." Adelia brushed the bead of sweat away with a remarkably steady hand. Her voice was even. A little too even. *Keep it together, Adelia,* they thought. *Just stay upright until he's gone.* "I had already guessed that you were a fool—you would have to be, to invite us to your home. But it appears that I overestimated you."

"Oh?" Parrish ashed his pipe into a tall, fluted vase next to his rocking chair. "How do you figure?"

"Adelia's retired," Hero murmured. They said it just quietly enough that Parrish could have pretended not to hear them—but he didn't.

"I don't give a piping hot damn," Parrish drawled, not looking away from Adelia. "She's coming out of retirement tonight."

Adelia's head snapped up. Hero had pushed off the wall and was standing between Parrish and Adelia before they knew what they were doing. "Tonight?" they snapped, louder than they'd intended.

Parrish smiled, showing a row of teeth that were so even they couldn't be real. Hippo ivory, probably, and recently fitted at that. Hero wanted to knock them out of his mouth.

"Tonight," he said, leaning over to look at Adelia. "You'll kill Mr. Burton tonight. Or I'll throw your baby into the Mississippi and let the ferals crush her soft little skull between their teeth."

Adelia didn't make a sound. Hero didn't turn to look at her—couldn't turn to look at her, couldn't risk the appearance of concern.

"Why tonight?" they demanded. "Why can't it wait for us to make a real plan?"

Parrish finally looked at Hero, his lip curling. His eyes were a startlingly bright blue, incongruous in his dishwater complexion. "Tonight is Mr. Burton's seventy-eighth birthday," he sneered. "He'll be feted here on the *Duchess*. There will be drinking and dancing and toasts and gifts and then do you know what will happen?" He waited, staring at Hero with lead-weighted malice writ plainly across his features.

"What? What will happen then?"

"He'll go back to the Bureau of Land Management headquarters in Atlanta. He'll sit behind his desk and he'll continue running the bureau into the ground, and I'll rot underneath him until the day I die." Parrish pulled at his pipe, fuming smoke.

Hero laughed, incredulous. "You must be joking," they said. "All this is for a job?" They shook their head and ran a hand across their face. "You kidnapped a baby for—what? For a *promotion*?"

Parrish leveled a cold stare at Hero. "I kidnapped the baby for the well-being of this country," he said. "Burton is the damned fool who let the Hippo Bill through."

"Congress let the Hippo Bill through," Adelia rasped from behind Hero. "The Senate let the Hippo Bill through. President—"

"*No,*" Parrish shouted, jabbing his pipe at Adelia. "They let the Hippo Bill become a *law*! Burton let it *through*! There are so many ways he could have stopped it—so many—you can delay *anything,*" he sputtered, then closed his mouth with a click of those false teeth. His jaw worked as he breathed heavily through flared nostrils. After a moment, he closed his eyes and ran a hand over his slicked-back hair, taking deep, slow breaths. Hero watched, fascinated, as he continued stroking his own hair, growing visibly calmer with each pass of his pale hand. "The man loves hippos," he muttered. "He thinks they're delightful. He let the bill *through* because he is an *idiot*. He'll never approve the extermination of the American variant of the species. And I can't for the life of me get him *fired*. If that disaster at the Harriet couldn't do it—no, this is the only way." He opened his eyes and nodded to Adelia. "So you'll kill him, *tonight,* and I'll be promoted into his position, and I'll clean up the mess he left behind."

"How?" Hero asked. "The hippos are here to stay. What can you do that he can't?"

"It's not what I can do that he can't," Parrish said. "It's what I will do that he *won't*. Those beasts are a menace, and he thinks they should be treated like—like *deer*!" His eyes narrowed. "I think they should be treated like the vermin that they are. And when I'm in charge of the bureau, I'll be able to declare a state of emergency, bringing the full might of the United States military down upon the Hippo Problem. We'll wipe them out within a few months, at the most. Each and every one. The farms will be shut down, and this long, embarrassing chapter in our nation's history will be over at last." He sniffed, smoothing his hair again, then muttered, "That includes your little pets, by the way. Enjoy them while they last."

Hero blinked. Their face felt numb. "You can't kill the livestock, too," they said. "That's insane, Parrish. It's madness. People will starve."

Parrish grinned, suddenly looking like a cat with feathers in its teeth. "People will have jobs."

"What?"

He ran a tongue over his teeth, then spoke to Hero in a tone that implied he was uncertain of their ability to understand. "I am currently the owner of ninety percent of the boats that are on the Mississippi, the Ponchartrain, and the Ohio River." He fondled the corner of a waxed leather folio that rested on his desk. "I'd like to be able to *operate* them. Once the vermin is out of the water, I'll be able to do so. Do you comprehend this?"

Hero shook their head. "Travers seemed to think that having the hippos in the water made his work quite a bit easier."

"Yes, well, Travers was a sadistic simpleton," Parrish snapped. "I'd rather not have to replenish my staff due to *grisly deaths*. His empire was one of blood and sweat." Parrish stood, tugging at the bottom of his waistcoat. "Mine will be one of money."

He gave Adelia a final, appraising look. "You have ten hours until the party begins, Miss Reyes." He jerked his chin toward a small silver bell that rested on the table next to his chair. "Ring that when you're ready, and my staff will show you to your quarters for the evening."

"What about me?" Hero asked.

"What about you?" Parrish snapped at them, his face reddening again. "I didn't send for you. I sent for *her*. You were not invited to this party, and I can't imagine a use for you. You're lucky I don't have you shot for trespassing on my property."

"Hero is with me," Adelia said, pushing herself up out of her chair. "They're my partner, and where I go, they go. And if you harm them, I will slit you open like a letter and read the contents to the river."

Parrish shook his head at Adelia. "I'd been told that you work alone. You're *supposed* to work alone."

"Your opinion is not of interest to me," she replied. "Now, if you'll excuse us. We have a plan to pull out of our asses."

Parrish stalked from the room, his pipe clenched in one white-knuckled fist. The instant the door had slammed shut behind him, Adelia collapsed back into her chair.

"Pollas en vinagre," she murmured, pressing her hands to her face.

Hero stared at her. "Partner, eh?"

"Sorry," Adelia groaned. "I was—it seemed like the right thing to say. I don't know. Manda huevos. Ten hours?"

Hero eased themself into the rocking chair Parrish had recently vacated, trying to ignore how warm the seat still was. They imagined Abigail, Ruby, Rosa, Zahra, Stasia—all dead, along with every hippo ever bred on U.S. soil. They couldn't wrap their head around it. "We'll figure it out."

"What did we bring with us?" Adelia asked, eyes still closed. "Just the one bag, right?"

"I grabbed what I could," Hero said. It had been a frenzy—they had shoved everything they could see into the bag, tossed it out the window. Some things had surely fallen out as they'd tried to half carry, half drag Adelia through the back alleys of Baton Rouge and along the winding road to Port Rouge. "And let's see—I've got . . ." They turned out their pockets, dropping a few paper-padded vials on the table, along with a waxed brick of explosive putty the size of a deck of playing cards.

"Plus your knives, plus my knives," Adelia murmured, kneading her temple with her fingers. "Ah, my head is *bellowing.*"

"Why don't we take a look at our 'quarters,' " Hero ventured. "Maybe you can get some rest? We've been traveling all day."

"There's no time," Adelia breathed, but her eyes didn't open.

"We'll plan after you've had a nap and I've had a bath," Hero said. "Nine hours isn't that much less than ten." They stood a few feet from Adelia and held out a hand. After a moment, Adelia cracked one eye, evaluated the hand—and took it. Hero helped her out of her chair.

"Alright," Adelia said. "Alright. One hour. But only because you wanted a bath."

"Oh, trust me, you could use one too," Hero said, reaching for the bell with a grin. "But I get to go first. *Partner*."

⬧

The bath was everything Hero had hoped it would be, which is to say the water was warm and mostly clear. There was even soap, and it was good soap, with some kind of smell to it. Hero couldn't put their finger on the smell, but it smelled much better than anything they'd been smelling over the last two months, so they lathered themself with it until their skin squeaked.

On the other side of a painted silk screen, Adelia was asleep. Hero knew that Adelia was still asleep because she wasn't muttering to herself about how she wasn't tired and resting was a waste of time. They endeavored to get out of the tub quietly—although they doubted that any amount of noise would rouse Adelia now—and reached for the length of linen that had been left for them to dry off with. It wasn't exactly soft, but it didn't scratch and it wasn't dry clothes over wet skin, which was nice.

Hurried footsteps sounded in the hall, and Hero pulled the towel around themself. They opened the door, startling the hell out of the maid who was about to knock on it.

"Oh! Oh, I'm sorry, I—uh, they told me—there was a lady staying here? Miss Reyes?" The maid blew a lock of curly red hair out of her face.

"She's resting. Did you need something from her?"

The maid held out another length of linen, this one folded into a thick packet. She spoke so quickly that Hero could barely keep up. "The chef for tonight sent these. She's, um. She lost a baby last month and she had some problems and the butler—he showed you up here?—well, he talked to her about what's going on with Miss Reyes and she said it sounds like Miss Reyes has the same problems she had. I don't know what she's talking about, but she said to bring this to y'all."

Hero took the cloth from the girl and unfolded it. They could hear Adelia stirring behind them. "Cabbage leaves?"

The maid shrugged. "She said to put 'em on Miss Reyes's, uh, 'inflamed areas.'" She started to edge away down the hall with the unmistakable air of someone who does not wish to discuss the matter any further. "Good luck!"

When Adelia had applied the cabbage leaves—a scene Hero did not witness, as they chose instead to take their time getting dressed behind the silk screen—she seemed to brighten. "I don't know if it's working or not," she said, "but they're cold, at least."

"Aha," Hero said, because there was not a single other thing they could think of to say. Adelia was sitting upright in the bed, and Hero perched awkwardly at the end of it.

"So," Adelia said. "The plan."

"Right. The plan. I took an inventory, and we have a good variety of poisons, although—"

"No." Adelia pulled her hair off of her neck and fanned herself with the flat of her hand. Her eyes were still worryingly glassy. "The plan for after."

"What?" Hero wondered if perhaps Adelia needed another hour of sleep before she would be coherent.

"We don't need a plan for the murder, Hero," Adelia said. "It will be simple. I will walk into the party and slit this 'Burton' fellow's throat. Or I'll hit him between the eyes with a throwing knife. Or I'll find a curtain tie and garrote him." She was studying the backs of her hands as she spoke, her eyes tracing the network of tiny scars that mapped them. "I will kill him the same way I would kill anyone else. No elaborate plan required."

"But how will we get him alone?" Hero shook their head. "You're not making any sense. You can't just walk into the middle of a party and kill a man—a *government official*. You'd hang."

"I'll hang anyway," Adelia murmured. She looked up at Hero, and her eyes were the clearest they'd been in days. "Gran Carter will find us, Hero. Yes? He has found us already. He will find me here—he is probably on his way already. And then he will capture me, and I will hang anyway. So I may as well do this job quickly."

"But—I don't understand," Hero said desperately. "I mean, I understand, but I don't—you're just giving up?"

Adelia smiled—a tired smile, but a warm one. A real one. "No," she said. "I'm not giving up. I'm making a plan." She looked back down at her hands, and Hero realized that they were seeing Adelia differently than they'd ever seen her. Even when she was about to give birth, Adelia had never seemed *nervous* before.

A cold finger of fear traced the scar just below Hero's navel.

"Hero," Adelia said. "I am going to kill Burton at the party, and then Parrish's demands will be met. Very shortly thereafter, Carter will capture me. I cannot outrun him, not like this." She gestured to herself—to her sweat-soaked hair, and to the damp patches over each breast where the cabbage leaves had made the fabric of her shirt cling. "I'm very sick, and I cannot run on my own. So . . . Carter will capture me, yes? We know this. And I will hang."

"But—"

"Let me finish," Adelia said softly. Hero bit their lip hard. They didn't want to hear the rest of this—there had to be another way. "I'm going to hang, but before I do . . . you can get Ysabel back from Parrish. He'll hand her off—he won't want to keep her, not once I'm captured and the job is done. He'll give her to you. And I need you to take her.

"Hero, I haven't—hm. How to say it? My life, for the past fifteen years, has been all about running. In all that time, I haven't trusted anyone but myself. That is"—she swallowed hard, still staring at her hands—"I haven't trusted anyone until these last two months. You had every reason to hate me—to *kill* me, even—but you didn't. You stayed with me. You helped me birth Ysabel, and you've helped me with her when you had no place helping me with anything. You've saved my life more times than I think you know." She cleared her throat. Hero blinked back hot tears; this was easily the longest they'd ever heard Adelia speak, and she was saying more than they could take in.

"You've been a friend to me, Hero. You've done so much for me, and now . . . I have to ask you for more."

Hero shook their head. "Don't," they whispered. Adelia looked up at them, her eyes brimming.

"Promise me you'll take care of Ysabel," Adelia whispered. "Tell her—" Tears spilled onto her cheeks, and instead of wiping them away, she reached out and grabbed Hero's hands. "Tell her I was a murderer, that's—she should know that, she should know why I'm gone. Tell her I was the best. She should know that, too." Adelia smiled even as her tears splashed onto Hero's hands. "But tell her this. Tell her that I was every inch her mother, and that I loved her more than I loved being the best."

She squeezed Hero's hands so hard that the bones creaked. Hero felt themself nodding, even as an ache filled their chest. "I'll tell her," they said.

Adelia nodded back, once. She released Hero's hands and wiped at her face with the linen the cabbage had been wrapped in. "Alright," she said with a loud sniff. "That's settled, then." She swung her legs over the side of the bed and stood unsteadily.

"Where are you going?" Hero asked, rubbing the collar of their shirt across their cheeks. It felt so sudden—the conversation was over, and their future was decided.

"If I'm going to meet Gran Carter tonight," Adelia called as she stepped behind the silk screen, "I'd like to at least be clean. I hope you saved me some soap for my last bath on this earth, eh, Hero?"

"You should have told me you were planning to die a little sooner," Hero called back. Their voice was still thick with emotion, but they managed to laugh as a cabbage leaf came flying over the top of the screen at them. "What am I supposed to do with this?"

"Shove it up your ass," Adelia shot back. "And then go find me a fresh bar of soap."

Chapter 10

Archie dipped her fingertips into the water and ran them across her hairline for the thousandth time, smoothing down the wisps of hair that seemed determined to curl at her temples in the humidity of the late-afternoon air.

"You look beautiful," Carter murmured, in a voice so low that only she would be able to hear it.

"Beautiful is not what I'm worried about," Archie replied, but she smiled at him anyway. "But merci."

"What *are* you worried about, then?"

Archie looked over at Carter, struck as always by how unconscionably handsome he was. The low, golden sun made his features almost glow. His rented hippo, Antoinette, was too small for him—the water nearly lapped his knees—but he rode with a grace that would have made anyone think he was a full-time hopper. "Getting into the party," she said. "You'll 'ave no problem—all you need to do is flash your star. And 'Oundstooth . . ." She glanced over her shoulder and ran out of words.

Houndstooth looked like himself again. And when he looked like himself, no party would turn him away, whether he had an invitation or not.

He'd changed into a suit that Archie had never seen him wear. She supposed he'd been saving it for a special occasion. She'd asked him if perhaps he wanted to change into it once they arrived at Parrish's barge, but he'd said that it would weather the ride there. So far, it had; the crisp collar of his plum shirt still stood tall and contrasted his white four-in-hand brilliantly, sending a tart spark of envy across Archie's tongue. He'd shaved and trimmed his own hair in the time it had taken for Archie to arm herself and oil the chain of her meteor hammer; he was immaculately combed, his moustache waxed into a razor curl. There was a light in his eyes—the light of expectation. The light of hope.

He winked at her from his seat astride Ruby's back, and Archie's heart nearly broke with relief.

"Why wouldn't you be able to get in?" Carter said, breaking into Archie's thoughts.

"I will," Archie replied. "I will. I suppose I am just worried about what would happen if I didn't."

Carter nudged Antoinette close enough to bump into Rosa. Rosa gave a snort, spraying creekwater over Antoinette's jowls, but didn't move away. "We won't be separated again, Archie," Carter said. "I mean it. I'm not going to run off chasing Adelia. This time, if I don't get her—and I *will* get her," he added, narrowing his eyes, "—but if I don't get her, I'm not going to run off after her. I swear."

"Don't make promises," Archie said with a sad smile. "Just keep them."

"Archie." Carter shifted on Antoinette's back, probably sore from spending so many hours in the saddle already. "I know you don't like me to make promises, but . . . I've been wanting to talk to you about maybe making some plans."

Archie stared straight ahead, watching the ripples in the water. "We 'ave a plan. We'll go to the party, find Adelia, arrest her, and let Winslow have ten minutes alone with her to find out where 'Ero is."

"That's not what I—"

A piercing whistle cut him off. Archie and Carter both

looked back to see Houndstooth staring at the water a few hundred feet away. He'd gone stock-still. One hand gripped the pommel of Ruby's saddle; with the other, he was reaching for the fully assembled harpoon that was strapped across his back. Archie started to call out to ask him what was the matter, but he raised a hand without looking away from the patch of water his eyes were fixed upon, and she fell silent.

For a long, tense minute, the only sound was Rosa blowing bubbles in the murky brown water. Finally, Houndstooth lowered his hand, shaking his head. He rode up next to Archie and Carter, still watching that patch of water.

"What is it?" Archie asked, looking between her old friend and the place he was staring at.

"I don't know," Houndstooth replied. "I thought I saw something—a wake—but then it was gone."

Archie patted Rosa's flank, and the three of them picked up speed, riding abreast through the widening creek. "A breeze, perhaps?"

"No, it was bigger than—never mind." Houndstooth rolled his shoulders. "I'm sure it was nothing."

"It's good of you to be so vigilant," Carter said. "You've got a keen eye, Houndstooth. We could use men like you in the service."

Houndstooth laughed and drew breath to say something that would probably make Carter regret his invitation, but stopped before saying anything, his head cocked.

"What is it now?" Archie asked, not unkindly.

"Do you hear that?" Houndstooth said, a smile spreading across his features.

"No, but then, my hearing isn't what it used to be. What is it?" Carter asked, looking around at the surface of the water. The three of them rounded a bend in the creek, and then Archie heard it: a faint ragtime melody that grew a little louder as Ruby, Rosa, and Antoinette proceeded through the water. After a moment, Carter heard it too—his face grew stern, and as Archie watched, a mantle of authority seemed to settle over his shoulders.

"That'll be the party, then," he said. One of his hands drifted up to check that his marshal's star was affixed firmly to the brim of his hat.

"Almost there," Houndstooth said with a giddy grin.

Archie didn't say anything at all. She checked that the chain of her meteor hammer was properly coiled. She loosened the straps on the knives that were sheathed at her shoulders, her waist, and her thighs. She unbuttoned the top button of her blouse. Then she leaned over, dipped her fingertips in the water, and smoothed her hair down again. Just in case.

The barge was bigger than Archie could have anticipated. The narrow stream that led up to it was too straight to be anything but man-made, so she'd known there was money at work, but it wasn't until she saw the thing for herself that she realized how *much* money. It was a floating mansion in the middle of a perfectly round private pond. Three ferrymen poled finely appointed party guests from the shore to the deck of the barge, where they were helped up by a servant in a coat and tails.

And there were so many guests. At least a hundred that Archie could see, and judging from the noise, twice that already inside. A loud cheer went up from somewhere within, followed by the sound of shattering glass and another round of shouts. Above it all, the music continued unabated—a powerful piano pounding out "The Wild Pottamus Rag." It was Archie's least favorite of the songs that had been written about the collapse of the Harriet Dam, not least because of the chorus: "And not a soul escaped alive, and not a soul escaped alive, hi-ho hop-whoa! And everybody died."

Not everybody, asshole, she thought tartly.

"Excuse me." A ferryman was stepping out of his boat and approaching them. Archie rested an easy hand on the hilt of the knife that hung at her waist. Out of the corner of her eye, she saw Carter slip the strap off his pistol with all the smooth subtlety of a gator sliding into the water.

"Yes?" Houndstooth said in an easy, friendly voice.

"I'll need to see your invitation, please," the ferryman said. "And you'll need to leave your hippopotami with the pond-hand." He snapped his fingers at a skinny, towheaded white boy in wading boots. Archie flinched, remembering another skinny boy who had wanted to be a hopper. She looked away from the pondhand before she could remember too hard.

"Of course," Houndstooth said, reaching into the breast pocket of his waistcoat. He paused, cocked his head, and reached into his other pocket. He made a show of checking his jacket, then swore. "Damn," he said, frowning at Archie. "You don't have our invitations, do you?"

"You were supposed to bring them," Archie said. She glanced at Carter, who nodded, then looked back at Houndstooth. "Don't tell me you don't have them at all, 'Oundstooth?"

He patted himself down, then shrugged. "I must have left them on the chifforobe." He looked up at the ferryman with a half smile. "I'm so sorry, my friend, I appear to have forgotten them."

"Alas," the ferryman said drily. "I can't let you in without one. Are you *certain* that you don't have an invitation? Just one would do for all three of you."

Houndstooth stared at him for a beat, then broke into a broad grin. "Oh, yes, of course. How could I forget?" He reached into his breast pocket again, and this time, he withdrew a bulging paper packet, tied with twine. "Here they are."

The ferryman took the packet and weighed it in his hand before nodding to Houndstooth. "Very good, sir." He snapped to the pondhand again, and the boy came running. "You may leave your hippos with Arthur and retrieve them again at the end of the evening."

"We'll take them around back ourselves, thank you," Carter said. The ferryman raised an eyebrow at him, but then, glancing up at the star on his hat, nodded.

"Very good, Mister Marshal," he said. He gave them directions to the paddock, then turned smartly away, greeting a set of guests that had arrived overland.

Archie guided Rosa into the pond, patting the hippo's white flank. "You were very brave back there, chérie," she cooed. Rosa's ears flipped back and forth as she slid into the clear water of the private pond. A cloud of mud bloomed from her hide, muddying the water around her. "Very brave," Archie added in a murmur.

The paddock was a loosely constructed ring of buoys with netting strung between them. As Archie, Houndstooth, and Carter approached, a second pondhand untied a length of netting and drew it aside. A few hippos were inside already, their ears and noses barely breaking the surface of the water. One flicked an ear at Ruby as she slid between the buoys and into the paddock, ahead of Rosa. Houndstooth pulled Ruby up short, much as he had in Thompson Creek, and stared.

"It can't be," he whispered.

"What's the holdup?" Carter called from behind Archie. Houndstooth ignored him, urging Ruby toward the hippo that had caught his attention—a runty grey one that had clocked Ruby as she entered the paddock.

"That's . . . that's Abigail," Houndstooth said. At the sound of her name, Abigail lifted her great grey head out of the water. "That's *Abigail.*"

Carter looked at Archie. "Hero's girl, Abigail?"

Archie nodded as Houndstooth took his hat off, running a hand through his hair. "I thought we left her back at Port Rouge," she said.

"We did," Houndstooth replied. "Or . . . I don't know, I thought we did. It was dark, we were in such a hurry, I didn't think to check—" He rubbed his eyes with one hand, looking old for a moment. "This doesn't make any sense at all. How would Hero have gotten ahold of her?"

"Are you sure it's her?" Archie asked. Houndstooth nodded slowly, then pulled himself up onto the dock that led from the paddock to the barge. Without looking back, he stalked toward the sound of the party.

"Will he be okay in there?" Carter asked as Archie dismounted.

"We'll find out," Archie said, staring at Houndstooth's back as the sound of his red hippo-leather boots pounding on the wood of the dock blended into the ragtime rhythm. "One way or the other."

The inside of the barge was dense with people. The crowd fairly bristled with knives, pistols, and fists. Archie pushed her way through, Carter at her back, and found Houndstooth standing at the entrance to the formal dining room. The long table was crowded with gifts, as thick as ticks on a dog's back—baskets of oranges, pistols shining with oil, long parcels wrapped in white paper. At the head of the table, the oldest man Archie had ever seen was hunched over a package, picking at the twine that wrapped it with a gnarled finger. He squinted at the knot with cloudy eyes, shaking his head, before pulling out a pocket knife and sawing through the twine. A young woman stood beside him with a sheaf of paper and an ivory-barreled pen; behind her was a stack of already-opened gifts, including an ill-advised model of the Harriet Dam as it had looked before it fell.

The young woman with the pen looked up just as Archie edged into the room, and Archie had to swallow a surprised laugh. It was Acadia, wearing a pile of false curls and a heavily ruffled corset that had pushed her bony frame into the approximate shape of a violin—all extravagant curves. She gave Archie a wicked grin before laying a possessive hand on the shoulder of the old man in the chair.

"I suppose that must be Mr. Burton," Archie said to Houndstooth, nodding to the old man. But Houndstooth didn't answer. Archie turned and found that he was no longer standing beside her. She whipped around, only to see him crossing the room, pushing people out of his way. A woman cried out as he shouldered past her, knocking her into a butler's tray of tall cocktail glasses.

"It's her," Carter said behind Archie. He was staring over the heads of the people in the crowd. "It must be. He must have seen Adelia—" Archie didn't want to hear more. She followed in Houndstooth's wake, stepping over the ankle of a man he'd bowled over, lifting her skirt to step over a puddle of gin on the floor. The quarters were too close for her to use her meteor hammer without putting the drunken party guests in danger, so she unsheathed her weightiest blade and shoved past a tall woman who had stepped into her path.

And then she saw Houndstooth. Some of the guests had wised up, clearing a path in front of the harpoon-strapped madman who was knocking people down. As Archie watched, her friend reached up and took his much-abused hat off, letting it fall behind him without so much as a backward glance. He strode forward and, as the crowd parted in front of him, grabbed one of the party guests by the shoulder.

They turned around.

Archie stopped in her tracks, feeling her mouth fall open, and stared. The music was too loud for her to make out everything Houndstooth was saying, but she didn't need to hear a word. Carter caught up to her just in time to watch with her as Houndstooth swept Hero into his arms. The air in the room stilled as he kissed them with the unrestrained fire of a man possessed by months of fear and searching and need and a tenacious, undying certainty that the person he loved was still out there, waiting for his lips to meet theirs.

"Oh," Carter said.

"Yes," Archie agreed.

"Excuse me," came a voice from beside her. Archie moved aside—out of the corner of her eye, she saw the tall, dark-haired woman she'd pushed aside a few moments before. The woman moved past, trailing the sharp smell of sweat and something sour.

Archie glanced back at the woman.

Then she looked again.

"Shit." She looked back at Houndstooth, who was holding Hero by the face, his forehead pressed to theirs. She looked up at Carter, who was watching the reunion with a familiar smile. "Fucking shit-arsed *fuck*," she said, and grabbed Carter by the elbow. She started to pull him after her, following the path of the dark-haired woman. Behind her, she heard Houndstooth calling.

She looked over her shoulder, met his eyes, and nodded. As she turned back, she saw him cast a regretful glance at Hero. She didn't need to watch to know that he was following her.

"What is it?" Carter asked beside her.

"It's her," Archie answered, gathering a length of chain in one hand and tightening her grip on her still-unsheathed blade in the other. "It's Adelia."

Chapter 11

Adelia's head swam. She heard a commotion behind her—but there was no time. Her fever was spiking again, her vision tunneling, and it was now or never.

Burton had to die.

She wove through the crowd, which seemed far too large for a government official's birthday party. She supposed that Parrish must have padded out the list with whoever he was accepting bribes from. She shook her head hard, trying to jar herself into focusing. *None of that matters,* she thought as she reached the door to the formal dining room. *None of it.* All that mattered was killing Burton and getting Ysabel into Hero's hands before—

A hand on her elbow.

No, she thought desperately. She shook off the hand and shoved her way into the dining room, barreling toward the head of the table. Burton looked up at her, his thick brows furrowed. She grabbed a length of cut twine from the table in front of him and stepped behind him in one fluid motion. A bead of fever-sweat ran down her back as she looped the twine around her palms, slipping it over the old man's head.

Now.

She heard the impact at first, more than she felt it—a crack from just behind her. She almost turned to look, but then she was falling, and a searing pain was in the back of her skull.

I've been shot, she thought. As she landed on the waxed wood of the dining room floor, she reached up with one hand, and felt her unbroken skull.

Not shot, then. She fought to remain conscious and won by the skin of her teeth. She started trying to scramble to her feet, but then hands were under her arms, and she was kicking as she was dragged back through the crowd, away from her only hope of getting Ysabel back.

—◆—

"You can't," Hero was saying. Adelia tugged at the cuffs that Carter had applied to her wrists. The chain rattled against the chair to which she was tethered, and everyone turned to look at her.

"Please," she rasped, staring at Hero. "You have to do it. You have to kill him. Please." She was drenched in sweat, her head pounding—her fever had finally broken, too late to matter. She couldn't reach back to feel whether her head was swelling where Carter had struck her, but she could guess.

"Why the hop-eared fuck would Hero do a thing like that?" Houndstooth growled, trying to lean back against a wall, then shifting again as his harpoon dug into his back. "This useless bloody thing, I swear—"

"Hero would do a thing like that," Hero said, making Houndstooth startle, "because it's the only way to get Ysabel back."

"And Ysabel is the baby, right?" Carter asked, pinching the bridge of his nose.

"I just don't understand why Parrish would kidnap Ysabel instead of just *hiring Adelia,*" Archie said. She was leaning against the plaster wall of the quarters that had been assigned to Adelia ten hours before.

"Because I'm retired," Adelia said. "He tried to hire me a year ago, and I told him no. And then he tried again, right before the

Harriet job, and I told him no. And then he tried to sabotage the Harriet job, so that Burton would look incompetent and get fired, and he wanted me to help him do it—and I said no then, too. I think he went through Travers after that. And . . . then Travers decided to go through me anyway. I kept saying no, Hero. They kept trying to make me kill, and I kept saying no." She closed her eyes, wishing there was a way that she could will herself unconscious. "And men like him . . . they do not like to hear that word." At least then she would be able to get some sleep before hanging.

She could hear Houndstooth pacing back and forth in front of her with the measured steps of terrible patience. "And you were 'retired' when you tried to kill Hero?" His voice was quiet enough to make her open her eyes again—a dangerous kind of quiet that sent a rare spark of fear through her.

"That's what I'm trying to tell you, Houndstooth," Hero said. They grabbed him by both shoulders, staring into his eyes. "Adelia didn't try to kill me. She saved me. Do you understand? That's why it's so important that she's retired. She *didn't kill me*. If she hadn't done what she did—Travers would have killed me himself. I was the one who was setting up explosives in the Harriet, wasn't I?" They shook their head. "He would have made *sure* I was dead long before the dam fell."

"Hero, please," Adelia said. "None of that matters. Parrish has Ysabel."

"She's right," Carter said. Hero looked at him with wide eyes. "None of it matters. Adelia has killed more men than I can name in an hour. Retirement doesn't change that."

"I've killed dozens of men," Hero snapped. "So has Houndstooth, and so has Archie. If you think you're in the company of innocents, Carter, you're much mistaken."

"I don't have a warrant for your arrest, or for his," Carter growled back, his finger under Hero's nose, "but if I did—and Archie's neither here nor there, you leave her out of—"

"Pardonnez-moi?" Archie's typically fluting voice was as low and dangerous as the rumble of an approaching avalanche. Carter waved a hand, still towering over Hero.

"You know what I mean," he said.

Archie took a step closer to him, her arms folded across her chest. "Explain it to me, chérie," she said, fury simmering in every word. "Perhaps I do not understand. You know 'ow I *struggle*."

Carter turned to look at her. "I just meant, you know. Once we're married and all, I can't be forced to testify against you, and as long as you don't get yourself into any more trouble . . ."

Hero took a quick step backward as Archie's face went still with cold rage. " 'Ow dare you?" Her voice rose with every word. "As long as I don't *get myself into any more trouble*?! As long as I—what was it?" She wheeled on Houndstooth, who threw up his hands in a please-don't-kill-me plea. "As long as I birth a litter of brats and spend my time chasing them away from the fine china, then I can be your wife? As long as I spend all of my time taking care of *you* and *him* and *every fucking one of you useless men*—va te faire enculer! Non," she shouted, turning back to Carter, to Houndstooth's evident relief. "You will marry me as I am, you will love me for who I *am* and for what I am *great* at—or you won't marry me at all, Gran Carter."

"Archie," Carter said, pleading in earnest now, "please, I can't . . . I can't marry a con. I can't marry a killer. I'm a U.S. marshal." He reached for her hands, but she snatched them away. "Please. I've worked my whole life for this star—"

He reached up to tap the star on the brim of his hat, but it wasn't there. Archie shook her head, holding up the stolen star. She'd taken it from his hat without him so much as flinching. "I've worked my 'ole life for this," she said, shaking the star at him. "To be able to do the things that I do—it gives me more than bread, Carter. It gives me *life*. Just like this maudit star gives *you* life. I would never ask you to give this up for me, *never*. And if you think I'll give up my life's work just to marry you, you are not *good enough* for me."

She slapped his star against his chest with enough force to knock him backward a few steps. Adelia closed her eyes over strange, hot tears. *Just finish me,* she thought desperately. *Fight afterward. You'll have time.* When she opened her eyes, Carter was holding both of Archie's hands, murmuring something that sounded like an apology. But before Adelia could get a good read on what he was saying, her view of the fight—or the aftermath, she supposed—was obscured as Hero crouched in front of her.

"Adelia," they said, "I'm not going to kill Burton." Adelia let her head sag, feeling a last trickle hope drain out of her. "But I will get Ysabel back." Adelia looked up. Hero was staring intently into her eyes. "I made you a promise, and I intend to keep it. Do you believe me?"

Adelia nodded without hesitation. She squeezed her eyes shut as another wave of pain washed through her skull, and when she'd opened them, Hero was gone. Archie and Carter startled apart as the door slammed—Houndstooth pushed his way between them, tearing out of the room after Hero.

Carter stared at Adelia, his hand still resting on Archie's arm. The fury in Archie's face seemed to have dimmed, although its ghost was still there, beneath the surface. "How are we going to get her out of here while the party's going on?" Carter murmured.

"It can wait," Archie said. She looked at Adelia with something close to pity. "She's not going anywhere."

Adelia couldn't help agreeing. She was so tired—more tired than she could remember being in a long time. She shifted, rattling the chains again. "Archie," she said, "can I make a request?" When Archie didn't say anything, she decided to go ahead with it. What did she have to lose? "There are some cabbage leaves on the night-stand there. Please—" She cleared her throat. "Could you please give them to me?"

Archie just stared at her.

"Please? I—what was that?" All three of them looked to the door as another scream rang through the early-evening air.

Carter grabbed Archie's hand. "I promised," he whispered, looking between her and the door. "And I meant it. You're more important to me than—than damn near anything. We'll find a way to make it work. I'm not leaving you again, I promise. I swear, Archie."

"Don't make promises, chérie," Archie murmured back. "Go. I'll watch her," she added with a glance toward Adelia. Carter handed her his key ring, kissed her fiercely, and bolted toward the growing sound of screaming guests. The moment he was gone, Archie grabbed the cabbage leaves and thrust them at Adelia.

"I can't do it myself," Adelia said, rattling the chains.

"What do you need done with them?" Archie asked, massaging her temples.

Adelia told her.

"No," Archie said flatly.

"*Please.*" Adelia felt a flush of shame—she was unaccustomed to begging. "I have had this infection since a few days after Ysabel was taken, and the cabbage leaves are the only thing that's helped. My fever has finally broken, but I don't know if it will come back without—*please,*" she finished weakly.

Archie pursed her lips. "I will not do this for you," she repeated. Then she knelt beside Adelia and, with a rattle of keys, freed her hands. "You will do it for yourself," she continued. "And if you try to run, I will kill you. Is that understood?"

Adelia rubbed her numb wrists in a state of mild shock. "Thank you," she breathed. Archie pressed the cabbage leaves into her hands, then stood at the door with her back to the room.

"What did he say?" Adelia asked, easing her shirt off.

"Hein?" Archie said, turning her back. "What did who say?"

"Carter. What did he say to make you forgive him?"

There was a long pause, long enough that Adelia almost repeated herself. Then, slowly, Archie answered. "I 'aven't forgiven 'im. 'E said all the right things, about respecting me and wanting to find a way that we can both 'ave our lives be what they are supposed to be, and 'ow 'e wasn't thinking straight. So, I've decided to give 'im a chance to prove 'imself. I think that's what love is— it's not about forgiving or forgetting right away. It's about deciding to give someone a chance to earn your forgiveness, eventually."

"And you love him?" Adelia asked.

"More than I know 'ow to express," Archie replied.

"More than the work?"

"No," Archie said. "Not more than the work. But I 'ope there will be a way for me to love them both at the same time. And if there is not—c'est la vie. I will live with 'eartbreak one way or the other."

"We're not so different, I don't think," Adelia ventured as she replaced the old cabbage leaves with the new ones.

Archie barked out a laugh. "We couldn't be more different if our lives depended on it," she said. "But that doesn't mean you deserve to suffer."

"Some people would say it does," Adelia murmured. She examined her swollen breast—it seemed less red than it had even that morning. The pain in her head was pulsing white and grey, but the pain in her breast had eased. *How timely,* she thought. *Perfect.*

"I am not 'some people,'" Archie said. They both went silent, listening to the sound of screams.

"What do you think is going on down there?" Adelia asked. As if to answer her, a bellow cut through the screams like a steam engine bursting through a snowdrift.

Archie spun around to face Adelia, who froze with her shirt half buttoned. Their eyes met, and a terrible knowledge passed between them as another bellow joined the first.

"No," Adelia breathed.

"Ferals," Archie replied. Outside the door to Adelia's quarters, footsteps pounded down the hall. Outside the window, a long, loud scream was cut short by a wet splash.

Chapter 12

Houndstooth caught up to Hero just as the first feral rammed into the barge.

"Fuck, fuck, fuck, fuck," they were chanting under their breath as they pushed the doors to the kitchen open. "Fuck, fuck, fuck—" And then, a sound of splintering wood and a bellow of rage blended with the screams of the party guests.

"Hero, wait—" Houndstooth caught Hero under the arms as they stumbled, then immediately stumbled himself. "We have to go," he said as they both found their feet.

"I have to get Ysabel," Hero said.

"No, Hero, we have to *leave,* you don't understand—"

Hero wheeled on him. "Don't tell me what I don't understand," they snapped. "You have no idea what you're talking about. You—I can't talk about this right now. There's no time." They turned back into the kitchen, which was nearly empty save for a sobbing girl with wild red curls and skin so pale that Houndstooth could see a blue vein at her throat. "Hey," Hero snapped their fingers in front of the crying girl's eyes a few times. "You, what's your name? Where's the chef?" When they received no response, they slapped her smartly across the face. The girl's sobs only got louder.

"Where is the chef?" Hero shouted into the girl's face over the sound of bellowing ferals. Houndstooth gripped the doorframe to steady himself as the barge rocked. Hero slapped the girl again.

"Where is the *chef,* tell me!"

The girl shook her head. "She's gone," she cried. "She left when the first feral got here, I'm sorry—"

Another bellow from outside—two, three, and then the barge was rocking again. A pot of something that smelled like damn good she-crab soup fell from the stovetop, spreading a fragrant, steaming slick across the floor.

From somewhere in the kitchen came a high keening sound.

Hero straightened. They let go of the girl, who immediately fled past Houndstooth, slipping on the spill. The noise grew louder, until it sounded like a grinding, grating wail.

Houndstooth realized what was going on just as Hero opened a cupboard and knelt in front of it with a cry of relief.

"Ysabel!" they yelled, reaching into the cupboard to retrieve the swaddled baby.

"How did you—" Houndstooth slipped in the stuff on the floor, catching himself on the oven as a new wave of screams rose outside. "How did you know she'd be in here?"

"The chef sent up cabbage leaves for Adelia," Hero said, clutching the screaming baby to their chest. "That girl with the red hair brought them up. She said that—shhh, Ysabel, hush—they said that the chef had been dealing with an infection like the one Adelia had, just last month." Houndstooth put a hand on their elbow to help them balance as they made their way back to the door. "It was a long shot, but . . . Ysabel had to have a wet nurse. If she hadn't, we would have been able to hear her crying all the way from Port Rouge." Even as they said it, the baby let out a fresh piercing cry. Houndstooth winced.

"We have to leave," Houndstooth said. "Please, Hero—it's not safe, not if the ferals are here."

"I know." Hero bounced Ysabel, and Houndstooth let it go, even if they hadn't been on the Harriet that terrible, blood-soaked morning when the dam collapsed. Even if they couldn't possibly know the danger they were in. "Let's get out of here." They stepped out of the servants' entrance and onto the dock with Houndstooth on their heels.

He watched them run along the dock with Ysabel in their arms, and he mercilessly crushed the question that rose in his mind—the question of why they hadn't been in touch. Why they'd stayed with Adelia, instead of coming to find him.

He clenched a fist as he tried not to wonder whether they'd missed him at all.

The pond was a horror to survey. Four ferals had found their way into the water—*just four,* Houndstooth thought. *So much chaos for just four.*

Chaos was the only way to describe it. At first glance, Houndstooth thought that all three ferrymen floated on the surface of the water; after a second look, he realized that it was one ferryman floating in three different places. The other two were nowhere to be seen, but the pink tint of the formerly clear water gave him an idea. Their boats had been reduced to splinters in the water; sections of the barge's railing were floating alongside their remains.

Houndstooth looked around Hero, trying to see the paddock, but it was out of sight. *Please,* he thought. *Please let it be whole.* He pushed away a mental image of Ruby, trapped in the paddock as a feral pushed its way in.

He looked back to the water, where a partygoer had seen fit to attempt a swim to shore. The three ferals in the water were still tearing at the severed leg of a ferryman, tossing it into the air as they rammed each other away from it. As Houndstooth watched, the man—blond, and lanky as hell, Houndstooth noted—swam for the shore. He looked over his shoulder at the ferals, who still hadn't noticed him. His eyes were a startling shade of blue.

Houndstooth recognized him with a jolt, and stopped in his tracks, his boots skidding on the wood of the dock.

"Parrish?" he called it out before he realized his error. The swimmer paused, turning to look at who had called out to him.

The ferals looked, too.

"Houndstooth?" The man—Parrish, it was definitely Parrish— was treading water, staring at Houndstooth incredulously.

Houndstooth hadn't believed it until then, not really—hadn't believed that the little blue-eyed boy, the federal agent he'd so deftly exhausted some four months prior, was truly the man behind it all. If Hero hadn't disappeared, Houndstooth realized, he would never have thought of Parrish again.

But Hero *had* disappeared, and somehow this man—the briefest of entertainments in a closed chapter of Houndstooth's life—was back.

"What are you doing here?" Parrish shouted. Houndstooth shook his head, didn't know how to answer. He automatically checked the water, a habit that had hardened over the last few months. He blinked, looked again.

"I'm here for Hero," he said. He went to gesture at Hero— but they were gone, out of sight ahead along the dock.

"Who?" Parrish called, still treading water, his arms making little splashes on the surface of the pond.

"Hero," Houndstooth said. "Hero Shackleby? They came here with Adelia Reyes?"

Parrish spat, looking over the water, his head bobbing as he kicked to keep himself afloat. "This ain't exactly the best time," he said—but he started swimming toward the dock Houndstooth stood on.

Somewhere to Houndstooth's left, Hero's voice called.

"I'm right behind you," he called back, watching Parrish swim.

Watching the water.

"Parrish," he said, not too loudly. "Watch out."

"What was that?" Parrish said, pausing in the water. Footsteps pounded along the dock—Hero was coming back—but Houndstooth couldn't look away from the water.

"I said watch out," he murmured, as four wakes shot along the surface of the water toward Parrish.

"I can't—damn it," Parrish said, pausing in the water, splashing again in an effort to hold still for long enough to hear Houndstooth. His seersucker suit clung to him, and Houndstooth was struck by just how bony the man was. "I can't *hear* you, Houndstooth, what did y—"

And then, just like that, he was gone.

He disappeared below the water with barely a splash—one moment, talking; the next, absent.

Houndstooth counted as Hero drew up short a few feet away. They watched the water with him. *One . . . two . . . three . . . four . . . five—*

And then he was back above the surface, arms thrashing, swimming desperately away from the triangle of ferals that had closed in on him. One surfaced, blood streaming from its drooping, whiskery jowls. Then a second—then a third. They shoved at each other, jaws gaping. Houndstooth spotted a shoe between the teeth of the largest one.

They fought each other and bellowed and Houndstooth half hoped that they'd be too distracted to finish the job. But then Parrish looked back over his shoulder, faltered, took in a lungful of water. He coughed and spat, and the feral with the shoe between its teeth turned.

It saw Parrish.

Parrish screamed as the three ferals, the smaller two closely trailing the largest one, closed in on him. They bumped into each other, snapping and bellowing. Parrish swam as hard and fast as Houndstooth had ever seen a man swim, and it looked as though he might just be able to outswim the ferals.

"*No!*" A raw scream sounded from the riverboat, and then a girl in a beautiful gown was diving into the water, false curls falling from her head as she jackknifed through the air. Her powerful jump had taken her far, and she entered the water close to Parrish, closer than the ferals. She swam toward him, water frothing before her.

"Acadia," Parrish shouted, choking on water. "Acadia, help—please—"

The girl had reached him, and she grabbed him by the collar, treading water. "Thank God," he gasped, "thank God, you have to help me—"

The girl planted a hand on his head and shoved with a mighty yell. His head disappeared beneath the surface of the water. The girl reached beneath the churn with the hand that wasn't drowning Parrish, and seemed to root around. After a moment, Parrish surfaced, sputtering.

Acadia held up a hand. She was clutching a waxed leather folio.

"No," Parrish said, grabbing for the folio and getting a mouthful of pond water. He was tangled up in his own suit jacket, which had come half off during his struggle. "No, you can't, those are—"

But the girl folded herself in the water, planting both feet on Parrish's shoulders. She pushed off, shoving him down below the surface of the water and springing away from him, and began to swim toward the shore, holding the folio aloft with one hand. And still, the hippos were closing in on Parrish.

He surfaced, choking. He looked after the girl and shouted hoarsely, but she didn't look back. He coughed a few more times before turning to see the trio of ferals approaching, too close for him to even consider escape.

He didn't even have the good sense to drown before they got to him.

Poor bastard, Houndstooth thought. *Three on one? He doesn't stand a—wait.*

He counted the ferals again.

One, two, three.

He could have sworn there had been four before.

The section of the dock that lay between Houndstooth and Hero exploded, shards of wood flying in all directions. Hero stumbled, nearly falling into the water as the dock shook with the force of the feral that was bursting through just a few feet ahead. It bellowed, then vanished below the surface of the water.

Houndstooth watched the shadow in the water as it circled, building momentum for another run at the dock. In front of him, a five-foot section of dock was gone, floating in fragments.

"Hero!" he called, even as he reached over his shoulder to unstrap his harpoon. "Run to the paddock! Abigail is there—"

"I know!" they called back. Houndstooth could only just hear them over the gurgling screams and thick tearing noises coming from the water, where the three ferals had reached Parrish.

And then the fourth feral was back, and Hero was running toward the paddock, and Houndstooth was bracing his feet on the dock although he knew it was a useless effort. He twisted the harpoon in sweat-slick fists, trying to find a grip that would make him feel ready.

The beast burst out of the pond near Houndstooth's feet, spraying water as it bellowed.

Houndstooth aimed the harpoon at the exposed roof of the feral's mouth. As he drove it forward, the feral turned its head to bring its teeth down on his leg. He dodged it so narrowly that he felt whiskers scratch his trouser leg—and then, the harpoon meet soft flesh.

Too soft.

The harpoon was jerked out of his hand, and as he watched, the hippo backed away with the shaft of the harpoon sticking out of from between its teeth like an absurd toothpick. It shook its head, but the harpoon was stuck fast in the back of its throat. Behind Houndstooth, another *thump* shook the dock. He tried to grab the harpoon, but the shaft was already slick with dark blood and the beast was jerking around too quickly for him to get a firm grip.

Something pounded on the dock behind him, hard and fast. Hero was already out of sight ahead of him, and Houndstooth was grateful for that because he wouldn't have wanted them to see him die this way. Sweat soaked his suit jacket, and he peeled it off before rolling up his sleeves. He drew his knife, clenching it between his teeth, and braced his feet on the edge of the dock in preparation. This was it, then: he bent his knees, ready to jump into the water so he could kill the beast in front of him before facing whatever was behind him. He took a deep breath through his teeth, closed his eyes—

"'Oundstooth, *no!*"

He turned as the pounding on the dock behind him got louder, and there was Archie, running toward him with her meteor hammer already swinging. She reached him just as he was stepping back from the dock's edge, and she swung the heavy hammer high before bringing it down with a crunch on the skull of the feral. She dragged it back by the chain, trailing rich red through the water, and wound it up to swing again—but the beast was already sinking below the surface of the water, its skull cracked wide, blood and brain matter floating on the pond's surface like oil.

"Archie—" Houndstooth's heart was pounding in his ears, and he and Archie stared at each other, breathless. "Where did you *come* from?"

She gestured up toward the second floor of the barge as she wound the chain of the meteor hammer around her waist. "I saw you fighting that thing, and I jumped. Are you alright? Where is 'Ero? 'Ave you seen Carter? What's—"

Houndstooth crushed her in a hug, letting his knife fall to the dock. She embraced him back, clapping him on the shoulder with her free hand.

"You saved my life," he breathed. "Again. God, am I so useless to need all this saving?" She clapped him on the shoulder again, gracious enough to not say *yes*. "Did you see that girl?"

"Who, Acadia?" Archie nodded. "She is . . . formidable, no?"

"Will she be okay?" Houndstooth asked.

Archie laughed. "I think she will be just fine, mon frère. For now, you'll want to worry about yourself."

They both stared at the hole in the dock.

"I don't think I can jump that," Houndstooth said.

"Nor could I," Archie said. "I landed poorly, I am afraid . . . I don't think my ankle could take another landing." Houndstooth looked, and saw that she was standing on one foot. "I think it is not broken, but it will be of no use today."

Behind them, screams rose from the barge as a feral bellowed.

"I don't think we can go back, either," Archie said.

A shadow appeared in the water. "Fucking *damn*," Houndstooth said. His harpoon was underwater, still clenched in the jaw of the dead feral. He knelt to pick up his knife as Archie hefted her meteor hammer with a weary arm. The shadow stopped in front of him—and without so much as a ripple, Ruby's head slid up out of the water.

"Roo?" he said, disbelieving—but there she was, his Ruby, out of the paddock and ready for him. Her saddle was soaked, but he couldn't begin to care. Behind her, a white splash, and then Rosa's ears flapped above the water's surface.

Houndstooth turned to look at Archie. "Hero must have opened the paddock." As they watched, more shadows filled the water. The ferals, still fighting over the scraps of the swimmer, didn't notice these new hippos until a moment too late—and then the real fight began.

"We 'ave to get out of 'ere," Archie said as the ferals' bellows were met and matched by the roars of the hippos who were attempting to pass them.

"I concur, my friend," Houndstooth said. He held Archie's arm as she stepped down onto Rosa's saddle with her already-swelling ankle.

"Houndstooth!" The call came from around a corner, and then Houndstooth's heart swelled because there was Hero, riding Abigail toward him at breakneck speed. They stopped next to Ruby as Houndstooth settled himself into her saddle, and then the three of them were skirting the frothing knot of ferals and hippos in the center of the pond.

Ruby shook her head and snorted nervously as she swam through the bloodied water. Houndstooth stroked her flank, murmuring to her in an attempt to keep her calm without attracting the attention of the ferals. As they reached the stream that led to Thompson Creek, Carter came running along the bank, one hand pressing his hat to his head.

"Grâce à dieu," Archie breathed—and then she held out a hand and Carter jumped into the saddle behind her, clinging to her waist as they rode away from the fray and into the safe waters of Thompson Creek.

They were a few miles down Thompson Creek when Houndstooth asked the question he'd been sitting on since Hero had ridden around the dock on Abigail's back. Archie and Carter rode a hundred feet behind them, squeezed together into one saddle. Rosa was slowed by the extra weight, and Archie had to set an easy pace to keep her ankle free of the stirrups. Houndstooth had been waiting to ask until he and Hero were far enough ahead that he could be certain the sound of his question—and of Hero's answer—wouldn't carry, even over the insect sounds that were rising with the dying light.

"Hero?"

Hero looked at him, and his heart faltered like a hop learning to walk. They looked exhausted, too thin from months doing whatever they'd been doing. Blood and sweat and mud spattered their shirt, and there was a cut on their arm that was too deep not to worry about. They rubbed a hand across their face, smearing the dirt that was smudged there and leaving a light streak across their cheeks.

They were the most magnificent thing he'd ever seen.

"I'm so sorry, Hero." He swallowed around something sharp, something like shame and anger and fear all stuck through his gullet. He was so sorry that he was choking on it. "I should have . . . I'm sorry."

"I'm sorry too," they said.

"What? No—"

"I'm sorry I yelled at you," they continued, as if they hadn't heard him. "I didn't—there was so much happening all at once, and the ferals—"

"It's alright—"

"—and I . . . seeing you, Houndstooth." Their voice broke, and they looked away, but Houndstooth could see starlight reflected in their eyes. "I thought you were dead. I didn't think I'd ever see you again, and I tried not to let myself think about it, but late at night when the baby would cry and wake me up and it would all hit me at once and—"

"Hero—"

"—I'm sorry." It had grown too dark for Houndstooth to see Hero's tears, and he was too far to brush them away with the edge of his thumb.

"It's alright," he murmured. "Or, it's not alright—none of it was alright—but I understand. I'm . . . I thought you were dead, too. The only difference was, instead of pushing the feelings away, I . . ." He paused, struggling to find the words that could describe the depth of his obsession with the idea that Hero *had* to be alive. "I lost myself in them. I said things, Hero. I did things that I didn't have to do. I hurt a man who didn't—he didn't need hurting. I hurt Archie. I hurt her, and I haven't even apologized to her. I don't know if she'll let me."

There was a soft splash as Abigail nudged her shoulder against Ruby's. Houndstooth reached out. He was too far from Hero to lay a hand on their shoulder, but his outstretched fingertips met theirs, if only for a moment.

"I think Archie understands," Hero said. "She knows what it's like to be far from the person you love."

Houndstooth looked over his shoulder at Archie, Carter, and Rosa, silhouetted in the moonlight. "That she does," he said. He cleared his throat. "Hero, I have to ask you something. I'm sorry, but I just—"

"What is it?" Hero sounded so small in that moment that Houndstooth wanted to cup them in the palm of his hand where they'd be warm. He cleared his throat again and reached out to see if Hero's fingertips were still within reach, but his hand met empty air.

"Houndstooth? What's your question?"

Now or never, he thought. He might as well ask, because the answer would be the same no matter how long he waited.

"I was just wondering," he asked. "Where's Ysabel?"

Chapter 13

Hero debated not answering the question. They were silent for a long time, and Houndstooth, bless him, was patient. He waited while they thought about lying to him, while they thought about ignoring him, while they thought about diving into the water and swimming away.

But in the end, they looked over and, in the dim light of the waning moon, saw him reaching out a hand. He was waiting for their fingertips to meet his—waiting so patiently—and they knew they had no choice but to tell him the truth.

"Adelia has her," they said.

Houndstooth was silent for a long time. Then: "How?"

"She came to the paddock," Hero said. They would never forget the look on Adelia's face when she made it to them. She had burst up out of the water along the edge of the paddock, levering herself over the netting. Hero had asked how she'd dodged the notice of the ferals, but she'd been too out of breath to answer. She'd held out her hands for the baby after scrambling onto the back of a hippo that bore the brand of a Port Rouge rental company. When Hero had handed Ysabel over, Adelia had looked like all of her illness and suffering and flight had been worth it.

"So, what—she's going to keep running?" Houndstooth's voice was gentle, and Hero couldn't hold back their smile.

"Well. I was going to talk to you about that."

Hero leaned forward to rub Abigail between the ears, remembering the sight of Adelia on her stolen hippo, fading into the shaded section of the paddock, as shadowy as Ruby in the water. She had been looking down at Ysabel with tears stream-ing down her face. Hero reached into their pocket and felt the smooth stone that rested there—a stone plucked from the bank of Thompson Creek, if they had to guess. With their thumb, they could almost feel the image that was etched into the stone. Two hippos, shoulder to shoulder.

"*Goodbye, Hero.*"

"*Goodbye?*"

"*This is the 'end of the line,' no?*" *Adelia hadn't sounded bitter in the slightest as she repeated Hero's words back to them.*

"*I—well, I don't—*"

"*It's alright, Hero,*" *Adelia had said, her lips brushing Ysabel's hair. "It's what we agreed. You would help me find Ysabel, and then we would part ways.*"

Hero had done many brave things in their life. They drew on all the courage they possessed. "Adelia, what if—Houndstooth and I. We're going to start a ranch. We haven't talked about it since before the Harriet, obviously, but . . ."

"*But you know he has not changed his mind about it,*" *Adelia had said, stroking Ysabel's wispy hair.*

"*I haven't changed mine,*" *Hero had replied. "And back before everything happened, we talked about it, he and I, and we were going to do it. I have my land, and now we have the capital from the Harriet job.*"

Adelia had been silent, absorbed in Ysabel. The green shadows of the paddock had fallen across her face, and Hero had felt a bone-deep certainty that they might never see her again.

"*I was thinking,*" *Hero said, a tremor in their voice. "We'll need a ranch hand. Someone who knows their way around. Someone who we can trust.*" *Adelia's silence had thickened then, had solidified into something taut and patient. Hero had waited.*

"*It would not be a good life for Ysabel, running and hiding all the* time," Adelia had finally said. "It would be good for her to grow up on a ranch. Around people who aren't killers."

"We're all killers," Hero murmured. "But we'd love her like family."

Adelia had looked up then, a slant of dappled light illuminating her wet face. "Like family," she'd said, and there had been something like a smile in her voice.

"Anyway. It'll take us a month or so to get there," they'd said, awkwardly rubbing the back of their neck. "And we'll have to do some work on Carter in the meantime, convincing him not to go get a new warrant for you and all. But maybe you can meet us there . . . ?"

"Maybe I can," Adelia had said. And then Ysabel had begun to stir, and a horrible scream had sounded from the pond, and they'd all had to leave, and Hero hadn't been sure if "maybe" meant "I'll never see you again"—not until they'd found that stone in their pocket.

"I was going to talk to you about that," Hero said again, and Houndstooth looked over at them. "But maybe it can wait until morning."

"Maybe it can," Houndstooth said. The silence between them was quickly devoured by the night-bugs and the soft splashes of Ruby and Abigail moving through the water.

Hero took their hand out of their pocket and, at last, reached toward Houndstooth. Houndstooth's fingers found theirs, and they rode like that for a time—fingers just touching, Ruby's and Abigail's shoulders pressed close. Just enough to remind each other that they were together in the dark, until they could look at each other in the light.

WORTH HER WEIGHT IN GOLD

Winslow's Problem

Winslow Remington Houndstooth had a problem.

The problem was Ruby.

She wouldn't get up. She was lying there with her head in the mud and making the most piteous noises Houndstooth had ever heard, and she simply wouldn't *stand*.

This was an especially bad problem for three reasons.

Reason One

Ruby was a hippopotamus, and when a hippopotamus doesn't want to get up, there is not a soul alive or dead in the great green state of Georgia who can make her get up. Winslow Remington Houndstooth, by his own account (and perhaps one or two others), was the greatest hopper in the South or anywhere else. But not even he could make a hippopotamus get up and go without her express permission.

Reason Two

Houndstooth was not a hippopotamus, and therefore he was not equipped to run faster and farther than the men who would soon be chasing him. He was a very fit man—any number of conquests scattered in his wake could have attested to that—but he was not fit enough to run fast and far while carrying a Bellerman High-Quality No-Lock Ultrafine Safe's worth of gold ingots in a large sack over his shoulder.

Reason Three

Ruby didn't care about reasons.

The hippo looked at Houndstooth with one doleful eye. She was hip-deep in the wallow outside Barley McMorrow's mansion. Her head rested on the edge of the wallow, and she wouldn't budge. She usually responded to his presence by heaving herself upright, and if that didn't work, the phrase "let's go" was always more than enough to get her going—but not this time. She'd been put and she intended to stay that way.

"C'mon, Roo," Houndstooth murmured, stroking her nose with one blood-spattered hand. "Get up for me. We have to go."

Ruby didn't shift.

"Ruby," Houndstooth repeated, giving the hippo a sharp tap between the nostrils. "We've got to *go*."

Ruby didn't blink.

"Bloody stubborn—*move!*" Houndstooth shouted into Ruby's face as loudly as he dared.

Ruby did not care for shouting.

In response, she opened her mouth and let out what was, for her, a soft groan. The bellow roused the attention of the sleeping guard on the front porch of McMorrow's mansion.

"Hello down there," the guard shouted, taking a few steps toward the wallow. "Help you?"

Houndstooth glared at Ruby. "We're just fine," he called up casually, trying to spread some Georgia over his Blackpool accent. "My girl here took a fancy to y'all's waller, and I can't make 'er git."

The guard hesitated, staring at the two of them. Houndstooth cursed himself—his accents were never accurate, and he was certain that he'd put too much Tennessee into his voice.

"Is that a Cambridge Black?"

"Fuck me twice in a row," Houndstooth spat under his

breath. Then, a little louder: "Oh, no, of course not—she's just got into that there dark clay, is all. Real slob, this'n." *There,* he thought, *that's a better accent.*

But the guard came closer, stepping down onto the broad green lawn that stretched between Ruby's wallow and the mansion. "I'm nearly sure—I saw a Cambridge Black when I was just a pup, and she looks just like one! I thought they all died when that fire—"

Houndstooth didn't listen any further than that. He didn't need to.

He'd been made.

"Ruby," he whispered," you need to get up *now,* love, or we'll both be lake bacon." With one hand, he loosed the leather straps that sheathed his two best knives; with the other, he tightened his grip on the sack of gold. Ruby gave him another grumble, her mouth gaping. Houndstooth dropped his sack into her saddlebag, the sound of ten thousand dollars in gold making a satisfying *thud* against the leather. He used his free hand to press on Ruby's nose, trying to make her close her mouth. "You'r'nt gonna want to come too much closer, now," he drawled loudly at the approaching guard. "She done went and got herself a bad case of hop-mites."

There was a noise from inside—shouts. *Damn,* Houndstooth thought, *they've found the bodies.* He thought he'd hidden them better than that, but he couldn't have accounted for *all* the blood trails.

The guard hesitated. "Where are you from, friend?" he asked, and Houndstooth laughed.

"Oh, here and there," he said. He laughed again, trying to cover the growing shouts of alarm coming from inside of the mansion— but the guard went very still. As Houndstooth watched, the man's gaze turned from him to Ruby, and back again.

Then, the guard turned tail and ran back up to the house, kicking up divots of grass behind him.

Ah, Shit

"You gull-blighted beast," Houndstooth hissed at Ruby. "Get up, we have to go, *now!*" There was no question, none at all, that the guard had figured out who he was looking at. Winslow Remington Houndstooth, creator of the best and rarest breed of hippo in the United States of America, notorious outlaw, handsomest heartbreaker in the American South—

Ruby bellowed, opening her jaws to their full 180-degree breadth.

She left her mouth open wide.

Houndstooth reached up to try to grab her nose and yank it down, but she pulled her entire head up at the last second and his hand landed on one of her long, curving lower tusks. She bellowed again, and this time, Houndstooth looked.

"Oh, no," he said softly. "Oh, Ruby, *no.*"

Ruby's Dentition

Ruby had a lot of teeth.

Being a Cambridge Black meant that she was different from other hippos in many ways. She was sleek—not thin by any stretch of the imagination, but more bullet-shaped than her peers. She was black as night, black as ink, black as a shadow. She was quiet when she wanted to be. She was faster than a secret spreading through a church picnic.

But her teeth were hippo teeth, plain and simple. She had the requisite number of molars to back up her bite, which was more than strong enough to turn a man's femur to pulp. She had eight incisors, two long and two short on the top and bottom of her mouth. The long ones jutted forward like extended swords: her fighting incisors.

All of these were in excellent condition. Houndstooth, like any hopper worth his resin, brushed and polished all of Ruby's ivory once a week whether she needed it or not. Her teeth gleamed white in the Atlanta sun, immaculate. Perfect.

Except for two.

Her tusks—the long, curving sabers that arced up out of her lower jaw to boldly dare anyone, man or bull, to come near her with anything less than an attitude of worship—were cracked.

"Ruby, no," Houndstooth repeated, gingerly running his hands along her lower tusks. A meandering grey line ran up the length of each one. "How did this happen?"

Ruby slowly, finally closed her mouth. She looked at Houndstooth and flipped an ear back and forth.

"Okay," Houndstooth said. "Okay, I see. I know it hurts, Roo." He stroked her nose as gently as he could. Out of the corner of his eye, he saw the doors of McMorrow's mansion fly open. Men flew down the steps of the veranda and onto the lawn, drawing pistols to aim at Ruby and Houndstooth. "Roo, love, if you can just manage for one more day," he cooed into her ear. "Just one more day, and I'll take you to see Dr. Bantou. We'll get you fixed up, sweet."

Ruby sighed heavily. Then, the enormous midnight bulk of her shifted, and she began to rise.

Houndstooth reached up as she was standing, wrapping his hand around the pommel of the kneeling saddle that was strapped to her back by a harness of mesh and webbing. He held his grey Stetson onto his head with his free hand and flung himself up into the saddle. The moment his knees met leather, he whipped his hat off and used it to slap Ruby's behind with just enough force for her to flick her tail at him. She took off like a cannonball, and before McMorrow's men could get a shot fired, Ruby and Houndstooth had disappeared into the waters of the Peachtree Lagoon.

Ruby's Romance

Ruby loved Dr. Bantou with a passion, and Dr. Bantou loved her right back.

Houndstooth and the doctor had a slightly different relationship.

"Mite-bitten huckster," Houndstooth muttered under his breath.

"What has this cruel, neglectful man been doing to you?" Dr. Bantou crooned into Ruby's open mouth. He tucked a large, glistening bunch of grapes into Ruby's cheek as he gripped each of her molars in turn, looking for a loose tooth to yell at Houndstooth about.

Houndstooth drew himself up with a lofty indignance that would have made his mother deeply proud. "I have been doing *precisely* what you told me to do the last time you extorted me for a fortune," he sniffed. "Anything that's wrong with her is your fault, I shouldn't doubt."

Dr. Bantou showed absolutely no sign of having heard a word Houndstooth said. He squeezed a melon slice over Ruby's gullet, then ran his juice-soaked hands over her gums and tongue. "And I'll wager he hasn't been feeding you enough, either," Dr. Bantou said conspiratorially. Ruby made a pleased noise in the back of her vast throat, and Dr. Bantou chuckled, dropping a pomelo onto her tongue. He withdrew himself from within biting distance and patted Ruby's nose. She immediately dropped her teeth shut with a *snap,* sending various fruit juices spattering across Dr. Bantou's long leather apron.

"Well," Dr. Bantou said, turning around and wiping his hands across his front. "She's in acceptable condition, other than the cracked tusks."

"I know that," Houndstooth snapped. "I take damned excellent care of her."

Dr. Bantou raised an eyebrow. "So excellent that you didn't notice those tusks for . . . what, a week?"

Houndstooth didn't mean to lose eye contact with the dentist, but he did. Just for a second. It was enough.

"Mmm, that's what I thought," Bantou drawled.

"I was on a job," Houndstooth snapped. "I was helping a friend to whom I owed a favor and my honor—something I'm sure you'd know nothing about."

"Well, whatever you were doing, you left her someplace too small and too boring," Bantou said. "She's been biting at boulders. Did you put her in a quarry somewhere? By herself, I gather?" Houndstooth clenched his jaw. Dr. Bantou's face remained placid. When he spoke, his voice carried the authority of a man who has had the upper hand all along. "They're bad, Houndstooth. I'll need to pull them out."

Houndstooth felt all of the blood drain from his face. "No," he breathed. "No, you can't. There must be some other way. Ruby's tusks, they're—they're her pride and joy, Bantou." He knew he sounded like a lunatic, but it was true. When Ruby basked with her mouth wide, the sun glinting off her beautiful white tusks, every other hippo that saw her would dip its nose below the surface of the water. Her tusks were beautiful, strong, fearsome. "What are our other options?"

Bantou clicked his tongue. "You won't like it," he said. "Better to just pull them out."

"What's the other option?" Houndstooth asked. His heart was racing. He kept looking at Ruby, who was merrily crunching on a watermelon. He tried to imagine her without her tusks, and tears welled up in his eyes.

"You won't like it," Dr. Bantou repeated. A broad grin spread across his face. "You won't like it at all."

"Let me guess," Houndstooth said. "It'll cost me?"

"Oh, yes." Bantou was still smiling. "And then some."

"How much?" Houndstooth asked.

Bantou's smile slid into a frown that was thoughtful, but no less smug. "Do you know, it's the strangest thing," he said. He studied his cuticles. "I heard a rumor this morning."

"How much will it cost me, you hop-shitted hunk of swamp grease?" Houndstooth spat. Bantou didn't flinch.

"It was the most curious rumor about a theft," he said. "Barley McMorrow's estate, I think it was. Have you ever heard of it?"

In the water, Ruby grumbled in pain. Houndstooth pinched the bridge of his nose. "I see."

"Yes," said Dr. Bantou, his smile returning. "I'd imagine you do."

Dr. Bantou Was ~~a Scoundrel a Charlatan~~ ~~a No-Good Son of a~~ Right

Four days later, Houndstooth returned to pick up Ruby from Dr. Bantou's infirmary. The infirmary was a broad loop of marsh, divided into individual paddocks to prevent recovering hippos from taking out their discomfort on one another.

Bantou wasted no time with insincere pleasantries. "She's doing very well," he assured Houndstooth the moment he approached the marsh. "The procedure went entirely according to plan. As routine as can be."

"Where is she?" Houndstooth demanded.

"I'll have my payment first, thank you," Dr. Bantou replied, stretching out a languid arm and opening his palm expectantly.

Grumbling, Houndstooth fished around in the sack he was

carrying. It was a large sack—too large by far for its contents. Houndstooth had to reach his entire arm into the sack before his hand wrapped around his quarry.

He withdrew a single gold ingot from the sack and clutched it tight. "Haven't you taken enough already?" he asked. Bantou didn't respond—he simply kept his hand out and steady. After a long, tense minute, Houndstooth dropped the ingot into Bantou's palm.

"Thank you," Bantou said with a cold smile. Then he let out a sharp whistle, and Ruby rose smoothly out of the water directly in front of them both. "Ruby, my lovely girl," he cooed, withdrawing an apple from his pocket, "show Mr. Houndstooth what we've done."

She opened her mouth for the apple, revealing her restored tusks. Houndstooth gasped involuntarily.

"They're beautiful," he murmured in spite of himself.

"I know," Bantou said, running a hand over his work. It was true—they were beautiful. Bantou had filled the cracks in her tusks using a fine cement, his own recipe. Then, to protect them, he'd affixed to each tusk a thin, supple sheath of pure, polished gold.

It had taken a lot of gold to do the job, though.

Almost the entirety of one Bellerman High-Quality No-Lock Ultrafine Safe's worth, to be precise.

"It's my finest work, for my favorite patient," Bantou said, smiling at Ruby. When he smiled at her, he was almost handsome, Houndstooth thought. The thought evaporated when Bantou turned to glare at him. "While I was working on her, I noticed something else," Bantou said. "You've been neglecting her flossing."

Houndstooth let his fingers play across the hilt of one of his knives as the dentist lectured him about tartar buildup. But then he looked back at Ruby, who was happier than he'd seen her in months, and he sighed. He settled in to listen to the dentist prattle on about Ruby's gums. *For Ruby's tusks, I'll let you live,* he thought. *For now.*

In the water, Ruby let her mouth hang open, the sun glinting off her new tusks. A tiny marsh bird landed between her fighting incisors, inspecting her mouth for morsels it might enjoy. It pecked once at her tongue, and Houndstooth caught a familiar glint in his old friend's eye.

Before the bird could notice its own reflection in the polished gold of her tusks, Ruby's teeth snapped shut. Bantou startled— his foot slipped on the muddy edge of the paddock, and he only just caught himself in time to keep from falling into the cloudy water. As he yanked his leg up out of the muck, cursing his ruined boot, a single white feather floated down to land on the brim of his hat.

Houndstooth smiled. She'd been worth every ingot.

NINE AND
A HALF

◄◄◆◆◆►►

"Eight."

"Non, il est neuf." Archie muttered more to herself than to Houndstooth as she brushed the fawn linen jacket of her suit with long, slow strokes. Houndstooth, in contrast, was attacking the black wool of his jacket as though it had offended him—which, judging by his scowl, it had.

"Eight," he snapped again. "And can you please enlighten me as to why I have to look like a bloody undertaker on this job?"

"Because, cherie, you are too recognizable and we must at least pretend that we are trying to blend in." She cast an eye to Houndstooth, who had discarded his shirt and was standing before his wardrobe with his suspenders hanging over his bare shoulders. He was examining a collection of brightly colored shirts and jackets in a range of fine cuts: his traveling clothes. His back was a constellation of assorted scars. "Must you?" Archie sighed.

"Yes, I must, Archie," Houndstooth snapped. "I must because you insist on dressing me like my grandfather's pallbearers. I have *pride.* I will not be seen in . . ." He gestured to the plain white shirt-front he'd slung over the back of a chair. "Whatever you call that."

"Nine," she said, ignoring him. " 'Ere." She crossed the room and prodded him in the back harder than was strictly necessary. "One." She jabbed the long, thin scar that wrapped around the ribs on his right side. "That is from when you fell off Ruby."

"I didn't fall off Ruby," Houndstooth sputtered. "I dismounted—"

"You fell and you almost impaled yourself and if I 'adn't

caught you in time, you would 'ave been a kebab." She flicked another scar, this one nestled under his left shoulder blade. It looked like a puckered star. "Two. The sheriff."

"Yes, alright, but—"

"I pulled fabric out of that wound with a pair of sewing scissors," Archie said, almost wistfully. "And you squealed like a 'ungry 'op. But not nearly so loudly as you did when I pulled out the bullet." She prodded his right shoulder blade, where a strange pair of parenthetical red welts marred the skin. "Three."

"You can stop now," he snapped, drawing a deep red shirt from the wardrobe and slipping it on. Archie nudged him out of the way of the mirror and began combing grease through her hair as she continued.

"The sheriff's son," she said with delight. "On the night before 'is wedding, was it not? I 'ave never seen so much pus in a bite wound, cher. You should 'ave made 'im brush 'is teeth before you took 'im to bed."

"His teeth were fine," Houndstooth replied with a wolfish grin. "I think it's my back that was dirty."

Archie cackled and finished parting her hair. She began applying a layer of gum paste to her top lip, and as she applied her mustache, their shared room at the unimaginatively named Riverside Inn was peaceful, if not quiet. The peace was half of why they'd chosen the Riverside, which was not known for its amenities, service, or comfort. Shouts from the riverboats that drifted past their window filtered in like birdsong.

The riverboats were the other reason they'd chosen the Riverside.

Houndstooth settled a flat-topped black boater onto his head, frowning at his reflection over Archie's shoulder.

"Four," Archie muttered, trying not to move her mouth.

"When you choked on the olive pit and I pounded your back until it was free."

"That doesn't count. You broke my rib," Houndstooth said, exchanging the boater for a grey bowler with a pheasant feather tucked into the grosgrain ribbon around the brim. Archie snatched the bowler from his head and replaced the boater.

"Better a broken rib than a blue-faced corpse, non?" Archie put the grey bowler onto her own head and admired herself. "C'est parfait."

Houndstooth crossed his arms and did not look at himself in the mirror. His black wool suit was long in the arms and loose through the thighs, and the hat was detestably plain. He looked entirely unremarkable. Archie wondered how long it would be until he stopped pouting about it.

"Let's go," he muttered, checking his pocket watch. He snapped the cover shut with a peevish click.

Archie slung an arm around him, pitching her voice half an octave lower than usual. "You look every inch the rogue," she lied.

"Flatterer," he replied with a sour smile. They locked the door behind them and Archie dropped the key into her waistcoat pocket.

The front door of the Riverside Inn opened onto a dock.

"Riverside" was both an exaggeration and an understatement. The inn was a glorified riverboat itself, huge and out of commission. The broken wheel had been left attached to the side of the inn as a sort of pirate flag, identifying the place as a Harriet veteran that had come upon the stubborn side of a crush of hungry ferals. The hull was sound, but the wheel was a lost cause, and so—like so many others before her—the riverboat had put down anchor and converted into a hotel. The back of the inn abutted the riverbank, and the veranda ended just one foot from the water.

Archie and Houndstooth emerged into the stifling noon heat and crossed the narrow wood of the dock to flag down a ferryman. Archie pointed to the approaching riverboat, which was arriving precisely on time.

"Are you sure?" the ferryman asked. She looked put out.

"Oui," Archie rumbled. "We are sure. Why?"

"Oh, it's just—trips from the shore to the bank boat are free," the ferryman said, pushing off from the dock with a long, slim pole. "I only get paid for casino runs and brothel tours. Unless you're hoppers? Hoppers gotta pay to get to the bank." A thin note of hope returned to her voice, but her long look at their decidedly non-hopper wardrobes was doleful.

"Afraid not," Archie replied breezily.

"Not us, no," Houndstooth cracked his jaw with the heel of one hand, then grinned at the ferryman. "We're tobacconists."

The ferryman's brow furrowed as she poled them toward the bank boat. "Tobacconists?" she repeated uncertainly.

"Yep," Houndstooth said. He tugged at his long cuffs. "Tobbaconists."

—◆◆◆—

"Tobbaconists?" Archie hissed at Houndstooth, once they were safely aboard the bank boat.

"It was the dullest thing I could think of," Houndstooth said with a shrug.

Archie shook her head at him. "You are ridiculous."

"I'm not the one pairing a lilac coat lining with a pea-shoot cravat," he sniffed in reply. "So perhaps we shouldn't go throwing around words like 'ridiculous' without assessing ourselves first, eh?" He leaned against the railing of the boat and gave Archie a purse-lipped once-over.

"Envy does not suit you," she retorted. She leaned forward and tapped him on the forehead with her index finger. "Five, six, and seven. Three separate times I 'ave kept you from getting your 'ead caved in by angry women with candelabras. You are making me regret the rescues."

"Are you still on about that? It's eight, Archie," Houndstooth said wearily. "I think I remember the number of times I've almost died."

"I'm surprised you remember anything, after that fourth candelabra landed. Which is eight, by the way," she added brightly. "When I sewed your 'ead shut before you bled to death."

"Let's get this over with," Houndstooth grumbled. "Before I sweat through every inch of this damnable jacket."

"Oh, le pauvre," Archie cooed. " 'Ow you suffer."

She lifted her pea-shoot cravat and fitted the top of it over her nose. It fluttered in a long triangle from her face to her collar, covering the lower half of her face, including her moustache. It was a shame to hide such a handsomely waxed moustache, but Archie was a professional.

Houndstooth pulled his own kerchief out of his pocket. Archie raised an eyebrow at him. "Really?" she asked.

"It's the plainest one I had," Houndstooth said, tying the kerchief around the back of his head. It was peacock-blue silk with pale pink pinstripes.

"Ridiculous," Archie muttered. She reached under her fawn linen jacket and withdrew a long-barreled pistol. Houndstooth reached under his sweat-heavy wool and withdrew a matching one. They nodded to each other, and Archie kicked at the door to the bank boat, and they burst inside. Archie pointed her pistol at the tall, broad-shouldered black man standing behind the counter. Houndstooth waved his at the bank boat's patrons—gamblers and madams all, none strangers to the sight of a pistol but none stupid enough to risk their lives for money they'd lose to a bad hand of cards the next day anyway.

"Hands in the air," Houndstooth drawled in a terribly thin Tennessee accent. "This here's a stickup!"

———✦———

Houndstooth tugged at his waistcoat. He suspected that, between the humidity and the ungodly amount of sweat he was producing, it was shrinking.

"You hot?" the banker asked him in a low, rumbling voice. His chest and shoulders strained at his white shirt, and the suspenders that held up the sleeves looked close to bursting. The man was sprawled in a chair behind the counter, but even sitting, he had an easy view of the bank. His customers were scattered across the floor, their hands resting over their heads. They weren't going anywhere, though—these were folks who had been banking on the river for a while, and they were used to the occasional robbery. They knew that if they kept their noses pressed to the worn wood slats until the excitement was over, they'd be allowed to return to their business soon enough.

"Me? No," Houndstooth answered, keeping his pistol leveled at the banker's face. "Hush. I'm fine."

"I'm hot," the banker said easily. "Hot indeed. It's muggy today, isn't it? Muggy and close and hot as hell. I can't imagine what it must be like for you in that wool, and with a kerchief to boot?" He shook his head and slapped his thigh with the flat of his hand. "I'd think a body would feel near enough to death."

"'E 'asn't been this 'ot since the ninth time I saved his life," Archie called over her shoulder.

Houndstooth made a *hsst* noise at her. "Now isn't the time—"

" 'E was dehydrated, you see?" Archie continued, shoving bundles of cash into a large brown saddlebag. "Delirious, almost. Tried to—"

"Please don't tell this story," Houndstooth groaned.

"—kiss me," Archie finished. "And that's when I realized that the fool 'ad been eating salt jerky all day and ignoring the fact that 'is piss was brown. I made 'im drink a saddlebag full of water! 'E slept for a day and woke up asking after 'Almondine.' 'There is no Almondine,' I told 'im, 'you were making eyes at Archie the whole time.'"

The silence in the bank was sudden and stifling. Archie paused for the space of a breath, then continued loading cash into the saddlebag as though she were hoping that the moment would pass unremarked.

"Archie," the banker said, rolling the name around in his mouth like a horehound candy. Houndstooth closed his eyes and waited, silently praying to a God he didn't believe in that the name wouldn't mean anything to the huge man. "That wouldn't be short for anything, would it?"

"No," Houndstooth said quickly. Too quickly. "It's just a joke we have. Archie, because Archie used to be my arch-nemesis."

Archie grimaced into the safe. "Oui," she said. "That's why."

"Really?" The banker looked between the two of them, his face credulous. "That is such a strange coincidence. See, just the other day I heard tell of a gentleman by the name of Archie who was knockin' over bank boats up and down this stretch of the river."

"You must have some competition," Houndstooth called to Archie, who was shoving cash into the saddlebag with increased speed now.

"But I do believe that name was short for 'Archambault,'" the banker drawled. "That wouldn't make you Winslow Remington

Houndstooth, would it?" he continued. "No, no, couldn't be. That fella's dapper as all hell, and you . . . well."

Houndstooth stared at him. "Well, what?"

"Not meaning any offense, now, but you do look like something a hop might drag up off the bottom of the river."

Houndstooth shot Archie a murderous glare.

When he looked back, the banker had drawn a matched pair of pistols. Both were leveled at Houndstooth.

"Now, friend," he murmured, softly enough that Archie couldn't hear. "Why don't you put your weapon on the floor there? We both know it ain't loaded, but I'd still prefer it on the ground."

"What makes you think it isn't loaded?" Houndstooth asked, dropping any attempt to cover his Blackpool accent.

"Because you're a hopper, Winslow Remington Houndstooth," the banker said. "And hoppers don't waste money on bullets what can't get wet."

"Alright, I 'ave all we can carry—" Archie stood, and as she did, the banker rotated one arm so that the pistol gripped in that hand pointed behind him. He wasn't looking at her, but the barrel was aimed unerringly at Archie's face. "What's this?" Archie said, yanking down her cravat to reveal a deep scowl. As she did, the fabric snagged on one side of her moustache, pulling it half-loose. She pressed her fingers to it, wide-eyed, and gestured to Houndstooth to keep the banker's attention.

"Who are you?" Houndstooth asked the banker, lowering his unloaded pistol slowly to the floor. "How do you know who we are?"

"I thought you'd never ask," the banker said, flashing a broad, dimpled smile. He waited until Houndstooth's pistol was on the floor, then kicked it away with one boot before turning his smile to Archie. She kept her hand pressed to the moustache.

The banker's dimples deepened. "I'm Gran Carter, but you can call me Marshal."

He stood, his pistols still pointed at Houndstooth and Archie. As he rose to his full height, his jacket fell open, and the light streaming through the windows of the bank boat caught the silver star that hung from his belt.

Archie swore and dropped her pistol with a heavy thud. She did not, however, drop the saddlebag full of cash.

"I'd be right grateful if you gentlemen would turn around so I can get your hands secured," Gran Carter said. "And don't try running away, now. It'll only make things harder on you. Besides, it wouldn't be worth the effort." He chuckled. "I've been a marshal for a long time, and I can tell you truthfully that there's not a man in America who can escape me."

"Oh," Archie said, her eye glinting wickedly. "Good."

She gripped the saddlebag full of cash in both hands and swung her hips in a wide arc, using the momentum from the movement to loft the heavy bag into an underhand pitch. It landed hard in the marshal's gut, and he let out a pained *huff* as he doubled over, his knees hitting the floor with a *crack*.

"'Oundstooth, throw me your jacket and run!" she shouted, her moustache pulling loose and dropping to the floor at her feet. Houndstooth peeled off the sweat-soaked wool and threw it to her, then turned and leapt over the bank counter.

"I'll be outside in three minutes!" he said as he darted toward the door.

"Make it two!" Archie called over the marshal's airless groaning. "Wait, 'Oundstooth!"

He turned in the doorway. "What?"

"This makes ten!"

"Nine and a half at best!" Houndstooth roared—and then he

was gone, out the door and over the deck rail, barely making a splash as he landed in the water of the river.

Archie chuckled to herself. She planted a foot on the winded marshal's shoulder and shoved him onto his belly, then tied the sleeves of Houndstooth's wool coat around his wrists. "These will shrink fast, Monsieur Marshal," she murmured. "I would not recommend a struggle—that would only make it worse for you. Wait for someone to cut you loose."

"Don't try to escape," Gran Carter growled into the floor. "You know I'll catch up with you sooner or later, Archambault. No man—"

"—can escape you, oui," Archie said. Then she leaned down and let her bare lips brush against the marshal's ear. "But Regina Archambault is no man."

Carter went still beneath her. "What did you say?" he asked.

Archie pressed her lips to his cheek. At the same time, she grabbed her moustache from the floor and dropped it next to his face. Then she stood up, grabbed the saddlebag, and stood on her toes to peer out the window. Houndstooth was just a hundred meters upriver—one foot planted on Ruby's saddle, the other planted on Rosa's. The two hippos were moving in perfect unison, bearing him toward the bank boat with uncanny speed. "My carriage awaits, Gran Carter. À bientôt."

She leapt through an open window and landed on the outer deck. The boat creaked with the sound of her vaulting the deck rail to land on her notorious albino hippopotamus. The real banker, disguised as a casino owner, cut Carter loose, and the Marshal eased himself off the floor, rolling his wrists. His eyes were shining, and he pressed his fingers to the place where Archie's lips had left the faintest hint of warmth. He toed the moustache that rested on the floor. It was a handsome moustache.

"Regina Archambault," he murmured to himself as the

patrons of the bank boat began to stand, brushing themselves off and buzzing about the robbery. Carter's fingers played over the silver star at his belt and he felt a shiver of admiration pass through his belly. "See you soon, indeed."

APPENDIX 1: TIMELINE OF EVENTS

March 1857: Congressman Albert Broussard proposes the Hippo Act, seeking $25,000 to import hippopotami into the United States in an attempt to solve the nationwide meat shortage.

July 1857: The Hippo Act is signed into law by an enthusiastic President James Buchanan.

August 4, 1857: President Buchanan cuts the ribbon on the United States of America's first hippo ranch in Alabama; declares the hippo ranching industry "open for business."

November 1857: The Federal Marsh Expansion Project begins, employing 40,000 men to dam sections of the Mississippi, creating a series of marshes so as to meet the great demand for "lake pig." The series of marshes are named "the Harriet" after Buchanan's favorite pet cow.

December 1857: The territory encompassing the Harriet and the hippo marshes are declared neutral, free territory in the Great Hippo Compromise. The Great Louisiana Hippo Rush begins. Ranchers stake their claims.

January 1858: Quentin Houlihan, a hired hopper on Samuel F. Greenlay's hippo ranch just outside of Baton Rouge, falls asleep on the job. His lantern falls onto a pile of rushes. The fire is put out, but not before the hastily erected fencing that surrounds the ranch is compromised. All 97 hippos escape into the bayou. None are recovered.

May 1859: During the Great Hippo Bust, ranches throughout the Harriet are plagued by feral hippo attacks and disease.

February 1861: President Buchanan, nearing the end of his term, signs off on the construction and staffing of the Harriet Gate, a measure intended to trap feral hippos in the Harriet proper and to save the remaining hippo ranches in the South.

March 1861: President Abraham Lincoln enters his office, declaring that he will fix Buchanan's mistakes. During his inaugural address, he promises that "the Bayou will belong to the hippos and the criminals and the cutthroats no longer!" Unfortunately, some things come up.

March 1865: President Andrew Johnson declares in his inaugural address that he will fix the one problem Lincoln couldn't. "The Wild South days are over!"

March 1869: The newly inaugurated President Ulysses S. Grant promises to clear the feral hippos out of the Mississippi "once and for all!"

March 1889: President Grover Cleveland declares the Southern United States under martial law, calling it "an unresolvable den of thieves, mercenaries, hoppers, and scoundrels"—but promising to maintain a steady flow of subsidies to the hippo ranches that feed the rest of the country.

ABOUT THE AUTHOR

Photograph by Raj Anand

Hugo and Campbell Award finalist **SARAH GAILEY** is an internationally published writer of fiction and nonfiction. Her nonfiction has appeared in *Mashable* and *The Boston Globe,* and she is a regular contributor for *Tor.com* and the *B&N Sci-Fi & Fantasy Blog.* Her most recent fiction credits include *Mothership Zeta, Fireside Fiction,* and the Speculative Bookshop Anthology. Her debut novella, *River of Teeth,* was published in 2017 via Tor.com. She has a novel forthcoming from Tor Books in spring 2019. Gailey lives in beautiful Portland, Oregon, with her two scrappy dogs. You can find links to her work at www.sarahgailey.com; find her on social media @sarahgailey.